BLIND TO THE SAVAGE FORCES
THEY HAD UNLEASHED, THEY
GROPED FOR SOLID GROUND . . .

DAVID DOLAN—Draft dodger, antiwar activist,
he returned after years of exile to exorcise the
nightmare of his brother Brendan's death in
Vietnam . . . to pick up the broken pieces of
his life.

CHENEY McCOY—A brilliant and celebrated
actor, he knew how to use a theatrical gesture
to get what he wanted. What he wanted now
was the love and loyalty of his adopted son.

EDDIE McCOY—She was Brendan's widow. She
had been David's lover and Cheney's wife. But
now she was a woman fighting for self-respect,
independence—and custody of her eight-year-old
child.

BREN—Patiently he waited at his grandmother's
house in Maine, sensing the gathering storm,
the perilous ground . . . unaware of how
easily everything he loved and trusted could
be changed forever.

FAULT LINES

"RICHNESS AND RESONANCE . . .
[CARROLL] TURNS WHAT MIGHT
HAVE BEEN A DOMESTIC MELO-
DRAMA INTO A NOVEL OF SUBTLETY
AND DEPTH."

—Christopher Lehmann-Haupt,
The New York Times

Books by James Carroll

MADONNA RED
MORTAL FRIENDS
FAULT LINES

FAULT LINES

James Carroll

A DELL BOOK

Published by
Dell Publishing Co., Inc.
1 Dag Hammarskjold Plaza
New York, New York 10017

Dell ® TM 681510, Dell Publishing Co., Inc.

ISBN: 0-440-12436-0

Reprinted by arrangement with
Little, Brown and Company

Printed in the United States of America

First Dell printing—February 1982

For Elizabeth

CHAPTER 1

It was important, Dolan thought, to approach as though nothing was wrong.

He walked with the same slightly hurried jaunt that all his fellow passengers used, as if the race through Immigration didn't end in the bottleneck at Baggage and Customs. There was no point in hurrying. He wanted to slow down and rehearse again what the officer might ask him, but his instinct told him to keep up the pace, to skip forward quickly and edge out the other travelers, as if he too had other planes to catch, dates to make, children to hug, gifts to give, a wife waiting at the gate.

He was ready for anything but what happened. The immigration officer hardly looked at him. He opened the passport, closed it and waved him through. Only the pressure from the passengers behind Dolan kept him going in stride. At Customs it was the same. The agent didn't even open his bag.

When Dolan walked through the large doors into the airport lobby where the welcomers clustered, there was, to his great surprise and relief, no one waiting for him.

Apparently he was home and, apparently, though

he expected a tap on his shoulder until the Manhattan Express pulled out with him on it, he was free.

He got off a second bus on the corner of Twenty-third and Sixth and saw the sign of the Chelsea Hotel shimmering just the way that beglamored name should have. The massive orange-red light hung over the lively hot street the way a bottle of the best liquor overhangs the dream of a man who sleeps in his clothes.

There was more to the night scene than Dolan could properly take in: the red blur of taillights, headlights, gleaming off the golden sheen of taxis on the run, green lights, walk lights, garish shop windows and, flooding everything, the fearsome glare of the giant arc lamps, high-crime street lamps which illuminated brilliantly while washing out all color and making the street and its people look filthy. Husks of men moved slowly from one doorway to the next. They slouched, as if against the hard light. Was there no darkness in American cities at night? Had it been so before?

Dolan watched them plodding, like old horses, under the weight of, not hunger but the memory of it. They kept their eyes down, not looking at him. One man in a dark coat brushed past, making for the doughnut shop. Dolan walked on. Others went down into the dark drinking dens, where their pale skins and stony yellow eyes and dyed hair and gruesome facial lumps would not show up. He could smell dried, stale urine. The street was heavy with it, always was in August, he guessed, but Dolan had not whiffed the stuff in years. He remembered the stench, and slowly suddenly, expecting to discover the additional odor of marijuana. His furtive introduction to the weed had taken place years before in the back stairwell up from the subway at Harvard Square; bums' piss and cheap dope, both alien odors to him now, could still suggest each other, and that amused him. He might have laughed, but his laughter would have been lost in the noise. Honking cars, loud Latin music, the roar of buses, sirens, a jazz trumpet—the sounds of everything but human speech hung over Twenty-third Street. Everyone Dolan passed was alone. The noises canceled each other and became a kind of silence, and the colors combined in the glare into no-color, white or black, but for the great exception toward which he was walking, the sign, like whiskey lit from behind, of the bright hotel.

The Chelsea Hotel was a massive gilded-era brownstone with wrought-iron balconies and elaborate Victorian lintels. It had been a graduate student's dream when Dolan had stayed there twelve years before. He hadn't been back since, but it wasn't hard for him to remember the appeal of the place. Everything had had its appeal in 1967. What attracted him to the hotel originally was its very name, because he was thinking at that time of writing his dissertation on More—"The Chancellor and the Bard: The Influence of Thomas More on William Shakespeare"—who loved to speak of his "pore howse" in Chelsea-on-Thames. More's house had been a great mansion, of course, but the New York hotel was faded, even by 1967. It had been a landmark since 1882, when Twenty-third Street was the Times Square of New York, and with age it had become picturesque and eccentric and had attracted artists and writers. Dolan could see why. It was inexpensive, but clean then, and the old building with its bay windows and wainscoted walls and molded ceilings and ornamented doorways was itself a work of art. There had been exhibits of paintings from the Art Students League hung throughout the hotel and here and there carefully printed posters had announced poetry readings and showcases, of which Dolan had attended half a dozen in two days, feeling certain the whole time that he was brushing up against the Arthur Millers and the Delmore Schwartzes of the seventies. But now, incredibly, the seventies were over and Dolan had no real idea who its Millers and Schwartzes had turned out to be, despite having collected stipends for teaching contemporary American writing. Perhaps that was why the impulse to stay at the Chelsea his first night back. He had to begin somewhere to discover what he'd missed.

The hotel's entrance canopy protruded across the sidewalk. It was askew because one of its supporting metal pipes had been rammed and bent. A green plaque by the door, weathered bronze, read, "The Chelsea Hotel, home in New York to James T. Farrell, Robert Flaherty, O. Henry, Thomas Wolfe, Henry Moore, Edgar Lee Masters, Dylan Thomas and Brendan Behan." Dolan did not recall seeing the plaque before. Was Behan dead in 1967? But they weren't all dead, even now. Farrell was still alive, wasn't he? Dolan remembered his mother finding *Studs Lonigan* in his drawer. She had surprised him with her search, but more by being familiar with the book and knowing about the rape scene. He remembered yelling at her, "The Irish celebrate their frauds! The rest they drive away!" How old was he then? Sixteen? When she said, "The book goes," he'd replied, "Then so do I." He'd hitchhiked to San Francisco and stayed there the entire summer.

Dolan laughed at himself, at his knack, now that he was home, for conjuring self-serving clichés about Irish exile. But he wasn't home. He was in New York. The Chelsea Hotel, home in New York to David Dolan, Junior.

It seemed suddenly foolish to be standing, suitcase in hand, reading the bronze plaque which, together with the crippled entrance canopy and dirty exterior of the hotel, suggested bad days and new management.

Dolan turned toward the threshold and saw faces peering out. Three Spanish-looking girls just inside the door were watching him. They were thin, raven-haired, wearing identical short skirts and spike heels and cheap purple blouses unbuttoned nearly to waists cinched with wide gleaming black belts. He thought they expected him to speak. Oo-la, baby. One smiled. Her eyes were huge almonds. She was very, very young, a child, he thought. He could see all but the nipples of her breasts through the slit in her blouse, tiny breasts which she displayed because they would not fill a garment yet. He stood looking at her, transfixed despite himself. She was measuring him and he knew it, not by looking him up and down, but by holding his eyes. He knew much more about life than she did; still he was conscious suddenly of his appearance, his tan corduroy jacket, his white shirt and maroon knit tie, his out-of-fashion chino pants, which had been creased in the morning but which were now rumpled and baggy after the long flight, his oxford tennis shoes, supremely modest, of the kind rarely seen in America anymore. Without so much as glancing at his clothes, she made him feel improperly attired. He straightened himself slightly, correcting his habitual slouch. He was six feet tall. He had auburn hair just long enough to cover his ears, which he had always considered too large. Otherwise he liked his face. He had an angular chin and pronounced bones under his eyes, which had, he knew, begun to show his weariness. He was thirty-five years old and showed it.

When the girl's two companions began to giggle Dolan realized he was blushing. If the girl was seventeen, he was twice her age. He was probably older than her father. In the glass of the window he glimpsed the brown shadow of her nipple and he knew despite himself it was the sweetest shadow he had seen in a long time, the sweetest because of the blatant innocence with which she offered it not to him but to the glass, and of course both he and she knew the trick of that. Innocence, to be irresistible, must be blatant. The girl was good.

He smiled at her, but stiffly, then dropped his eyes to the forward edge of his suitcase, which he maneuvered past her and her friends. The fragrance of their perfume cut him. He knew that she was watching him as he crossed into the lobby, and he could picture her vividly because of that perfume. He thought he would never forget it, it was so awful, but by the time he had walked six paces into the bright lively room, it was gone. The Chelsea lobby had an overpowering odor of its own, just as cheap, just as awful, worse, because in addition to perfumes and the musty smells of ratty Victorian furniture there were those of alcohol and the distinct additional odor of fresh disinfectant.

The lobby of the Chelsea Hotel shocked him. This was not it at all. Two huge canvases with rotund naked figures in screeching acrylic dominated the walls, jarring the room with their mediocrity. Dolan knew craftless junk when he saw it. Even the person who painted them knew it; he or she had not bothered to stretch one of the canvases free of wrinkles. The two crude canvases had the same function as the plaque outside, to proclaim in a loud voice that this was an art hotel. Only in an art hotel would such bad art be displayed.

Strange-looking people were also, as it were, hung here and there around the room, defining the place further. They were not what he remembered either. They were queerly dressed, vacant-eyed girls, males with young bodies and old faces, a pair of junkies leaning together in a corner, a sexless figure sleeping it off on a shabby couch. Art is anything, they seemed to say, done by crazed, desperate liquor-ridden sensitive souls. Art rides close to the edge of madness and death. The broken characters in the frayed lobby were, he knew suddenly, caricatures, victims of the dream of the Chelsea Hotel. In Stockholm their cousins wrestle with each other in mud-pits in nightclubs before patrons who pay to feel better about themselves, if only in comparison. Dolan did his best thinking in those places.

He crossed to the registration desk acutely conscious of the eyes of the place which stared and dreamed at once, the way the eyes of inmates do. The man at the desk behind the bars of his squirrel cage was as loony-looking as any of them. He was missing an ear. The inmates had taken over. Come home, America! For this?

"Hello," Dolan said. He put his suitcase down on a spot where the ancient orange rug was worn through. All that Samsonite, all those Lillian Hellmans and Jack Kerouacs. But she'd have stayed on the East Side, and he'd have had a knapsack. "I'd like a room, please."

The clerk stared at him with hound's eyes, showing such a round sad face with its two days' growth above defeated shoulders in meager blue lapels that Dolan knew the man's misery was counterfeit, an act, like Jackie Gleason's Poor Soul. Vincent van Gogh was a creep like this, but with talent.

"How long?" the clerk asked, and Dolan knew suddenly that he could answer either in hours or years.

Just then three boys in bolero hats swung out of the elevator chattering away in Spanish. Dolan turned to watch them, their asses twitching in tight black pants which swirled at the ankle over shiny high-heeled boots as they pranced across the lobby. They wore purple blouses with puffy loose sleeves. A pair of them held hands. Dolan understood as they joined the three girls at the door that they were a troupe of Latin dancers, and he longed suddenly to see them perform. He thought of leaving his bag and dashing after them, but then his eyes locked on the almond eyes of the girl who, despite the distance, sent her signal.

It panicked him. He was not prepared for his emotion. Men in their middle thirties are still young, but in the way that Sweden is still a monarchy. Remnants are there to be clung to and made much of, but still they are remnants. It was all very well to mourn the passing of time and regret growing old, especially when one's life had not turned out to be what one wanted at all. Dolan could muster regret with the best of his kind. But that wasn't it, or not merely it. The girl bothered him because she seemed to be offering him something he had never had and had never missed having: utter simplicity. She was shooting arrows at him. He imagined her looking that way at her father and her father not hesitating to spank her and then, despite all taboos, to force himself on her. She would be sublimely indifferent to the outrage of it.

She could make herself so clear, even from across the lobby. I see you, mister. I like you. I look at you with my eyes and I show you everything.

"How long, mister?" the clerk repeated.

Dolan turned back to the desk.

As he did so the dancers left. The girl was gone.

"A few nights," Dolan said nervously.

"Thirty-five dollars a night," the clerk said, dangling a key. "Cash in advance."

The price shocked him. In kronor, that was one hundred and fifty. For that you could stay in the Hotel Östermalm with a huge room on the Stockholm harbor overlooking ships and yachts across to the Royal Palace. Dolan's hand shook as he reached for his wallet. He couldn't afford this place for more than a few days, this foul sty.

Christ, he hoped his job lead paid off. A good lead, it was why he'd stayed over in New York instead of going on to Boston. It did make sense for him to be here, didn't it? He had to push down on his desperate feelings. Money was not the issue; his life was. But money was the source of his anxiety at that moment. The job would help with that, and it would be a signal to the courts of his hard-earned respectability. The job would be a place from which to begin everything else. He decided to call the man first thing in the morning. Meantime a night's rest, time to think, to establish an agenda. He would make a list of things to do the way he had as a boy when conflicting impulses had threatened to take him in opposite ways at the same time. A list would reassure him, calm him, make him see how the terrible blank future might save him from his past.

He paid the clerk for one night and followed him. The passage from lobby to room was so labyrinthine that Dolan wondered if he would be able to negotiate it later alone. The clerk was an indifferent guide. At one point Dolan asked if famous writers ever stayed there anymore, but he spoke to the severed ear and the clerk seemed not to hear. They rode the elevator, climbed a flight of stairs and, after tracing a way through the dark corridors turning constantly, they came to a door at the end of a cul-de-sac. Dolan stood aside while the clerk applied the key. On the neighboring door in front of which Dolan stood a hand-lettered sign warned: "The fuckers are coming!" He was aware of a revolting taste in the back of his mouth, third-degree nausea, that and a sudden, inexplicable desire to invite the pathetic clerk into the room for a slug of vodka.

Look, I got some questions I want to ask you, he could have said. Where has he gone, Joe DiMaggio? Why didn't Nixon go to jail? Can you still get cream from the top of the milk? The clerk's presence posed a problem Dolan had not foreseen. He wanted to talk to somebody. Anybody. On the plane he had made it a point to sit by himself and had regretted it even before takeoff. He wanted to talk to someone in English and then ask if he, Dolan, had an accent of any kind. He wanted to tell someone that, yes, Sweden's suicide rate is nearly double that of the United States, but its murder rate is about a fifth. Dolan was afraid that if he spoke it would be pure nonsense. A fifth of vodka, thanks. Any kind. When had he ever had cream from the top of the milk? The fuckers are coming, eh? The clerk, once Dolan's door was opened, turned and left without a word and without waiting for a tip.

Dolan closed the door behind himself and leaned against it. What was it that struck him first? The odor. The room smelled like the alcoves of the street, like the stairs up from the subway in Cambridge. Obviously a previous and recent occupant had urinated in the corner. Dolan slapped his breast pocket, took his cigarettes out and lit one. He smoked a Danish brand. He wanted the smell of it more than the taste.

The light switch was two buttons, one over the other. He punched it on, then put his hand to his face and looked at the dingy room, the exasperated bed, the chair with soiled foam rubber showing through a hole in the fabric of the cushion, the gray draperies that blocked a floor-to-ceiling window. He tried to remember what view of the city his room had had when he'd stayed at the Chelsea before. The Chrysler Building. He'd been able to see the Chrysler Building. At night they lit it, didn't they? For a hundred and fifty kronor they should light it. He stared at the draperies. His thumb leaned against his right cheekbone and the rest of his hand cupped his cigarette and covered his mouth and chin. He stood like that for some minutes enjoying the smell of the smoke and the idea of himself in such a pitiful place after years of rooms that smelled of fresh oil on perfect wood.

He affected an opaque expression as if he were being observed. It showed nothing of what he was thinking. Pictures of New York flashed before him, fancy cafés and sweeping vistas of the Park with hansom cabs and plumed horses and strollers by the bookstalls on the Avenue and long shot of the glittering skyline as if the draperies concealed a view from Brooklyn Heights or the Palisades. The King of Crete looks out on his city from the center of its maze, which is the point of being at the center of a maze. Knossos teaches that to see things whole one must lose one's way in the midst of them and then, only then, open one's eyes. Dolan took his glasses from the inside pocket of his jacket and hooked them around his face, preparing himself for the Chrysler Building, illuminated, and more. He crossed to the window and in one swift motion jerked the heavy draperies back.

Ten yards across the airshaft a man humped a woman in a patch of light, their window which displayed them. Her toenails were painted and as her lover ground her, those red spots jerked about in circles like bees. The man was grunting. The woman's thighs around his waist were fat. She was saying, oh, oh, oh.

Once Dolan walked into the bathroom of the B.U. dormitory he and two hundred other radicals had seized as their headquarters after Kent State—"Strikedorm" they called it—only to see a couple ball-ing in a shower stall. He watched them writhing behind the frosted glass and listened to the water splashing them. Then he went to the sink, washed his hands, dried them meticulously, undressed, crossed to the shower stall, opened it and said, tapping the exhausted dripping boy on the shoulder, "May I cut in?" And since it was the new age and they were as stoned as he was, they let him. In that water the girl's legs kept slipping from his waist and he couldn't get his leverage, new age or not. The memory unsettled him. How little everything cost in those days. What a glib, facile, shallow time. With what grandeur had he strolled through it, a leader of the movement, on his way, as he saw now, to the long sleep from which he'd just awakened.

He thought of flipping his cigarette across the airshaft, imagined them engulfed in flames, her saying, "Wow, honey, you light my fire!"

Dolan wanted them to know that he was there, watching them. He coughed once. They did not hear him, though the windows were open. The motor of a bus roared from far off and he seized on it, something to focus on other than the copulation, which should have seemed ludicrous or exciting, but was only suddenly threatening because of the other memory it was forcing on him.

Night after night he had lain curled on a couch listening through the thin wall to a man and a woman fucking discreetly inches away from him. They were not strangers. When Dolan was first on the run he hid for weeks at his younger brother's apartment. He was not prepared for Eddie Brewster, who struck him as far too fast, bright and lovely a woman for Brendan. Not that Dolan didn't regard his brother with affection. Everyone did. Brendan was a large-hearted embrace of a kid, but Dolan never expected him to snag that quite remarkable woman with whom, it seemed to David, he himself had more in common than Brendan did. While listening to the stifled noises of their lovemaking, Dolan admitted to himself one night that for the first time in his life he envied Brendan.

That feeling complicated what happened, but he insisted to himself it didn't cause it. He hatched a plan for his escape that involved assuming his brother's identity while driving to Canada. He shaved his beard and had Eddie cut his hair to look like Brendan's. And then Dolan took off in Brendan's clothes, in Brendan's car with Brendan's skis strapped to the roof. In his pocket he carried Brendan's wallet, his identification and two hundred dollars of his money. And at his side, the ultimate disguise, Brendan's woman. At the border, for the agent's sake, she sat close to him and let her hand rest on his knee.

If Dolan made a mistake with her in Quebec wasn't it because she shared his sense of their affinity? Hadn't she responded to his proposal that she travel with him as his skiing partner with the same suppressed eagerness with which he offered it? Even in those glory years of free-spirited anarchy, his behavior with her after all his brother did for him made him uneasy. Since Brendan's death the memory of it had become a kind of crystal spur that stabbed whenever he slowed down enough to think of it.

He focused again on the couple across the airshaft. He reminded himself that in a similar situation somewhere in Durrell a voyeur laughed. But it didn't seem funny. What he was watching reminded him of a dirty movie and it embarrassed him the way pornography did. Such a concise summary of his life—the unmoved observer whose cold eye rendered everything profane.

He reminded himself that nothing was required of him. It was not a crime he was witnessing. What was the girl's name who was murdered in the street and no one went to help her? Kitty Genovese. Kew Gardens. All those detached observers, cold eyes. At rallies up and down the East Coast in the late sixties Dolan gave rousing speeches saying Kitty Genovese was being murdered again, stabbed repeatedly, but in Asia, not Queens, and someone had to cry enough! Resist! Stop the slaughter! Cry no! The killing stops here! But where, exactly? he would have asked now. And how?

He turned away from the lovers. And now, smashing out his cigarette in the tin ashtray on the table by the bed he did laugh quietly. He flopped diagonally across the bed, laughing. For years he had dreamed in his sleep-of-a-life of coming home. And now he had. Come home, America! He resolved not to think about it, but he couldn't help it.

He heard them again, slam-banging on their mattress, bouncing, squeaking, the male grunting away and then the woman, finally, crying with perfect hooker's pitch, "Fuck! Fuck! Fuck! Oh, baby, fuck!" and on and on, "Fuck! Fuck!" fading, fading, fading to a whimper until, "Ooooh, babeee!" Cut. Wrap. Thanks, kids. Dolan wondered if she fooled her john, if he cared. The fuckers were coming? Wasn't everyone? And to think that for three years at one of the great universities in Europe he taught a course entitled The Absurd Hero in American Fiction.

Soon the couple across the airshaft noisily dressed and left. Dolan got up, closed the draperies, turned the light out, undressed to his underwear and lay down rigid under the sheet. He always thought of sleep as the tunnel two miles down the highway, visible from the hill. He made for it, gunning, but got nowhere.

A mind's jumble of memories, names, faces, feelings pushed sleep off; Kitty Genovese, Eddie Brewster, Strikedorm, Brendan, Brendan's kid, Boston University, the sanctuary at Marsh Chapel where he put a flame to his draft notice, the cheers of the crowd, the police swinging their sticks, the screams, the blood, the panicked mob, his flight to Quebec with his brother's woman, the dawn scene in her hotel room, his mistake. Dolan tried to snap the memories off. It had been years since he was at their mercy. He closed his mind against all of it.

But Artie Rose. Suddenly he thought of Artie Rose.

He turned the bedside lamp on, picked up the phone, got the desk clerk, who informed him that long-distance calls could not be charged to his room. He hung up, turned the light out and resolved again to sleep.

But he remembered Artie, his short friend, straining to drape an arm around his shoulder, tears in his eyes, saying, "Doe, kid, call me, get in touch with me, let me help you." And then Artie had kissed him on the cheek just as the police began pounding on the chaplain's door. Dolan had said he would, then climbed out of the window.

He turned on the light again, called information in Boston. There were four Arthur or A. Roses, but only one was listed as an attorney.

"A collect call for Arthur Rose from David Dolan. Do you accept the charges?"

"Who?" It was a woman's voice and she sounded as if she'd been asleep.

Dolan looked at his watch. It was two o'clock. What the hell was he doing?

"Arthur Rose from David Dolan," the operator repeated.

"This is Arthur Rose," a man said impatiently. "Who's calling?"

"David Dolan," the operator said.

"From where?"

"New York City."

Dolan wanted to interrupt to say, "Artie, it's me!" Or, "Operator, never mind."

When Rose spoke now there was caution in his voice, and suspicion. "David Dolan?" He paused, then said, "Yes, operator, I accept. Let me give you a credit card number."

While Arthur Rose recited a number Dolan tried to think what he was going to say. Why this mad impulse, this rude puerile late-night call? But he knew why. He'd never expected to get past Immigration. He'd thought they would come to him. They hadn't, and now he didn't have a clue what to do. Artie was his lawyer. Artie would know.

"Doe? Is that you?"

"Hi, Artie. Yes, me. No one calls me Doe anymore."

"No one calls me Artie."

Dolan propped himself up with a pillow, aware of

a quite physical surge of relief. Affection for this old friend threatened to undo him. He found it difficult to speak.

"You're in New York?"

"Yes. I just got back."

"From where?"

What did Rose mean, "from where?" He didn't know? "From Sweden," Dolan answered.

"You've been in Sweden? You mean all this time? I thought you'd come back years ago."

"You know better than that. You know I couldn't. I'd have called you if I had."

"How are you, Doe?"

Dolan was shocked at his reaction to the obviously heartfelt simple question. It moved him, and he almost said, "Not good, Artie. I need help." Instead he took a moment to get hold of himself.

Before Dolan spoke Rose went on, "God, it's great to hear your voice. Those were our best days, weren't they?"

"Artie, I called to ask you something. What kind of shape am I in?"

"Christ, Doe, I haven't seen you in, what, eight years?"

"I mean legally. What kind of shape am I in legally?"

"You haven't resolved all that stuff? It's still hanging?"

"I told you. I've been in Sweden." Dolan paused. "I've come back to straighten things out."

"You tell me then, Doe. What do you think?"

"I spoke to the legal attaché at the embassy in Stockholm. He thought I wouldn't have any trouble. They're not prosecuting draft cases anymore."

"Draft cases?" Rose's voice took on the hint of an interrogator's edge. "What about the . . ."

"Isn't there a statute of limitations or something?"

"Yes. Seven years."

"Well then. Maybe they've dropped it." Maybe that was why they hadn't met him at the airport.

"But you were indicted. The grand jury nailed you. You know that. Did you tell the legal attaché that you have outstanding indictments?"

"No."

"Christ, Doe, you should have. A draft offense is nothing."

"Nothing?" With sudden agitation Dolan lit a cigarette while he talked. "I spent all this time on ice for nothing?"

"Conspiracy, Doe. Arson. Incitement to riot. Those are not nothing."

"But those had nothing to do with me, and you know it. I didn't conspire. And all I burned was a fucking draft notice. And the riot was what the police did, not me."

"A cop was blinded in one eye, permanently."

"Jesus, I didn't know that." Dolan knew only that pandemonium had broken out in the chapel after he'd fled.

"You were going to turn yourself in. No one expected you to take off. A symbolic act of resistance. It was supposed to be symbolic."

"Hey, Artie, wait a minute. You told me to split. You of all people. You said they'd throw the book at me once the shit started flying."

Rose fell silent.

"Right?" Dolan inhaled nervously. He was perspiring. His pillow was damp behind him.

"I don't remember it that way, David. But you didn't call to nitpick history with me."

"History? Maybe history for you, but not me. I called to ask you what my legal jeopardy is."

"I don't know."

"I've just come back from Sweden, Artie. What the hell." The man's affection had moved Dolan, and now his reticence was making him angry.

"You should presume the indictments stand. Presume you are regarded as a fugitive. Legal attachés at most embassies are FBI. Didn't you know that? You're lucky you weren't arrested at Immigration. You should turn yourself in."

"I need a lawyer."

"Yes. You do."

"I want to know what I'm charged with before I turn myself in. I want to know what the hell I'm dealing with." Dolan paused. "Will you help me?"

"I'd love to, David, but I don't know what I could do. I'm not in litigation anymore. You need someone who's on top of these things. I'm in real estate now, Doe. I negotiate mortgages. I'm not your man."

"Artie, I'm feeling . . ." Dolan had to force himself to go on ". . . fairly desperate. I just want to get a job. I want to see my parents. I want to meet my brother's kid. I want to start something of my own, a life, for Christ's sake. I have to clear this shit up. You've got to help me." Dolan looked around the room. "You ought to see the dump I'm calling from."

"Don't tell me."

"What?"

"Don't tell me where you are."

"Why?"

"Because it could prove awkward."

"For you or for me?"

"For both of us."

"You'd call them. You'd tell them."

Rose didn't reply.

"Well, Jesus, Artie, it has been a long time, hasn't it?"

"Maybe someone in my firm could help, from our criminal staff . . ."

"Your firm? Your criminal staff?"

"As opposed to civil."

"You're civil?"

"Yes."

"Just barely, Artie. Good talking to you." Dolan hung up. His hand shook as he stubbed his cigarette out, but he felt a surprising calm as he leaned back against his pillow. He was on his own. There were hard things to find out and to do, but he had begun. The result of his first act was disastrous and disorienting—it was foolish of him to have expected Artie Rose to be still what he was, a leftie and a friend—but Dolan was reassured by the simple fact of his having acted at all. His season of passivity, perhaps, was nearly over.

He got up, crossed to his bag, took out his papers and read again the letter of introduction from his mentor at Uppsala to the professor at NYU. The generous praise relaxed him. His prospects were not all bleak. And then he read for the millionth time the letter Eddie Brewster had written him years before. It was a brutal, accusing letter, written in her first grief. It required a response, but Dolan had never been able to make one, perhaps because he'd been trained as a child to ask absolution of no one but the priest. But he didn't believe in priests anymore. He didn't know how to ask forgiveness of anyone. He folded her letter carefully. Its creases were nearly worn through.

And then he took a pencil and on the envelope of her letter made his list: jail, family, job. Each word was like a small stone dropped in his mind, sending ripples across its surface, disturbing it, but with a quilt of crossed diamonds which in the right light was lovely. Jail. Family. Job. A lawyer. The professor. His parents and Eddie Brewster. Despite their obvious priority, he let the first three go and went to sleep thinking of her.

CHAPTER 2

The boy could not take his eyes from the white sea-birds. Their movements fascinated him. In the pattern of their flying they kept tying each other in knots. They dove at the waves, then pulled up at the last minute like bombers. If they'd had vapor trails, like bombers, they would have messed the sky with impossible tangles. He tried counting them, but their darting made that impossible. He got as high as nine but knew there were many more than that. Now six and a half years old, he had been counting into the hundreds since he was four.

At home the gulls were cleaner, it seemed to him. He had a large collection of feathers, but that morning the birds hadn't dropped any on the rock where he stood. If he could only find some Atlantic feathers soon, he would know for certain whether the Pacific gulls were whiter or not. One thing, though, about this ocean: low tide was better. In California low tide just meant the pebbly part of the beach was showing. But here, when the water fell away, the very bed of the sea was left, with its blanket of brown seaweed draping the rocks. Blue mussels clung at the bases of the rocks and there were periwinkles and sea snails and the white cones of the barnacles and the fleshy crabs which the gulls were diving for, even as the surf continued to wash over the creatures nestled at the farthest edge of the tidal zone.

He thought standing on the boulder was like being a giant looking down on a forest and watching everything that lived there. He had come out early to see if he could tell the exact moment when the tide changed. He wanted to watch it coming in. He wanted to see the rockweeds gradually stand up as the water flooded over them. He wanted to see the limpet snails leave their homes. His grandmother claimed that with high tide they left their places on the rocks and went swimming around for food and then before the tide fell again returned to the exact same spot, without anybody telling them where it was. Homing instinct. But if snails had it and pigeons, why was it so easy for kids to get lost? He wasn't supposed to be out on the boulders. His grandmother had told him he could get trapped when the tide came in. She knew a lot, but she wasn't the only one. The rock he was on wouldn't be cut off from shore until lunchtime. Each tide took six hours. He had never noticed that in California. His grandmother was still asleep in the huge old red house on the ledge behind him. What she didn't know wouldn't hurt her.

He tried counting the birds again and got up to seventeen. He knew they would disappear at high tide when there was nothing to feed on. He wondered if they could see him. Their eyes were sharp enough, since they could spy fish underwater or crabs hiding in the seaweed, but they might think he was just another rock if he kept himself still as stone, like a statue. He was very good at statues, which was a favorite recess game at the Masters School in West-

wood, but he was supposed to start second grade in
September but probably wouldn't since he and his
mother had left L.A. and his father in May. Now
they lived in New York City. He had been hoping all
summer that they would go back, but they hadn't. Instead his mother had made him come to Maine without her. He didn't like Maine that much. The water
was too cold. There were no beaches. The seagulls
were dirty. He missed his mother, who had stayed in
New York.

On the day he left she had walked him across Central Park to his grandmother's apartment—he and his
mother lived on West Seventieth Street in the apartment he had been a baby in, and his grandmother
lived in a penthouse on Fifth Avenue. On the way he
had made his mother stop and take him on the carou-
sel and then to the zoo and then, in the empty baseball diamond, he had made her play a game of
statues with him. They took each other's hands and
began to circle slowly leaning more and more away
from each other and spinning more and more swiftly
until they were going around and around. He
couldn't take his eyes off her face for two reasons.
The way not to be dizzy was to pick a spot and stare
at it. And her face was so beautiful. The faster they
went the more she laughed and the tighter he
squeezed her hands, knowing full well that at any second they would shoot apart, hurling each other into
space. They did. Now the game said that each one
stop falling away instantly and hold perfectly still,
but both of them froze so that—and this could not
have been an accident—they could each watch the
other to see who cracked a muscle first. Bren McCoy's
reason for getting his mother to play this game with

him had been to stop everything. Leaving California
and his father had been enough. Once he froze his
position there in the park he swore to himself that he
would never move; if his mother didn't move either,
then he would not have to go to Maine without her.

He knew it was impossible for them to stand still
near second base until the end of time or until winter
or even until it got dark, when they would be
mugged. But his secret hope was that they would be
like statues long enough for her to get it in her brain
just how much he needed her. It all depended on
holding perfectly still. And so he did. Perfectly. For a
while. Then he moved. He was the one to move. He
raised his hand to scratch his forehead because that
was a trick he used to keep from crying, or to keep
his crying from showing. If his mother would leave
his father—he found it impossible not to think this
thought—why wouldn't she leave him? And if she was
going to leave him, what better way than to send him
off with Gram to Maine?

When he moved, even though on purpose, she
yelled, "Gotcha!" and pointed at him and danced
around him like a Tibetan priestess. When he wanted
to he could stay like a statue for hours. In Tibet statues were the guards, he'd read, of happiness. But he
did not show her how sad she made him. He let her
think the game was all he wanted. The rest was his
secret. He backed away from her rigidly, as if he were
a statue moving, a tin soldier, and that made her
laugh. He could always make her laugh.

The tide had turned and he had missed it. The
mussels were already flooded over and the surf was
swirling in on the brown seaweed. The birds must

have noticed him because they had moved along the
shore to the next jutting point. He stood there staring after them. He was aware of the waves sliding in
off the little hills, their swells, glittering and regular,
and he thought, at least they don't know I'm here.
They think I am a rock. They think I am a statue.
He looked at the ocean carefully to see if he could
catch it at something. In California one could see sailboats and freighters. Here in Maine, two days before,
Bren had seen a seal pop up right off the point and
look at him. His grandmother had told him there
were seals, but he had not believed her, but there it
was. He knew a seal when he saw one. He hadn't
been to Pacific Marineland seven times for nothing.
When he saw his father, it was one of the things he
would tell him, that he saw a real seal in the ocean,
not a tank. Now what he wanted was a dolphin, a
porpoise, or preferably, a whale. His grandmother
said that by August the water off Hunter's Island
might be warm enough, so he kept his eyes peeled.
Sometimes when he wore his cape and his sword he
called himself the prince of whales. He'd give anything to see one, a sperm whale or a sulfur-bottom or
a killer whale. He loved their names.

For the first time that morning he noticed the
wind. The tips of the black spruces on the next point
swayed in it and Bren thought, not for the first time,
that it was eerie how he could feel a breeze on his
face and at the same time see it bend things far away.
The birds gathered in it and rose and sank in it. Bren
thought the seagulls were trying to form themselves
into a ring against it the way all creatures do when
danger threatens. He could tell from the way they
fought it, like bombers fighting each other, that the

birds thought the wind was their enemy. Bren didn't like it either. He did not like anything that could touch him without him seeing it. He had always wanted to be able to make himself invisible. That, it seemed to him, would be power. The wind had that power. And statues had it.

That was not exactly true. Statues did not have the power to be invisible, but they had the power to be unnoticed, which, he thought, was just as good. For example, there were hundreds of statues in Central Park and no one noticed them. But Bren noticed them, and he did not believe that those statues could not in their secret way see him. He wondered if the wind could see him. He decided for the hundredth time it could, and that was why from across the water where it bent firs the wind dove at him like a train locomotive in a movie.

His father was in movies, which is why he had to stay in California where they make them. His mother said she didn't like California and that was why she moved Bren back to New York. But he wasn't dumb. What she didn't like was his father, and that was why they moved, even though Bren tried to talk her out of it, and then tried to talk her into going back in September so he could still make second grade. She said he could do second grade just as well in New York, but he couldn't. He would have tried talking her into liking his father again, but he knew it didn't work that way. It was simple. He understood. She had liked his father until he hit her. Then she stopped liking him. Bren had seen it from the stairs. His father had screamed something at her, poking his finger at her eyes. Bren remembered that his mother had pulled her face back from his finger as far as she could without actually taking a step, and even he, young as he was, understood why holding one's ground could be important. But she couldn't get her face away from his finger, and so she brushed at it with her hand, and that was when his father hit his mother. The sound of his hand on her face was like a clap. He did it again, and Bren felt the blows as if they were falling on his own face. He understood instantly that his father had been made so angry by something he, Bren, had done, and that his mother was protecting him. His father had screamed at her, and Bren knew that his father was screaming about him and his mother had defended him, and that was why that terrible fight hit them like a tidal wave from Japan.

The third time his father hit her, Bren cried out, "Stop!" But he didn't move from his place on the fourth stair. "Stop, you two!" His mother and father were shocked that he was there, and they both turned toward him with horror on their faces, and he felt very small. He had done something terrible, only now he knew what. He had snuck down the stairs and listened to them and looked at them when they thought they were alone.

That was the second time ever he had wanted the power to make himself invisible. His parents' stare lasted only for a minute, but it made him feel as if he didn't have his pajama bottoms on. The first time happened one day at school at the end of snack, when he had gone to the toilet, which was in a little room the size of a closet just off the cafeteria. He didn't like going to the toilet at school because he was always afraid something would go wrong. That day something did. After he had gone, he turned the doorknob just to make sure it was going to open when he needed it to. The doorknob didn't turn. He became frightened. He tried turning the knob with both hands, but it wouldn't budge. He looked and felt for a lock or a latch but could not find one. Before he could think about it or stop himself he was calling out, crying Miss Riordan's name, saying, "Help! Help!" and banging on the door with his fists. Suddenly the door jerked open. Mr. Beattie was standing there looking angry, and behind Mr. Beattie were all the second graders who'd come down for their snack. Only when they started to point at him did he realize to his horror that his pants were still down around his ankles. He hadn't even flushed the toilet, which Mr. Beattie did then, leaning past him.

It was an emergency and Bren knew it. He had only a fraction of a second before the class would start laughing at him. He had to make them think he wanted them to laugh. Mr. Beattie was bending over him, pulling up his pants. Bren squeezed his head between Mr. Beattie's arm and side and crossed his eyes like an idiot, twisted his face and touched his tongue to the tip of his nose. Not many of them could do that. The second grade laughed hard and Bren's shame left him, but still he would think of that moment later as the first time he wished he was invisible. Now he often did. He wished the wind, which he couldn't see, could not see him, and he wished the ocean couldn't. He wished the ocean would behave as if he were not there. He wanted a whale. He wanted at least the seal again.

"Brendan!" his grandmother called from the porch of the old house which was so big he felt alone in it even when he wasn't. There were no other houses nearby, only the lobsterman's shack by the paved road a mile through the woods. Bren liked that it was an island, even if Hunter's was too big to really feel like an island. You could not get to it except by the ferry, which was a cranky old boat that could carry fifteen cars.

"Brendan!" she called again. He pretended not to hear her. He didn't move. He was a statue.

When Bren asked his grandmother why they called it Hunter's Island, she said it was the old Indian name for it and that the island had been a hunting ground once. But she had just made that up and he knew it. Still he had pretended to believe her. Later she gave him an arrowhead, which she claimed to have found in the flowerbed in front of the house and which, in any case, he saved.

"Brendan Dolan!" she called loudly.

It irritated him when she called him that. His name hadn't been Brendan Dolan since his father adopted him. His name was Brendan McCoy. But would he have to change his name again if his mother never went back to his father? Dolan was the name of his other father, the one he never knew, the one who died. Or would his name be Brewster like his mother and grandmother?

She called him again, but this time with only his first name. His grandmother didn't like his father because he wanted them to stay in California. Bren wished that everyone in his family had the same name. Maybe that was part of the problem. He considered ignoring his grandmother until she got it right.

"Come have breakfast, dear!"

He was hungry. He turned and waved, then scampered across the rocks toward the rickety stairs that would take him up the cliff to her. The huge red house loomed behind his grandmother. It looked like a barn, but a white banister around the edge of the roof and an enclosed cupola on the roof's peak made it look too fancy for a farm. Bren liked the house. With its four bedrooms on the third floor and three on the second, each with its closets, there were dozens of nooks in which to feel secure. He liked the living room because of its great stone fireplace and the black iron woodstove in front of it. He liked the bay window overlooking the sea because he could stand in it and feel like the captain of a great ship. The porch surrounded the house on three sides and wicker benches hung from rusty hooks which squeaked when he swung them. On the fourth side of the house, jutting back toward the woods, was the kitchen with its low ceiling and black stone sink and long table. It smelled of flour. Though the kitchen had no view it was a snug room, the coziest, and therefore Bren's favorite.

"We'll have waffles, dear. What about that?"

Bren assumed a pose with his legs wide apart, one knee crooked forward and his arms open and his head at an angle. "The falcon," he announced, "loves his waffles." He stretched out the "o" sound in *love,* and rolled his eyes to it.

"The falcon," Mrs. Brewster replied, "better wash his face and brush his teeth."

Bren made for the door with his arms outstretched like wings, but his grandmother surprised him. She didn't laugh at his jokes like other people did. Kids were supposed to be snappy and funny like t.v. come-

dians, weren't they? Why didn't she laugh? The falcon at his waffles. Bren thought that was funny.

He let the screen door slam behind him, knowing
the sharp sound irritated her. In Bren's opinion he
and his grandmother would get along better if someone else was there. Pretty soon his two cousins from
Cleveland were supposed to come. They lived summers in a town called Blue Hill. It was in Maine too,
his grandmother said, but not on an island. Bren
would have preferred to visit them, to see for himself
if the hill was blue, but he was glad they were coming, even if he didn't like them that much. He
needed help.

Bren felt that the most important thing was being
strong. He knew that his grandmother was worried
about him because when a kid's parents break up the
kid tends to blame himself. Bren and his mother had
talked about it. She said it wasn't his fault and he
sometimes believed her. But it wasn't her fault, he
knew that, and he didn't think it was his father's
fault, except for hitting her.

Bren had decided that he should do all that he
could for everyone, maybe that would help. That was
why, even though he didn't want to be there, he was
trying his best with his grandmother. It was hard,
though, with just the two of them. He took more
waffles than he thought he could eat so he wouldn't
have to make up things to say.

"More syrup, dear?" she said.

"Thank you," he said, nodding. He had already decided to accept anything she gave him because that
was what pleased her most.

"What did you see from your boulder?"

"I'm sorry I went out. You told me not to." He paused, expecting her to forgive him. She ate her waffles and said nothing. "I saw the lippets."

"Limpets."

"I saw them on the rock, but I didn't see them leave."

"Only in the water, only in the tide," she said.

"Have you seen them do it?"

"I've seen them leave."

"Have you seen them return to the same exact spot?"

"No. The scientists do, though, dear. You and I couldn't tell them apart. But they do it. Each snail returns to the same exact spot out of thousands. It's one of nature's miracles. Pick up your napkin, sweetie."

"How do the scientists know?"

"They mark them. They put tags on them."

"Name tags?"

"Sort of."

"How do they know their names?" he said, giggling. She gave him a look. "I know they don't have names. But how do they tell them apart? Different colored tags probably. Or numbers. Do you think we could mark one, Gram?"

"Sure we could. A little drop of fingernail polish would do it. Good idea." She brightened at his interest and he began to relax.

And then the telephone rang. Two quick bursts, that peculiar Maine ring, efficient and haughty.

"It's Mom!" Bren cried. "Can I get it?" He didn't wait for permission, but dashed into the living room. "Hello!" he blared. His affection, impatience and the pain of missing her all rushed out in that one word.

"Hello, son," his father said in his clear, round voice.

Bren was shocked. "Dad!" he cried, but regretted it immediately and turned to see if his grandmother had heard. Of course she had. She was looking at him with her head at a certain angle, upward, so that her eyes were staring right at him and her ears were ready to snatch whatever they said to each other. Bren turned away from her. "Dad?" he repeated, but uncertainly.

"I can't hear you, buddy. Speak up." His father called him "son" sometimes, but mostly he called him "buddy," as if that was his name. He never called him by his name though, not Bren or Brendan.

"Where are you?" Bren asked.

"I'm in New York. I came all the way back here to see you, and what do you do but skip out on me!"

Bren felt a rush of anger at his mother. This was why she'd packed him off to Maine. "I'm in Maine, Dad, at Gram's."

"I know it, dummy. I called you, remember?"

"Oh, yeah," he said, and then he blurted, "I miss you, Dad."

"I miss you too, buddy."

"I had a dream about you."

"A good one, I hope."

Bren didn't say anything to that. It had been a sad dream. It was one of the nights he'd wet his bed, which, luckily, he hadn't done at his grandmother's house yet.

"Is your mom there?"

"No, she's not. Just Gram."

"When's she coming back?"

"She's not here, Dad. She's in New York."

"You're up there by yourself?" There was a sound in his father's voice that Bren thought was alarm, and that was part of what began to panic him.

"No," he said too loudly. "Gram is here."

"Oh," his father said, and then there was a long pause. And then he said but with a completely different voice, "Look I think I can get tickets to the Yankees. Want to? I'll take you into the locker room and we can see Reggie again. What do you think?"

"Sure. Except . . ."

"Except what, buddy?"

"I have to stay here with Gram."

"Is she right there?"

"Dad, I need to ask you."

"What, ace?"

"Do you still like Mom?"

"Like her? Oh, I love your mom, kiddo. That's why I wanted to talk to her. You don't think I called up all this way just to talk to you, do you?"

"Yes."

"Course I did. Listen to me, son, your mom and I just hit some fast water, that's all. Remember our canoe trip?"

"Yeah?"

"Remember those rapids, how scared we got?"

"I wasn't scared."

"But then it smoothed out just like before, right? Well, that's how it is with people sometimes. That's why I came back East, to get you guys and bring you home. You got school, right?"

"Yeah."

"Second grade, right? There you are! You have to come home. You got to be in school in a couple of

weeks and I got to take you out and buy you some
new pencils to chew on, right?"

"Right."

"OK. And if the Dodgers win it, we'll all go to the
Series together. I promise. Your mother can root for
the Yankees. You and I'll root for L.A. Deal?"

Bren did not answer.

"Deal?" his father repeated.

Bren had turned to look at his grandmother. She
was standing right next to him.

"How long are you going to be up there, son?
Where's your mother?"

Bren could not answer him. Tears were streaming
down his face. He thought the most important thing
was to be strong, but he couldn't. He couldn't be
strong anymore. He buried his face in his grandmother's apron. She took the phone away from him
but he didn't care. He just sobbed and sobbed.

CHAPTER 3

Cheney had an impulse to slam the phone down on its nickel-coated cradle, but he checked it, hanging up swiftly but gently. The boy's sobbing was not what made him angry. It made him want to dash to Maine and hug the kid. What in hell was Eddie sending him off to Maine alone for? But Cheney knew, and that's what made him angry. He put a dime in the slot and dialed her number. All week he'd been getting her tape machine and leaving messages. When she didn't call, he'd guessed she was in Maine. But she was in New York and without Bren. Maybe he could see her. He'd ask her to lunch. He'd be very nice. After the third ring someone answered, but he knew it was the machine even before the tape began.

He hung the phone up, again calmly. He thought of calling Maine again and speaking to Eddie's mother, but she disliked him and he found it impossible to deal with her. He wondered why, though any Freudian, putting it together with the fact that he had bypassed Montana for twelve years to avoid his own mother, could have told him. Frazier had, in fact, dozens of times.

He found it difficult to turn away from the pay phone, as if the machine were some girl he'd been having an affair with and now that it was time for them to separate they could not do it cleanly. He'd intended to say to his son—the more Eddie denied it the more resolutely Cheney thought of the child as his own—that he loved him.

He was in the greenroom of the Actors' Studio, a flaking theater on Forty-fourth Street two blocks west of Broadway. It had been a revival church once, and its auditorium and rooms, despite their faded worldly pallor, still had the feel of a place in which only the saved might truly be at home. Cheney had done his training there years before and cherished fond memories of it as the cradle of his career, but he felt uneasy at being back. The Studio, like a church, had always made him feel unworthy. It surprised him that it still could.

Cheney was not happy with his work so far on *Richard III*. The scene they were about to rehearse was the one in which he kept losing his flow. When work was off the mark, the very walls of the Actors' Studio had disapproving eyes. On a film set everyone loves you if you remember your lines, and stay inside the chalk marks and muster any feeling whatsoever. Here, though, nothing counted but the real thing. Cheney had been anxious to test himself against the place. He pretended to thumb his nose at its pontifications, but in fact it had taken him a long time to work up the courage to come back. He wanted to impress the Studio with his work. If he'd been trying all week to get Eddie, he knew it was because somehow she and the kid were what kept derailing his ability to concentrate. He turned away from the phone decisively, as if from her.

It was not quite nine o'clock, and the room was filling up with actors arriving for the rehearsal. Some hovered at the coffee urn barely looking at each other through their dramatically ruined eyes and creased faces. These tended to be the older actors who had never become stars but who had worked more or less regularly for years, mainly in earnest downtown productions but occasionally, some of them, in flashy uptown shows. There was a cultivated weariness about them, but also an ill-kemptness that was genuine, not studied. One man had not bothered to comb his hair; it was a wild tangle of gray. He had not shaved in days. A couple of women whose youthful good looks had already failed them shared a cigarette. Both had figures still, but their features had softened and their faces had lost their definition.

A chubby woman poked her face into her coffee repeatedly, like a bird at water. No one spoke to her. Her jeans bulged with her weight, and that alone seemed enough to account for her standoffishness, her hostile bashfulness. The actors by the coffee urn smoked, and a cloud hung in that corner of the room. At the opposite corner the young ones congregated, looking fresh, clean, alert, having jogged. They seemed slightly embarrassed that they weren't, say, in California. They were not smoking. They were not drinking coffee. They were uniformly good-looking. They knew that when they had made it they would come back to the Studio now and then too, pretending, like McCoy, to be just one of the company.

Reah Whitson was playing Lady Anne to Cheney's Richard. She wore French jeans, a denim vest over a silk blouse and expensive high-heeled boots. She approached Cheney from behind, slid her arm around his waist and said softly, "God give your Grace both a happy and a joyful time of day."

"Kind sister, thanks," Cheney said without thinking and he kissed her on the forehead, barely touching it with his lips, but burying his nose in her blond hair, which smelled of herbal shampoo. "Since I cannot prove a lover to entertain these fair well-spoken days," he whispered, "I am determined to prove a villain. Dive, thoughts, down . . ." he stooped slightly as he said this ". . . to my soul." And he took hold of her shapely buttock and squeezed.

"Why, sir!" she yelped. But she lived for such assaults, and he knew it and knew better than to disappoint his leading ladies. Even this one. Reah Whitson was no one's idea of a serious stage actor, but Cheney had suggested her for the part himself. They had recently finished a film together and he liked her. When she acted, only the camera and its angle existed. Reah had no capacity for robust speeches or Renaissance gestures, and that was what would make her exceptional as the widow of the Prince of Wales. She would enact Lady Anne simply, directly, without grand statements, because all she knew of acting was the close-up. Peter Garvey, the director, had wanted Janet Field, a Joe Papp regular, but Cheney had insisted on Reah. The production of *Richard III* was a mere benefit for the Actors' Studio that would run only three weeks, but Cheney wanted it to showcase film actors. Hollywood does Shakespeare! Damn right! Let New York try to dismiss it as that!

Reah still had her arm around Cheney's waist. He had barely noticed her, despite his grab, and she knew it. "What's wrong?" she asked.

"Nothing, sweetheart," he answered, but then added, "My son."

"He isn't well?"

He fingered the change slot in the pay phone. "No, he isn't well at all." When he looked down at Reah—at six-three he was eight inches taller than she was—he saw her expression of concern and he realized that without even intending to, he had lied to her for the effect such a statement would have. Behold C. Superstar McCoy, folks, tall, handsome, prime of his life, top of the heap, about to rehearse the greatest scene in theater, but preoccupied not with the fact that for more than a week he had floundered miserably in his search for the character he was playing, but with his ailing little boy. Trouble is—he nearly said this out loud—the little boy ain't ailing and ain't his.

"You're a good father, Cheney," Reah said.

"Good fathers, sweetheart," he said, making for the stairs to the auditorium, "are the worst kind."

On the bulletin board at the bottom of the stairs a full-page ad from *Variety* had been posted, and it showed a closeup of a man's face which, because obscured by shadows, was ominous and threatening. Bold letters announced grandly that Universal's big new film would be ready for Christmas. When Cheney recognized the dark, expressionless face as his own—the designer's effort at arty abstraction had nothing to do with the work Cheney had done—he shuddered. Hollywood; shadows, smoke, mirrors and trapdoors. "Cheney McCoy. The Most Significant Work of His Career!" Could the East Coast snobs be right?

He took the stairs two at a time and was relieved that no one had come up to the theater yet. The only light was from a single bulb in the balcony, which cast an eerie glow forward over what had once been the sanctuary and was now the stage. A great white staircase was the entire set, and Cheney climbed it too. At the top he lay down with his arms at his sides and his eyes closed. The staircase itself was what his mind clung to; Richard climbs it during the action of the play, each step one of his victims. The higher he goes the smaller he becomes until, at the top where he is crowned, he dies not of a wound but of his fatal loss of stature.

Cheney tried to clear his mind. He slowed his breathing and began consciously to relax. He'd neglected his exercises over the years, had considered them self-conscious and stilted, but now he began to contract and release his muscles just as he'd been taught to as a young actor, beginning with his face, neck and shoulders and ending with his ankles, feet and toes. He could feel the tension draining out of him. He contracted and released opposite pairs then, right arm, left leg; left shoulder, right thigh, and on through the halves of his body. Even as he performed the old routine, the phrases of its theoretical under-girding came back to him; external attention, inner attention, inner motive forces, the sense of truth, emotion memory.

Why was Shakespeare's Richard eluding him? Where was the block? At what point in the action of the play was he losing the tempo rhythm of his character?

He opened his eyes. He would create a small circle of concentration around himself. He was at the top of a staircase. What? What? A staircase.

*　　*　　*

A staircase. A cry. "Stop! Stop, you two!"

Bren was crouched behind the bars of the staircase which led up from the living room, and Cheney felt his cry as a blow to the groin.

He looked at Bren for a long time, and then back at Eddie. She had her hands over her face and he knew that he had hurt her. When she looked at him, it was as if he were Charles Manson.

He closed his eyes. It humiliated him to find his thoughts returning again and again to Eddie. It was months now since she'd left him, since their fight. He wanted to be done with her, wanted the divorce to be over with, wanted to forget about her. But if that was so, why was he dragging the suit out by insisting it be heard in California? But of course he knew why. For Bren. By law California courts gave children into the joint custody of both parents unless there were compelling reasons not to. In New York sole custody was still more customary and much more easily obtained, especially by the mother. Eddie knew that, and that was why she'd reestablished residence there. But the boy was legally as much his as hers.

Cheney's feelings about Eddie were chaotic. Her withdrawal had threatened him enormously and left him confused about every thing but one, his love for Bren, the simplicity and purity and strength of which shocked him.

He opened his eyes to stare at the ceiling. He was lying not on the top stair of the set then, but on the leather couch in Frazier's office. "We were fighting," he said, "about whose dog Pronto is."

But his memory fooled him, because it wasn't Frazier who replied, but Eddie. She said coldly, "I will not clean up his piss."

They were standing on opposite sides of a dark stain in the Persian rug in the living room. Eddie was wearing a floor-length blue caftan. She was barefoot, dangling her sandals by their straps from her left hand. They had returned from a party in Belair, both a little drunk, to find Pronto's mess. Cheney had asked her—nicely, as he recalled—to clean it up while he went upstairs to check on Bren. She refused.

"Goddamnit, I always clean it up," he complained. "You never do."

"I would have housebroken him."

"Christ, Eddie, he's twelve years old."

"The rug is not grass."

"It rings his bell. It's not his fault."

"Then he should stay outside."

"You heartless bitch. You resent him because I got him when I was with Francine."

"Bullshit."

Cheney remembered distinctly how she had turned away from him. He reached across the stain after her and grabbed her arm. She resisted him. Inadvertently he pulled her onto the dog's piss and, because she was barefoot, that made her furious. She danced off the moist circle as if it burned. "Let go of me, Goddamnit!"

"I want you to clean it up." Cheney knew even then that that decision to press her would explode in his face. Eddie was not one of the nubile teenagers who fetched coffee on the set, but her feisty verve was why he'd fallen for her in the first place, wasn't it?

"Let go of me, Cheney." She'd lowered her voice to show him that she was in control of herself, a trick of hers which fueled his anger.

His anger.

Cheney lifted himself on an elbow, as if that would take him closer to what he was feeling.

But then he heard someone enter the theater from below. "Someone's working up here," he called.

"Cheney, it's me, Reah."

"Give me five minutes, sweetheart. Tell Garvey to keep people downstairs, would you?"

"I thought we might . . ."

"Kind lady, please."

He heard her leave and then resented her having yielded to him. Why couldn't she defy him? She had as much right to an early crack at the stage as he did. But she wouldn't dare stand up to him. Only Eddie would. Cunts all.

His attention had strayed. He turned his head to stare at the light in the balcony. He would fix his concentration on that. He decided that the lightbulb was a flying insect; he raised his hand slowly, swatted at it and caught the thing in midflight. Richard might be physically deformed, but he is quick. Cheney had already decided to play him with only the barest limp, a nearly imperceptible slouch. He wanted it to be ironic and ominous when he described himself as rudely stamped. He intended that his deformity would grow, however, until, in the last act, its ugliness made England see without illusion who its king was.

Illusion.

"I was under the illusion," he said to Frazier, "that we both shared responsibility for our household."

"Was that the issue?"

Cheney shook his head.

"What was?"

To his horror he felt his chin quiver and his hands

clutched at each other futilely as he tried to fend off what he knew was coming.

"Are you angry at her because she hasn't conceived your child?"

Cheney shook his head. That wasn't it at all. Leave it to shrinks to reduce everything to impotence or sterility. Why couldn't Frazier understand that as far as he was concerned, Eddie had already given him a child? It did not matter that Bren was fathered by some soldier boy just before shipping out to Asia, never to return. What mattered was that, to his infinite surprise, the child had captured him utterly. He'd never been happier than when the adoption'd become final. The thought now of losing him filled him with the most intense emotion of his life. But what emotion?

Cheney knew that Frazier was watching him carefully. In all his years in analysis he had not wept like this. That it was a genuine outpouring of feeling did not prevent Cheney from watching himself too. An actor learns from his life.

"Can you tell me what you're feeling?"

Cheney opened his eyes to look at Frazier's ceiling, but it was gone. He lay there on the top step of the great stage staircase, right at the edge of what he needed to know, but it eluded him. His train of memory kept deflecting into the sequence of his feelings on Frazier's couch because they were once-removed from Eddie. Even in therapy he was incapable of facing directly the rage and the guilt and the humiliation that she had caused in him. He could not bring himself to articulate that memory, not for mental health's sake, nor even, apparently, for the sake of art. At first his explosion had terrified him because it threatened his marriage and therefore his access to Bren, but by this morning, the suppression of his sense-memory frightened him more because it threatened his ability to act.

"Cheney?"

It was Reah again. He closed his eyes.

"That's five." She began to mount the stairs toward him slowly.

Cheney lay quite still. He would give her nothing.

"What, do you tremble?"

At first he thought she had read his nerves, but then he realized she was reciting the beginning of Lady Anne's speech after the bearers of her father-in-law's coffin had fled, leaving her alone for the first time with Richard.

"Are you all afraid? Alas, I blame you not, for you are mortal." Reah stopped and kissed Cheney on the forehead.

"Who you calling mortal?" he said without opening his eyes. But he opened his arms and she slid into them, lowering herself on him so that her body sealed his. He had a strong, lean body for a man in his late thirties. They had slept together half-a-dozen times during the making of their film, lightheartedly enough considering both had recently split up with other people. But New York and this play were a world, if only weeks, away from that, and they were both aware of their inability to relax with each other. Cheney knew that his own tension had nothing to do with Reah, but she didn't know that. On the contrary, she assumed she was losing her chance with him.

"I wanted to ask you something," she said softly.

Her lips were by his ear. It was like talking to him in bed. "About the scene. I'm off base."

"You are playing it too shrilly, sweetheart, as if you only hated him. You hate him, but you also want him."

"Not at first."

Cheney let his hands rest together on her ass, lightly. "At first. It just takes you a minute to admit it. You know the tricks. So does Lady Anne. You're throwing acid, Reah, perfectly. I want you to lick cream at the same time. Show him your tongue."

Her body seemed very simple to him, and suddenly so did her part in the scene. "I want you to seduce me." Even as he said this, Cheney felt his penis come erect, and was aware for the first time in a while of the sharp sensuality that existed between them. The weapon they would use against each other in the scene was sexuality.

"No, Cheney, I'm serious about this." She started to pull away from him, but he held her.

"Do you remember that night in Malibu?" Cheney saw her naked. She was perfectly made. She had a way of taking him in her mouth and using her teeth on him, not quite biting, that had surprised him. The pleasure was in being led so close to pain. She did it wonderfully. "Do it to me again."

"What, now?" She tried again to lift herself, but he held her. "Cheney, Christ!"

This was it exactly. Richard makes Anne do the outrageous at the most inopportune time. "Come on! Quick!" Cheney got up and led her down the stairs and then around behind them. The stairs, like bleachers, formed a cave below, and that's where they went even while other case members drifted into the auditorium.

"This is really crazy," she whispered. "I won't do it."

He kissed her, letting his tongue play in her mouth against her teeth. He put his hands on her shoulders and pressed gently.

She pulled her mouth back. "No, Cheney! No!" But her second "no" became a low groan as she surrendered to his pressure and her own sudden excitement. Slowly she slid down the length of him until she was on her knees and, despite herself, tugging furiously at his trousers.

He sensed her resentment, even as she complied, and he knew that that too could work for them. It was pitch dark under the stairs, and Cheney had to guide himself into her mouth. "Think of it as a Studio exercise, sweetheart."

If called upon to justify what he was doing with Reah, Cheney McCoy could not have done so. He would have joked about getting his rocks off, and yet it was right. His every intuition told him it was right. Cheney nearly always looked askance at his motives, but in preparing to go onstage he trusted himself absolutely in the way an athlete trusts his reflexes. He knew without question when something was going to work. "Trust me," he said to Reah and apparently she did. She applied her expertise; blood and sperm were rising in him. But he had to trust her too. It was his prick, after all, between her teeth.

"Start over," Garvey ordered.

A dozen cast members returned from the shadows to the bright center of the stage and arranged themselves as the funeral procession. They did so sharply, promptly, without a hint it was the tenth time through the beginning of the scene. The play hinged on the confrontation between Anne and Richard. The business of the procession, the carrying of the coffin and the panicked *exeunt* of the bearers could not be allowed to distract from that confrontation. Garvey had been choreographing their movements.

They did it one more time and had it. The cast sat in the darkness then to watch Cheney and Reah work. Peter Garvey stepped between them, sipping at his coffee. "This play," he said slowly, "opens fast. This somber procession with the dead king is interrupted. This widow's grief for her husband's father is interrupted. England is interrupted. The world is interrupted. This scene has the power of lightning across the sky, and the knot it illuminates we spend the rest of the play untying." Garvey stopped and sipped his coffee.

Reah was looking at him attentively, respectfully. She had taken her vest off and her silk shirt was outside her jeans, but still buttoned to her throat. It made her look chaste and therefore voluptuous. Cheney was listening to Garvey without looking at him. He knew that the speech was less an instruction than a ritual transition into the next, more difficult, phase of the rehearsal. Still he found it irritating. He had to force himself to pay attention, not to Garvey, but to himself. Eddie's face, her blank stare, popped repeatedly out of the dark at him, but before it told him what he needed to know, it faded, and there was Garvey still talking.

"This scene takes twelve minutes to play. In our script it covers nine pages, in the Folio, four. In a

couple dozen snatches of wily dialogue we go right
into the bowels of evil itself. All moral values are re-
pudiated, decency exploded. Why? Because in forty
tidy speeches this bastard who will murder his own
brother and his own young nephews will convince
this widow, all of whose menfolk he has murdered, to
become his lover, to give it to him any way he wants
it. Now if there's a problem so far," Garvey said without missing a beat, "it's with you, Cheney. You're not
focused."

Cheney nodded, but he was in the living room with
Eddie again, still. Every thought of Eddie came
wreathed in a sense of his own failure. He loved her.
He lost her because he could not control his simul-
taneous hatred of her. Focused? Of course, he wasn't
focused. He didn't need Garvey to tell him that.

Garvey was still instructing him. "Your impact on
us and on her is diffuse, lightning perhaps, but sheet
lightning. I want bolts. I want flashes. I want to smell
sulfur. OK, do it." Briskly, Garvey walked downstage
to his chair that was half in the light. On the back of
the chair was stenciled in blocks the word *Lee*. It was
the chair Strasberg used in the Studio sessions and it
was uncommonly bold of Garvey to sit in it.

Reah and Cheney faced each other across the bier.
They would play this with the corpse between them.
Both looked relaxed, loose, though Cheney, secretly,
couldn't have been more agitated. Reah's hands swiveled at the ends of her limp arms, her start-easy-stay-
easy trick. Cheney had his hands in his pockets and
was staring at his feet.

Garvey snapped his fingers once.

Reah stiffened her back and was Lady Anne. "Foul

devil, for God's sake, hence, and trouble us not; for thou hast made the happy earth thy hell . . ."

Garvey listened with his eyes closed. She was so un-British, yet speaking as if that convoluted rhetoric were how she talked at home. She'd have to do it louder, though.

Lady Anne began their fencing with thrusts that nipped Richard repeatedly. She baldly accused him of murdering the king and he denied it, backing off weakly. Richard was speaking with a slight lisp that none in the audience had heard before.

Garvey liked the lisp and made the note, *Keep it slight*. He liked the irony of this trim, elegant-looking man verging on the obsequious.

His fawning denials were, of course, Richard's first trap, to let Lady Anne feel superior in their duel, and he sprang it suddenly by admitting that, indeed, he had killed the monarch. In that turn the moral order was shaken, less by regicide than by the refusal to disguise it or apologize for it. And then he was ready with his thrust. He leaned across the coffin. "Let him thank me, that holp to send him thither, for he was fitter for that place than earth."

To which Lady Anne replied quickly, "And thou unfit for any place but hell."

"Yes, one place else, if you will hear me name it."

"Some dungeon."

"Your bed-chamber."

That stopped her but only for a moment. Soon she was saying, "I would I were to be avenged on thee."

"It is a quarrel most unnatural, to be revenged on him that loveth thee." Cheney reached across the bier to her, but she drew back.

"It is a quarrel just and reasonable," she replied,

trembling, "to be revenged on him that killed my husband."

But Richard was silky. "He that bereft thee, lady, of thy husband did it to help thee to a better husband."

"His better doth not breathe upon the earth."

Richard turned away from her, giving her his back. Cheney had not done that before. This was new territory for him too. Neither of them was quite in control. But Cheney maintained the familiar, cocky tone. "He lives that loves thee better than he could."

"Name him." A brisk order.

"Plantagenet."

That was her husband's name. What was this? Was Richard playing with her? Was her husband not, in fact, dead? "Why, that was he." She relaxed some, and it showed in her body. That was her mistake.

"The self-same name . . ." He still had his back to her. He was in no hurry. ". . . But one of better nature."

Was her husband back from the dead? Resurrected? Was she to have a life again? She resisted the urge to step closer. "Where is he?"

He faced her, smiling. But the smile on that face was wrong, and he was practically ugly at last because of it. "Here," he said, meaning, I am a more accomplished lover than your husband whom I killed.

The script required that the actress spit at him then, and so Reah did. But she drew back from her act immediately, as if it terrified her.

Richard stood before her with her spittle on his cheek. He said nothing. He let his eyes fall to her breasts, the oldest view there is, and it excited him. He had stopped breathing. He felt a desire so great that Shakespeare's silence could barely contain it. He knew that she wanted him as much as he did her.

As he brought his eyes up again, he moved his face the few inches to touch her. That seemed peculiar to Anne until she realized that he was rubbing the spittle from his face back onto hers. He did so artfully, touching her only on the cheek with his cheek, but so erotically it was as if he had trailed his tongue all over her. She trembled, and he knew he had her.

In the part of himself that was watching his work, Cheney was pleased. His move had been the perfect adaptation. It heightened the sensuality of their encounter and made it impossible for her to resist him. When had sex ever seemed so vile or so inviting? He could take her, he thought, right there, on the coffin of her husband's father.

Richard said, "Never came poison from so sweet a place."

For a moment Reah could not remember her line and she began to panic. The spittle trickled into the corner of her mouth. It was her own, but the taste of it reminded her of his sperm, and that detail gave her not only her line but the emotion it required. "Never hung poison on a fouler toad!" And then with her first true spontaneity as the princess, she spat at him again, this time directly in his eye.

Cheney grabbed her arm, but he was stunned. The bitch surprised him. Toad? What did she say, Toad?

He pulled her toward him, but she resisted. She did not want to step onto Pronto's stain, but he forced her. "Goddamnit," he screamed. "Why not?"

"Because," Eddie said calmly and slowly, "the fucking dog is yours. The child is mine."

First, he looked at her without hatred, with no display of feeling.

Second, he brought his free arm up and slowly swung it at her. He remembered the high-pitched animal noise she made even before he struck. He remembered the sting in his hand and that memory, that sense of his own burning palm and fingers, unleashed the flood. He hit her again, even while holding her and preventing her escape. At last a vivid, immediate, total recall of that instant transformed him. His desire was simple and overwhelming, not to hurt her, but to kill her. He hit her again, the most fearsome blow yet. She would have fallen, but he held her upright for the next one. He was going to kill her with his hands. He had no idea how many times he struck her.

"Stop! Stop, you two!" the voice called, the most familiar voice in Cheney's head. He froze.

Cheney checked himself and turned downstage. He did not expect to see Bren at the staircase in the living room because he knew where he was. He was creating the physical body of his role. He had his finger on the pulsing blood of Richard III. He had not snapped. He was working from an aroused emotion back to its stimulus, its root, and he had found it. He had freed it, the exact truth. Exhilaration surged through him, even as his rage subsided. When an actor applies an intense past emotion from his own life to a character he enacts on stage it is a creation, not a madness.

Reah was looking at him with horror. In the part of himself watching, he thought perhaps they should stop so that he could explain to her that this was what made stage different from film, that it was the business of the theater to be dangerous. He wondered if she was hurt. He knew he had hit her awfully hard. The moment had taken him by surprise too. He wanted to reassure her that he would refine it next time, apply stagecraft to the actual blows.

But before he could, she went on, nobly, he thought, as Lady Anne. "Out of my sight! Thou dost infect my eyes!"

He let go of her arm and stepped back to admire her, but then it was her hatred that lay tangibly between them, like that coffin, like that stain. Even her hatred moved him. Its intensity matched his and it made them one. He took the dagger from his belt and handed it to her. Yes, he killed the king. And yes, he killed her husband. And then he told her what should have ruined her, that he did so because of her beauty and his love for her. He, the most despicable of creatures, was preparing her to betray her husband. Anne hated Richard but she also wanted him, and both knew it. "This hand, which for thy love did kill thy love, shall for thy love kill a far truer love."

Then he took off his shirt and drew close to her to offer her—her blade—his bare chest. Very quietly and gravely he said, "I lay me naked to your deadly stroke and humbly beg for death upon my knee."

Cheney knelt. He had arrived at Richard's truth—this bastard played for keeps, would risk anything—had arrived at it gradually, logically, by the force of his own will. He had stretched his creative powers to the utmost and was at the height of his own talent. Cheney felt his own triumph. He could barely contain it within the role, and he knew again why he was an actor. As Richard, he was now ready for anything.

According to the script Lady Anne was to raise the dagger to strike, but find herself unable to.

But this Lady Anne had never breathed before. The script counted for nothing. She did not hesitate. No sooner had Richard's knee touched the floor than she struck at him over the corpse, slashing at his face, the blade just missing his eyes by inches. She pulled back and gathered strength and lunged at him. Two can intend to kill.

An actor does only what is necessary, no more, no less.

Cheney moved slightly and therefore lived.

He caught her hand and bent it back until it seemed about to snap and only then did she drop the dagger. He picked it up and held it at her face.

When he had let go of Eddie in the living room, having been saved by the child's cry from committing murder, he did not know what to say. He had stood before her mute, stupid. He could have used Shakespeare.

"Take up the sword, you bitch," he said, "or take up me."

She could have spat at him again, but didn't. She kissed him. He was a brute, an animal, a monster. She kissed him passionately because she was like him. Therefore when he offered his ring as his response to her kiss, she accepted it. It sealed their union.

When she went off, indifferent now to the burial of the king—she did not give the corpse a further glance—it was to Richard's chamber that she was going. She was not going there to be defiled—that had just happened—but to be annihilated. She walked upright, in full possession of her dignity, as if to hand oneself over to despair incarnate were the most natural thing in the world. She walked offstage like that, admirably, to Richard's bed. She might have been walking to the block.

Richard watched her go and wondered, not smugly, "Was ever woman in this humour wooed? Was ever woman in this humour won?" He looked after her with triumph and with sadness. There was no virtue in the world. He wanted her less now that she had surrendered to him. But, alas, one must eat what oysters one has opened. He picked up his shirt and followed her, but he hesitated before exiting when he saw his shadow, saw the slight lurch in his gait. One shoulder was higher than the other, and his head was at the barest angle to his chest. The transformation of his body had begun.

Garvey and the cast did not applaud them. They sat and watched the empty set in silence. They knew something unprecedented had happened, something dangerous and ugly. They were the theater, though, and they would forgive anything if it worked on stage.

CHAPTER 4

The sun is too hot already for this nonsense, she thought, slamming one foot down in front of the other. She had to complete one and a half more circuits of the reservoir and would easily if she could just keep her mind out of it. Her body devoured the exercise. But her mind had its own opinion. Eddie frankly hated the idea of herself as a jogger. She was not a health enthusiast, wouldn't think of downing Perrier and made a point never to discuss the fact of her running. She had only been doing it since she'd returned to New York, as a way of getting a jump on her days, which she was now spending at her desk. Writers never move except to make their coffee and urinate, and that was the simple problem to which running daily in Central Park was addressed.

And so, even in such mugginess, it was awake at eight, untie the sheets, her sleeping partners, and fumble into gym shorts, bra, T-shirt and Pumas without socks. Hit the sidewalk moving, making for the Park, following the cinder bridle path from the Tavern-on-the-Green to the track around the reservoir. Once around that lake was a mile and six-tenths. Three laps plus yardage to and from West Seventieth Street made more than five. In her next life, she told herself, she would still start her days running, but she would be the only one who did so. It was typical of Eddie that she could both jog and disdain all joggers. She wouldn't have thought of doing it but for the pleasure she took in the rigor of the thing, in the pain of it. She was twenty-eight and pleased after too long a period of physical inertia to be back on speaking terms with her body.

It irked her to feel on display when she ran, and that feeling was new. Men in New York felt free to stare at her breasts then. It was her theory that some creeps ran around the reservoir the wrong way, counterclockwise, exactly to leer at the bouncing women runners who, docile, invariably took it clockwise. She'd considered thwarting the oglers by running counterclockwise too, but men who stare at breasts would stare at buttocks, even hers. She wasn't going to adjust her routine for them. Sometimes she could hear runners slowing down to fall into step behind her, and she knew they were seeing her naked. In Los Angeles men rarely looked lewdly at women, but that was because women in L.A. were everywhere and always on display. Flesh was the trees of the place. Southern California's creeps ogled themselves, not runners. One could feel utterly alone and unnoticed in almost any situation out there; the advantage to West Coast life, and the agony. Once Eddie had thought herself a passably attractive woman. Five years in nymph city had left her feeling plain and, on some days, ugly. But still she hated it when men leered at her.

She could hear a man behind her now. She had the feeling that he was the one who'd eyed her as he passed, stimulating these thoughts, and that he'd come about to run at her pace about ten yards back.

But that was silly. They were not bold. Men who leered openly were harmless. They were insulting, infuriating, demeaning, demented, but harmless. The people who hurt you sneak up on you. You never see them. Was he drawing nearer? He seemed not to be. She slowed her pace a bit to get him to pass, and even as she did so she chided herself for letting him bother her.

New York took getting used to again. The city made her feel continually defensive and vulnerable, which bothered her because she'd grown up there. She had looked forward to watching Bren shed the timorousness of a chauffeured suburban kid for the cocky nerve of a city boy who insists on taking the subway to school alone. Not that one ignores the dangers, but that one is not paralyzed by them. One uses Central Park all day long, for example, but goes nowhere near it, not even in a taxi, after dusk. One jogs in one's T-shirt and running shorts with her thighs exposed—her legs, including her thighs, are her only terrific feature—but she lets her eye meet no one else's. If a man is running too close behind and one begins to worry, one slows down and lets him pass.

But he was not passing.

She considered her options. She was just going by the elaborate Victorian pump house at the uptown end of the reservoir. Ordinarily that was her favorite part of the track because there, as she turned with the oval, the midtown skyline came back into view and she still savored everytime a thrill at seeing it. But the track at that point was bordered by a tangle of shrubs and trees, and it was remote from streets or playing fields. There were no other joggers nearby.

The rhythm of the footfalls behind matched hers exactly. She could not risk stopping, not there. She could not risk slowing further. She was trying to remember how big he was, but couldn't. The easiest thing in the world would have been to conjure up a vivid picture of him dragging her into the bushes and flashing first his knife, then his prick. She forced herself not to think of it. She could taste panic, that brown nausea, the first small wave of it lapping her throat. She pushed it back. She was strong, she told herself, and smart and had her wits.

She poured it on suddenly. She ran, thinking, Run like a breed of animal! Run, puma, run! A puma is a cat, she recited to herself, tawny brown in color, without spots, found from Canada to Patagonia. It is called also panther, catamount, cougar and mountain lion. If it has an escape route it will, when challenged, take it. But it is known for its cunning, the wisest of all cats, and it will not, unless coerced, settle in New York City, or take exercise in Central Park.

She could hear the man behind her. He was sprinting too. It was not her imagination now. There was a perverse relief in having confirmed that the creep was after her. She found a real, physical threat less intimidating than unfounded, paranoiac fears. Better to be mugged occasionally than send out for groceries or ride an exercise bike at home.

Only a hundred yards ahead the shrubbery fell away and the landscape assumed a more tailored character at the promenade to tidy Fifth Avenue. Her head was humming with the spasms of her effort. It seemed to her she was running very fast. Perhaps he couldn't catch her even if he wanted to. Perspiration streamed into the corners of her mouth. She liked its taste because she took it as a sign that her body was coming through for her. For once her body, not her mind.

She drew even with the promenade that led to the very avenue on which, a dozen blocks down, her mother lived. That recognition gave the turf suddenly the old mystical edge in her favor. She needed all the edge she could get. Her left side was splitting with pain. She had sprinted full out for nearly three hundred yards. She was going to have to stop.

A pair of joggers were approaching from ahead. The man behind her was still coming fast. She slowed and could hear him breathing. It sounded, as disembodied breathing does, obscene. Her anger had pushed back her fear. She could stop abruptly, turn, and wave her finger in his face. She could kick him in the groin. She could curse him. But those are things done on impulse, not reflection; it was too late.

A middle-aged couple drew abreast of her from the opposite direction, wrong-way runners but accidental ones, a short man who resembled Frank Perdue, and his wife, who looked like his Marie. They both wore garish yellow T-shirts with the word *Cancun* emblazoned over a setting sun. They showed their surprise when she greeted them as if they were neighbors of her mother's, but they greeted her back, as people do, and made room for her when she changed directions and slid into stride between them.

She did not look directly at her antagonist as they passed him, but she observed him acutely with her peripheral vision and was able to size him up quickly. He was just shorter than she was, perhaps five-seven. He was wearing a bright Hawaiian shirt and baggy trousers, but with sneakers. A dubious jogger. He was terribly winded and seemed to be halting. He was raven-haired and dark-complexioned, an Hispanic. Why couldn't he have been white? She hated the ease with which New York inflamed her racist feelings.

He was staring openly at her and she knew it, but she jogged along with Frank and Marie and tried to chat with them, though she could hardly breathe. Having laid eyes on the man, she found it impossible to think of him as a mere creep or of herself as some kind of mountain lion. How relieved she was that she had not tried to take him on and grateful that the couple seemed not to mind her presumption in joining them. She did not look back until they'd rounded the northeast turn to approach the pump house. No one was behind them. She strained to look all along the track. There was no sign of the man anywhere. She said goodbye to the couple and slowed at last to a walk. They waved at her and pressed on. After walking a tenth of a lap she stopped and leaned against the chain-link fence, hooking her fingers through it, and staring at the jagged skyline. New York, she said to herself, panting—catamount, eh?—New York.

Usually after her laps she jogged casually back to Seventy-second Street and then walked the last two blocks, but not that day. She was drained. Her legs shook, her hands trembled in the chain links and her chest heaved for breath. She remembered watching the boys at football practice in high school vomiting on the track after wind sprints. At the time it had seemed just another of the ways in which boys were crude.

As she recovered herself and began to walk, she realized that despite her exhaustion, she had still taken pleasure in the efficiency of her body. It had rescued her, and that seemed suddenly an unexpected inner landmark from which to get her bearings. She was not an innocent anymore. She was a survivor. It takes courage to value one's life from the inside, and that, it seemed to her, was what she was finally beginning to do.

The decisive act of leaving California had given her a claim, she was beginning to realize, on that courage and perhaps on a kind of wisdom. Her marriage had been a crushing defeat. She wished she could dismiss it as a mere blunder, as if, confusing flair with beauty and romance with love, she had wasted only her senior year and not half a decade. And it was a loss of more than time, of course.

She had loved her husband with a shocking intensity of feeling which, she could admit, had not faded. It underwrote her resentment of him now. Life with Cheney had cost her her self-confidence and her belief in her own gifts. Though hard to remember, in the beginning it had seemed the reverse of that. He rescued her from the shadow that Brendan's death had cast on her. Grief can stop even a young life cold in its tracks. It had taken a Cheney McCoy to get her going again, and she loved him for saving her. But a Cheney McCoy casts a shadow too, a colder one, a more deadly one than young widowhood, because a Cheney McCoy promises life to the full, then leaves you empty.

She had left him. She was on safer ground now, her own turf. Next time he called, she decided, she would talk to him. She would meet him for lunch, even. She would be friendly as hell. Bren was safely away. Soon she would be legally a resident of New York again,

and Cheney would not be able to touch her. Therefore they could be adults with each other. She was
ready to deal with him. Bring on the swaggering, ur-
ban punks, she thought, with their antenna-whips
and switchblades and surly looks and filthy mouths.
They don't threaten me. I've gone my rounds with
the champ.

South of the Delacorte Theater she saw the man
again. She recognized his Hawaiian shirt. He was in
front of her with his back to her and seemed oblivious that she was coming.

She immediately cut across the grass toward the
path that led out of the Park. She knew that she
could not go directly to her apartment if there was
even the slightest chance of his following. She had to
get to Central Park West. This time, if she let her
panic in at all, it was going to destroy her. She
maintained absolute control over every muscle. She
didn't run. He was still faced away at a distance of
about fifty yards. She watched him as she walked. She
felt a new flow of perspiration in the palms of her
hands, but she took that now as a sign that her body
was getting ready again for what it had to do.

She was nearly at the street when he turned. He
showed no sign of recognition or surprise as he
started running toward her, which meant that he'd
known she was coming. He was wily and coy.

She crossed from the Park to the sidewalk a minute
before he did and went directly to the nearest parked
auto. As if she'd done it a dozen times before, she
snapped the car's antenna off with her two hands and
turned on him.

He stopped short. "Hey, baby," he said, holding his

hands up in front of him, "I only wanted to ask you something."

What struck her were those hands, how long and thin they were and how they shook, and his eyes, which were placid and friendly despite his obvious agitation. That incongruity made her understand he was extremely dangerous. She pointed the tip of the antenna at his face and held her ground. She resolved to conform to the picture in her mind of how this was done.

"Hey, no shit, baby, I just wanted, you know, to talk with you." He took a small step back. That was his mistake.

She picked that step up, moving at him. "Talk with me?" she said, slowly, scornfully. "The idea of talking with you would never have occurred to me. I never knew that scummy, maggot-eating rodents like you could talk." The man sucked back from her and she followed. "I thought all you could do was crawl around other people's garbage. Why aren't you hanging around the bushes waiting for some old bum with no legs to come along on his board, huh? So you could jump him for his wine, isn't that right? Or the cork from his last bottle so you could suck on it. You made a mistake this time, scum-bag! You know what you got? You loser! You asshole! You got yourself the New York City Police Special Decoy Squad and you are fucking under arrest. Get your hands onto that wall!" At that she lunged at him, pushing his left shoulder so that he fell against the waist-high wall that separated the street from the Park. He leaned over it with his back to her.

"Hey, man," he whined. "I didn't do nothing."

"Shut up, mother-fuck!" She slapped at his pockets,

pretending to search, but if he'd had a weapon he'd have never taken that first half-step away from her. "Now you wait here while I call for the cage on wheels. If you move a muscle I'll kill your ass. You hear, mother-fuck?"

He didn't answer.

She garroted him with the antenna and choked him sharply. "I asked you, you hear, mother-fuck?"

He nodded vigorously.

She let him go, turned and walked across the street through traffic. Half a dozen people had been watching. She ignored them. When she reached the far curb she turned back and he was gone.

Now she should collapse in tears, get hysterical, scream for help? No.

She saw a flash of the guy's shirt as he tore across the Park, and she felt sorry for him. She swatted absently at her leg with the antenna.

The antenna. She looked at it. Where had she learned that? *Kojak?* All those evenings alone at home, babysitting Bren while watching cops push punks up against walls. Angie Dickinson, Jesus Christ, *Policewoman.* She swatted at her leg again, still watching the bastard run—*Hawaii Five-O*—until he dropped over a hill. And then it hit her, what she'd done. *Mano a mano* she'd whipped him with the curl of her own wit, snapped that metal rod with her hands, snapped the mother-fucker's cocky nerve in two. Where had that come from, not the trick, but the will? The vitality? The surge of power?

When Cheney had beaten her that night in May, she had simply taken it from him. That outburst of his, its cruelty, its violence at long last, and how it spilled over onto Bren, was what enabled her to leave him. She knew that she would do anything to protect her son. What she didn't know until now was that she could so briskly protect herself.

She thought of running after the bastard, to thank him.

Instead she walked the half-block down to Seventy-second Street to the neighborhood grocery where she bought her paper on the way home each morning.

"Johnny!" she said loudly, entering the store. It was out of character for her to attract notice to herself. The small old man at the register always responded kindly to her shy greetings, and now he displayed his surprise to be hailed so boldly and by her. "Guess what I just did!"

"Stole an antenna."

Eddie waved it. "That's right. I beat off a mugger."

"A mugger! Girl, you all right?"

"Never better, Johnny." Eddie knew that her expansiveness depended not only on the adrenaline rush, but on the shopkeeper's being, in fact, a stranger. "I need twenty bucks. Can you give me twenty on account?"

"Am I a bank?" he said, but he opened the drawer.

"I owe the guy," she said, gesturing with the antenna.

"Give him ten." He handed her a ten-dollar bill.

"No, twenty, Johnny. He saved my life." In more ways than one, she thought. When had she last scored such a victory? God, she felt good. The old man gave her twenty and an envelope, on which she wrote, "You saved my life. Thanks."

She went back to the car off which she'd snapped the thing, left the envelope under the wiper and then jogged home, carrying the antenna as if it were the Olympic torch.

Her plan was to keep moving. She was going to shower, shave her legs, wash her hair, put on her beach robe, make some coffee, take it to her table, sit and start writing. What juices she had going! With Bren in Maine nothing would distract her. She had been slugging away since June on her novel, an old-fashioned romance about a love affair between a soldier and a schoolgirl who marry in a fit of passion just before he ships out to a war from which he will not return. A novel, of course, about Brendan, and her decision to write it had been a deliberate one. What better way to recover from Cheney than to recapture an image of the person she had been before she'd needed him or even met him? If she returned in her imagination to what was unfinished about her first marriage, perhaps it would enable her to finish with her second.

In the shower Eddie lathered herself, humming something from Richard Rodgers, and tried to clear her mind to write. But it was Cheney she kept thinking of, not Brendan. Cheney still governed her. Brendan was long gone, a vague figment. But that was why she could write about him. Ironically, her second novel was supposed to save her from Cheney; her first had been the occasion of their meeting. Even while she hummed the show tune, she pictured the Warner lot where they'd met for the first time during a break in the shooting of *Quick Study*.

"So you're Tammy Holt," he said when they were introduced. Tammy Holt was Eddie's heroine, a Sarah Lawrence girl who fell in love with a failed playwright and ghost-wrote a play for him. When it turned out to be a smash hit on Broadway, his success ruined their affair.

"No," she said, "unless you're Roland Barry." In those days she had taken to thinking of herself as Françoise Sagan; that youth, that great success, that air of a tragic past.

"But," he said, still holding their handshake, "you went to Sarah Lawrence and you write like her and you're too young to be so talented."

Eddie blushed. All true. She tried to pretend that his flattery was not pleasing to her. He was Cheney McCoy, after all. "But are you selfish and despairing?"

She shuddered in the shower to remember that she had put such a question to him, and playfully. She remembered his reply. "Is that how you see the bloke? I wondered."

"I see him as a Roland," she'd said. "Rolands are Ronalds who can't spell."

It amused Eddie to recall what value she'd put in those days on smart talk. She'd lost her knack for it completely, and didn't know whether that was a sign of maturity or just another one of the ways in which he had demoralized her. Had she quit writing because of him too, or was that because of her baby? She'd written *Quick Study* while she was pregnant. Her escape into that fictional Manhattan romance had enabled her to cope with the news from Vietnam. When Bren was born she'd wanted to do nothing but take care of him. When she married Cheney and moved West she slid into a life of ease the decadence of which she didn't recognize until it was all she had.

Since leaving Cheney she found that her most frequent thoughts of him were of their beginning. One memory in particular was like a wound now that their marriage was over. She tried to deflect it by turning the shower fully on cold, but when she looked at the nozzle shooting water down on her she saw it as the propeller of his Cessna.

They were flying low over the desert. She had resisted his blatant overtures up till then, but, when a labor dispute on another film shut the lot down, she agreed to an afternoon outing with him because she'd never flown in a small plane. She liked the way the plane seemed to ride with the wind, not over it, and she liked, despite her reserve, being in the cramped cockpit with him. She had not been with a man since Brendan, nearly two years.

"I want to show you something," he said, and then pushed the plane over in a sharp dive that frightened her. But the poise with which he landed it on the flat rock edge of a desert plateau reassured her. She complimented his skill, and he told her that he'd learned to fly from his father, who'd been a bush pilot. When they dismounted, the heat which blasted them was suffocating, and the vast desert terrain disoriented her. She let him take her hand and lead her to the edge of the plateau, a cliff hundreds of feet high overlooking miles of red clay and mauve fingers of sand knuckled here and there by arroyos and buttes.

"It's beautiful," she said. The vistas of the Southwest always rendered her breathless.

"It is," he replied, "but that's not why I brought you out here."

He stooped with his back to the view and began to

gather the spiny desert shrubs into a small pile. He spoke solemnly, reassuring her and instructing her. "This was a sacred mountain to the Apache. They were nomads, but they had their holy places. They believed they could commune with the spirit world from a height like this, so squaws from camps hundreds of miles away came here on pilgrimage when their braves were killed in battle." Cheney did not look at her as he said this. He finished preparing the brush in silence, then he faced her and said, "The smoke from the fires they built bore messages to the spirits of their dead husbands."

Eddie would always remember the difficulty with which she asked him, "What messages?"

"One of two. To prepare for her coming to the spirit world to be with him." Cheney let his eyes drift out over the desert. Those women threw themselves from the cliff.

"Or, to commend his spirit into the care of the Great One. The smoke bade her love farewell." Those women turned their backs on the cliff and lived.

Cheney's simple statement of those alternatives made Eddie see them clearly for the first time as her own. Of course she knew what he was doing, but it moved her that he, a stranger, should understand. "How did you know?" she asked.

"About your husband?"

She shook her head. "About me."

Eddie was acutely aware of Cheney's celebrity status. It humiliated her to be impressed by it, but she was. That a famous movie star should have informed himself about her made Eddie feel a gratitude which toward anyone else would have been exaggerated.

Cheney struck his lighter. It flamed and he handed it to her. From anyone else such an initiative would have been insultingly presumptuous. From Cheney McCoy it was profoundly stirring, as if his very fame freed her to respond to him.

Eddie stooped and lit the brush, liturgically, as if it were a pyre. In a way it was. Eddie had never seen Brendan's body or burned it or buried it. She stepped back as the fire caught and watched the smoke curl away in the soft wind.

The memory of that moment could embarrass her, because it seemed in hindsight a glib gesture, a too easy one, all out of proportion with the long burden of her loneliness. In her time as a young war widow she had avoided her grief first by the dream exercise of her trendy novel, then by the joyous routine of caring for her baby. Now this stranger was facing her with the choice she had yet to make. Admit her grief and let it go, or throw herself from the cliff like those Indian women. A simple choice, a direct one. Later Cheney would claim as an actor to be a connoisseur of choices. His rule: live directly or die.

Eddie turned to him and said sadly, "I loved him very much. It's been hard to say goodbye."

He touched her cheek. "Your faithfulness and loyalty are beautiful to me." Had he always known her?

It was the most natural thing in the world to go into his arms. In his eyes she was neither the tragic heroine her family wanted to protect nor the slick first novelist her publishers were promoting. In his eyes she was, she sensed, the woman she wanted to be.

It was utterly unexpected. A few days on the West Coast to watch them film her book had become the occasion of her life's beginning again. She had expected Cheney McCoy to be a movie star whose polished surfaces she would instinctively distrust, but she found herself enthralled by him. She was as bowled over by his fame as anyone, but also he was a strong, kind man who knew exactly how to touch her.

She remembered quite distinctly the details of that, their first lovemaking, the odor of the smoldering mesquite nearby, the wind blowing tiny sand flecks against her naked body, his body muscled and gleaming with perspiration. The warmth of his skin as he lowered himself on her released her lust. Not since she was a virgin had sex seemed so exquisitely full of promise, but he moved slowly. Before coming inside her he traced with his two forefingers the lines of each feature of her face, and she felt that tracking so intensely that it seemed to her each nerve and vessel and pore and secret had opened itself to him. Her eyes and nose and mouth and chin and facial bones had never seemed so beautiful to her. Later she would love him for himself, his prodigal generosity of body and soul, as still later she would hate him for it. But that day she loved him only for his perfect rescue of her capacity for desire. Cheney brought her with him to a height from which, though they leapt repeatedly, she did not seem to fall for a long time.

The pulsing water-jets had both lulled her and sharpened the pleasure of her victory over the Central Park mugger. She was ready even for Cheney, and her memory of their beginning helped her feel almost benign toward him.

But then instead of water she felt the sting of his blows on her face as if it were happening again. His violence at the end was the perfect counterpoint to his initial, almost psychic sensitivity. His violence was what broke her inertia. When she woke the day after he beat her up—the harshness of that description fitted her mood—she found that he had taken Bren away. She understood then, for the first time, that Cheney could hurt her only through her son. That was when she resolved to leave. By the time Cheney returned with Bren that night it did not matter that they had been to Disneyland or that they'd brought her Crackerjacks.

The phone rang and from the shower its bell sounded as if it were ringing in someone else's apartment. She wished it were. She turned the shower off and listened to the phone ring again. She forced herself to think. Perhaps it was Barney, her agent, calling from California with news of the movie deal. It made Eddie nervous to have him selling the option before she'd written the book. She didn't want the writing of her story to be corrupted by the selling of it and would have refused to discuss the negotiations with Barney, but for one thing. She had instructed him to insert as an explicit condition of sale that the actor Cheney McCoy would have no part in the film version of her novel. Her nightmare was that Cheney would avenge himself on her by landing the role of the character based on Brendan. Barney thought she was being paranoid, but she'd insisted that he call her at each point in the negotiation.

She walked into her living room without bothering to dry herself or put her robe on. The phone rang a third time as she approached it, and she heard her answer machine click on. As if that were a click in her mind, she froze. It couldn't be Barney; on the Coast it was only five A.M. Perhaps it was Cranston, her best friend. Her roommate at college, Cranston was so glad to have her back in New York that she called practically every other day from Port Washington, where she lived in a fieldstone ranch with a broker husband and three babies so contentedly it was shocking. It bothered Eddie to have become one of those people who were unnerved by the happiness of their old friends. But Cranston never called in the morning.

It had to be Cheney.

Eddie listened to the recording of her own voice announcing her number and inviting a message after the beep. She listened to the beep. And then she heard not Cranston and not Barney and not Cheney, but a tinny, strange version of her mother asking her to call immediately.

Eddie broke in on her before she disconnected.

"Hi, what's up?"

"Cheney called."

"When?"

"Just now, a little while ago."

"What did he want?"

"I'm not sure. I didn't talk to him."

"Bren talked to him? You let Bren talk to him?"

"Sweetheart, he answered the phone. I thought it was you."

"I only call at night, Mother. I work in the morning. You know that."

"Did I disturb you? I'm sorry."

"Of course you disturbed me. What did he say?"

"It won't help for you to be angry. Calm down. Nothing has happened."

"How did he find out Bren is there?"

"I don't know."

"Is he coming up?"

"He didn't say that. Sweetheart, there's no reason for you to be agitated."

"The point is, I didn't want Cheney talking to him or seeing him, and the lawyer said if Cheney took him there's nothing I can do here until the court sets the hearing, and even then, since his countersuit's in California . . . Damnit, I'm not even a legal resident in my own state and won't be for months, and he can do anything he wants with Bren if he gets him."

"Calm down, Edna. Listen to me. I only wanted to tell you Cheney called. He talked to Bren for five minutes about the Yankees and the World Series."

"What about the World Series?"

"I don't know. What does a father say to his son about the . . . ?"

"Cheney is not Bren's father! Please!"

"I'm sorry. Of course he isn't."

"And what he says is a promise he'll take him to it. Is that what he said? He'll take him to the Series?"

"Yes. I think so."

"I'm coming up."

"Edna, sweetheart, the World Series isn't for months. You shouldn't . . ."

"I'll try to catch the afternoon plane from Logan."

"The last ferry's at four."

"Then I *will* make that plane. Pick me up, all right? And bring Bren. Don't leave him there alone."

"Of course."

"See you later."

"Goodbye, dear. Don't worry."

Eddie was crushed. The son of a bitch had destroyed her buoyant mood by means of a simple phone call, and not even to her. She leaned on the phone after hanging it up as if to push that news backward through its wires. Paranoid? Of course she was. That was no mugger in Central Park but an aging hippie, a shit-faced panhandler. Where was his weapon? How exactly had he threatened her? She could hear cops laughing at her, snickering. Likewise Cheney. He was no more going to Maine to kidnap Bren than the Russians were. Eddie was at the mercy of her figments, but utterly. Admitting it did nothing for her. She turned away from the phone table and toward that quite familiar contempt for herself from which, now, the morning's hopeful energy seemed a pathetic lapse.

She saw herself in the mirror over the oval table on which she and Bren ate their meals. The image of her body, still beaded with water, appeared to her neither athletic nor womanly nor possessed of any dignity or charm whatsoever. Her breasts were small and her skin was pale and her face drawn. She was far too thin. How could she ever have expected that body to hold a man's attention? How would it ever again? Her life with Cheney, despite its beginning, had turned into one long physical humiliation, beginning with his great lie that she was beautiful, stunning, a marvel to behold. He had waited for her to believe him fully before he began to undermine her illusion. His increasingly blatant affairs with other women had offended her not because of her notions about fidelity in marriage—hers were conventional, but loosely held—but because they made her feel sexually and physically unworthy, not only of Cheney but of the world he had introduced her to. In California women are only enemies to each other, and Eddie could feel defeated even by the brainless nymphs who displayed themselves at swimming pools.

Now the memory of their lovemaking on the cliff above the desert was a rebuke. She touched her face the way he had, with her two forefingers, tracing each feature. But then she remembered, against her will, the other time she'd watched him do that. It was on a movie set and he was naked, gleaming not with perspiration, but glycerine, courtesy of makeup. He displayed his sensitivity and kindness, but toward some actress, not her. With what awful recognition had she seen those moves of his, even craning through the crowd of technicians and cameramen and script girls and errand boys, beneath the glare of lights, amid the crush of equipment and the tangle of wires. She'd been under the mistaken impression that they closed the set for sex scenes, and wondered at first if Cheney's exhibitionism was what shocked and angered her. Or was it that he did in public and to another woman the very things he'd done to her? She'd thought of those gestures, his tracing of features, as a treasure of her own, like cherished valentines. If she considered them sacred and private, why shouldn't he? But she knew why. Everything, even the sacred and the private, was at the service of his art. But that could not justify the violation she felt, the abuse, the betrayal. She watched carefully as he touched that woman and kissed her and mounted her.

In some part of herself she was convinced by what he did, and impressed. He deserved to be celebrated. He was good, but her capacity to admire his work was obliterated. Far from mere jealousy, Eddie's clear, strong emotion came from her sudden understanding that she had made a terrible mistake. She was in the wrong world with the wrong man. She was wrong ever to have trusted him, his gestures, his kindnesses. Not that they were false, exactly, or that he was maliciously deceiving her in, for example, making up the business about the Indian women communing with the spirits of their warrior husbands—and certainly he had made it up—but that he was so utterly dedicated to artifice that when he achieved it, it became all the reality and all the truth he needed. He would not understand her problem. More mattered to her than epiphanies, and she was certain that some things between men and women should never be exploited, even for art. As that actress had begun to enact her orgasm—she was good at it, but so were hookers— Eddie turned and left the set knowing that one day, with the same numb horror, she would leave Cheney.

Eddie dressed quickly because she wanted to get going, but also because the sight of her naked body in the mirror had so depressed her. She put on sandals, jeans and a red cotton shirt, packed a bag and then started for her work table. But she stopped and looked about the room, remembering the day years before when she'd found the apartment. She could recall a wedge of sunlight falling across the floor and remembered taking it as a sign of welcome. She could recall the shimmering lace pattern of the shadow from a locust tree in the courtyard, how it overlaid

the sunlight at an angle. It struck her suddenly that
the locust tree was gone; until then its absence had
not registered. She crossed to the window that opened
onto the rear. She looked for a stump of that tree but
where it should have been was a brick patio with an
arrangement of black wrought-iron furniture. The
West Seventies were coming into their own.

Eddie was disappointed in herself that she had not
noticed the tree's disappearance and remained there,
as in penance, musing for a moment. Locust trees,
they say, are splendid city trees. They shoot up in va-
cant lots and corners, grow fast, slim and tall, make
the most of what sunlight the buildings don't block,
cast delicate, filtering shadows of their own, shower
the bricks and decks with green rain early each spring
for twenty-five years or so, then die and are cut down
and removed with little trouble while you are out of
town or at Bloomingdale's. They are companions,
meanwhile, which require nothing, not tending, not
pruning, not feeding, not space really or even much
in the way of soil, and they lack elaborate muscular
roots to disturb the cellar walls. Not trees, at all, but
saints. They are the way people expect each other to
be but never are. I should have married that tree, she
thought.

There are eight million stories in the naked city,
and as many burglars. It was just as well the tree was
gone. Nobody could climb up it now into her place.
Her refuge, her sanctuary.

How Cheney had complained periodically what a
waste of rent it was. They hadn't used it when they
came to New York, because he preferred hotels. She
knew he regarded the apartment as a symbol of what
she withheld from him. She always denied it and

stopped even visiting the place from their hotel, but she never thought for a moment of giving in to him and letting it go. Now she understood why.

Ironically she had exercised no such caution in relation to Cheney when it came to her son. She had kept her New York apartment and its phone in her own name, but had joyfully stood by a year after they were married while her three-year-old took the name McCoy.

Her mistake had dawned on her slowly, and for several reasons. The more of a person Bren became, the more she understood that he was not coin with which to repay her debt to Cheney. She could not "give" one human being to another, even in that benign way. In California, people passed each other around like hors d'oeuvres, and it horrified Eddie to think she had done something similar with her son.

But it didn't matter anymore. Her job now was to protect Bren from Cheney's revenge. She understood it too well; since she had begun by using her child to repay Cheney, why shouldn't he end by using Bren to repay her?

There was no sanctuary from these feelings. The safety of her rooms meant nothing. Eddie called the limousine company. Then while she waited for the car she sat at her table and stared at the pages of her manuscript. She had written an entire chapter in a week. It had released her to have Bren away and it made her feel guilty to admit it.

Maybe she shouldn't go to Maine? What if she called the Actors' Studio and asked for Cheney and challenged him directly? Was going off in a rush like this insane? Her mother thought so. Would Cheney McCoy just walk out on rehearsals of *Richard III*?

But Eddie knew he would if it suited him to. He would do anything. She could predict exactly nothing of his behavior, and that was what made her vulnerable. She felt a rush of the old helplessness. That morning's exhilarated triumph was gone completely.

She forced herself to read the top page of her manuscript again, a description of the army post in Alabama to which, in a fit of passion, her book's young woman had followed her man. Eddie took a Flair pen and, simply to counteract her inertia, changed two words and was about to write a new line when she remembered Barney. He was going to call, and at her insistence. She had to be certain he got that clause in the agreemnt. She had to protect everything from Cheney.

She went to the phone and recorded a message on the answering machine and then, as she finished, the doorbell rang. The limousine.

She looked at her manuscript and panicked. She had not intended to bring it. Her only copy, it represented the one act of will she'd been able to sustain. Not only was it subject crucial to her but on the writing itself—the very words on paper—hinged her one hope for reasserting an identity of her own. The sheaf of pages representing months of work and her new life seemed all too vulnerable sitting there on her table. What if the mugger from Central Park had followed her? What if, to avenge himself, he set a fire?

The doorbell rang again and her panic doubled. She could not leave those pages in her apartment. She could not leave them in New York. The rapists and the muggers and the arsonists were in New York. And so, as far as she knew, was Cheney.

She put her manuscript into a brown accordion folder and resolved, simply, not to let it out of her hands until she got to Maine.

At her door she saw the antenna on the table. Had she really threatened a man with that? Or had she dreamed it?

Suddenly she realized that she was terrified.

She was going to Maine for her son, to save him, and for her mother, to be saved.

CHAPTER 5

Dolan waited as patiently as he could. It was his own fault for arriving early and for not having made an appointment. He was sitting in a brightly lit corridor near a door marked "Ethnic Studies." He already liked NYU, he decided. With its Village brownstones nestled between looming glass high-rises, it reminded him of Boston University. Only in looking back was he able to see how happy those years at the Back Bay school had been. Now that he had actually taken steps toward reclaiming a place in normal American life, he realized how much he wanted it. Wanting with such intensity was a new experience for him, and it made him nervous. He was smoking his fourth cigarette when an extremely tall man of about sixty came down the corridor. Burdened with an old-fashioned satchel, he walked stoop-shouldered but quickly, and he breezed by Dolan and through the door as if Dolan wasn't there. Dolan guessed he was Professor Littleton.

Minutes later the secretary opened the door and invited Dolan in. As he approached the professor's office he realized to his horror that his palms were sweating. He shifted his folder of papers to his left hand in order to wipe his right on his pants.

Professor Littleton stood as Dolan entered his small office. "Mr. Dolan!" he said cordially, and he smiled briefly as they shook hands. "Sit down, sit down. This is quite a surprise. Kyllberg sent you, the girl said."

"Yes, sir." Dolan handed over the letter of introduction from Dr. Kyllberg, the Chairman of Literature at Uppsala. It was Dolan's ace, and it seemed strange to be playing it first. While Professor Littleton read, Dolan put his own glasses on, then sat, composed, to wait.

Finally Littleton looked up. "This is very impressive, Mr. Dolan."

"Thank you, sir."

"But you're American."

Dolan smiled, perhaps inappropriately.

"It never occurred to me when I wrote him that Dr. Kyllberg would recommend an American. Are there many at Uppsala?"

"A few, mostly in medicine. I was the only one in literature."

"He says you're the first scholar to specialize in Lagerkvist."

"I'm sure you know that the academic tradition in Europe prohibits dissertations about living people. Pär Lagerkvist died in 1974, just as I was getting underway." Dolan winced inside. He hadn't meant that death was a stroke of luck. "I happened to be the first of several to complete my work. Frankly, I think the committees were a little embarrassed that I was." Dolan handed the professor another page. "Here is a précis."

"Ah yes," Littleton perused the paper, then put it aside. "My favorite thing in Lagerkvist is the empty locket."

Dolan understood that the older man was both showing off and testing him. He nodded. "In *The Holy Land* Giovanni carries it with him everywhere for years."

"Indeed. I take it to be a symbol in Lagerkvist of human institutions, the church, the family, the nation, and how men cling to them long after whatever meaning they may have had evaporated." Professor Littleton paused, expecting Dolan to agree.

Dolan thought at first that the professor was having him on. His brief excursus seemed a perfect parody of the academic manner. "Frankly, professor, I prefer a more modest reading of that symbol. The locket was precious to Giovanni simply because of whose image was not in it. The very emptiness of the locket referred Giovanni to his beloved."

Professor Littleton eyed Dolan over the steeple of his hands. He had hard features, and Dolan found his silence intimidating. After a moment he said, "Doctor Kyllberg indicates you were offered a permanent position at Uppsala."

Dolan withdrew two more pages from his folder. "Here are the courses I taught, both as an assistant and as an instructor."

Professor Littleton took the pages, but otherwise ignored them. "Why didn't you take it?"

"As you said, I'm an American. In order to stay in Sweden beyond eight years, I'd have had to apply for citizenship."

"Eight years? You were there eight years?"

"Nearly, yes, sir."

"May I ask why?"

"Uppsala is one of the great universities in Europe."

"I mean why Sweden in the first place? Why not Cambridge or Bologna?"

Dolan took his glasses off, wondering at what point an interview becomes interrogation. He decided to take the question head-on; he had nothing to be ashamed of. "I went to Sweden, professor, because I couldn't stay in Canada. By 1972, when I left the United States nearly a hundred thousand draft-dodgers were already there, and the Canadian government was withholding status from new ones."

"David Dolan. I read about you, didn't I?"

Dolan shrugged, but that vestige of his notoriety disturbed him. Fame, when he had it, had seemed unnatural and inhibiting to him. "I spent 1973 in Stockholm working against the war. Then . . ." Dolan paused, to overcome an indecision ". . . my brother was killed in it, so I quit. When in doubt, go back to school." Dolan grinned, but Littleton only stared at him.

"Your brother was killed in Vietnam?"

"Yes." An image of himself careening drunkenly up and down the back streets of Stockholm filled Dolan's mind suddenly, but only for an instant.

"I'm sorry," Professor Littleton said.

Dolan looked away from him. An old sadness sneaked up on him. He was good at winning over professors, but this one surprised him by responding to his casual verbal résumé not with a question about his having been a draft-dodger, but with sympathy for the loss of a brother.

Littleton turned his attention to the synopsis of the courses Dolan taught. " 'The Absurd Hero in American Fiction,' " he read. " 'The Idea of Time in

Faulkner's South.' " He looked up. "These are not courses in Swedish literature."

"I lectured in Swedish, of course."

"But you didn't teach Swedish literature as such."

"No sir. That's what I was studying."

"And you received your degree . . . ?"

"This spring." Dolan offered his *vita*. He'd been accepted as a Ph.D Candidate at Boston University in 1969 after earning his Master's there. He'd graduated *summa* from U. Mass. Boston in 1965, and had been valedictorian at the Cambridge Latin School in 1961. Not bad for a street kid from the wrong side of Cambridge, the son of a trolley mechanic.

"I'm afraid the opening we have is in Swedish literature. I was hoping you had experience in that."

The professor's statement jolted Dolan. "Swedish literature is my field exactly. I'd appreciate an opportunity to demonstrate my grasp of it."

"Why did you pick Lagerkvist, if you don't mind my asking? In the land of Strindberg and Lagerlöf and Karlfeldt and Nelly Sachs, isn't Lagerkvist a bit, well . . . ?" Littleton shrugged, a perfect dismissal.

It was a mistake to feel defensive. The question was a test. Dolan knew that the surge of anger he felt could ruin him. He tried to speak calmly and intelligently. "As you know, Lagerkvist won the Nobel Prize in 1951 . . ."

Littleton's rude laugh interrupted him. "Yes, for *Barabbas*. The Swedes have to give the prize to one of their own every few years. *Barabbas* was a movie script."

Dolan felt as though he'd been slapped. Yes, the novel had been made into a pious, grunting Anthony Quinn spectacle like *The Robe,* and it had permanently undermined Lagerkvist's reputation abroad. But in fact his novel was short, unsentimental and agnostic. Dolan first read it shortly after the news about Brendan, and it had shocked him with its relevance to his own situation. Barabbas was haunted throughout his life by the knowledge that another had quite literally taken his place at the gallows. Dolan was not haunted by some strange rabbi who died a mystical death for the edification of the ages, but by his brother who was blown to pieces by a booby trap that had their family name on it. If Dolan had not fled to Sweden, he'd have hit that booby trap and Brendan, sole-surviving-son, would never have been drafted. Barabbas the acquitted? Dolan the exempt.

Professor Littleton's snobbish dismissal of a book which had changed Dolan's understanding of himself seemed profane. Why was he so desperate to stay in the academic world? Wasn't the abstract unreality of this conversation one of the things he had decided to escape?

"In my opinion, professor, Lagerkvist's Barabbas is a figure whose great stoic restlessness Camus would have understood."

"You know your Camus, do you?"

"I know that he regarded Lagerkvist very highly."

"I'm sure he did. I'm sure we all should. My problem isn't with Lagerkvist."

"Your problem. I'd begun to suspect you had one."

"Don't misunderstand, Mr. Dolan. My problem isn't with you either. You're a very impressive young man. My problem is with my funding. Our program is underwritten by a variety of grants, federal, state and private. We have professors from fourteen different ethnic strains. It's not only the concentrations we offer that make us a model, you see, but whom we employ."

"I don't understand."

"If you were Swedish or Swedish-American ..."

"I must be thick. Are you telling me that Irish need not apply?"

"You're being Irish has nothing to do with it."

"I speak perfect Swedish, professor."

"Mr. Dolan, this is very awkward for me. It never occurred to me that Uppsala would recommend . . ."

". . . Its most prestigious graduate."

Littleton shook his head. ". . . An American."

Dolan's anger overtook him. He was a traitor to his country, after all. Even though Littleton had no way of knowing it, he was still a fugitive. What did he expect?

He tried to keep his anger from bubbling into self-pity. Neither was useful now. It was more important to understand exactly what was happening and why. Despite his essential understanding of what the professor said, it was impossible for him not to relate the rejection to his own situation as a man strangling in loose ends. Even if the interview was ending badly he could learn from it. "My mistake," he said, "was in referring to my status as a draft-evader. Isn't that so?"

Littleton answered with a quiet, neutral tone that, curiously, despite what he said, defused Dolan's emotion. "It is my own view that citizens are properly obliged to defend their country, but that's irrelevant. I don't care a whit about your personal preferences, and the war in Vietnam is ancient history, long enough ago in fact to begin to suspect what a failure of nerve it was to have abandoned democracy in that part of the world. But I'm sure you went into exile for reasons you considered fitting. You seem a serious man."

"*Exile* is a word I never applied to myself."

"Exiles have achieved great things for culture over the years. Joseph Conrad. James Joyce."

Dolan laughed. "In my opinion Conrad was at sea too long, and Joyce found Dublin mystical because he lived in Paris."

Littleton continued. He knew what he was doing. "Exile is a great theme in our department. I've written about it myself. Exile is not emigration. It is a disorientation of time, place, language, loyalty, and it nearly always results in an in-turning of mind which can lead to both a kind of detached passivity as well as breakthroughs in the imagination. My conclusion from my reading is that a life without a country is not life on an island of virtue, but the opposite of that, a kind of moral paralysis. But the very marginality of exiles has become a most important metaphor, an image of the contemporary. Forgive me. I rattle on."

Dolan nodded and stood. The man was a perfect specimen of his kind. His abstract and windy analysis had cut Dolan, but also it had efficiently disarmed their confrontation. Dolan put his papers back in their folder. As he turned to leave, Professor Littleton stopped him. "Where do you go from here?"

Dolan heard the question with alarm. "Why do you ask?"

"Perhaps I could recommend you."

Yes, Dolan thought, and perhaps you could call the FBI. "My plans are somewhat up in the air. Frankly, I'd allowed myself to count on you."

"I'm sorry."

Dolan resented the man's kindliness because it short-circuited his anger. "Yes. So am I." They shook hands and Dolan left.

His disappointment was intense, but suddenly not paramount. His thought of the FBI with an accompanying momentary panic preoccupied him. Did they in fact know he was back? Were they in fact looking for him?

He crossed into the park at Washington Square, insisting to himself that he had nothing to fear. Once he had a lawyer he'd be fine. Hadn't the draft-dodgers and deserters all returned by now? Weren't they all free? The professor had said it himself: ancient history.

The young derelicts hanging around the fountain in the middle of the park reminded Dolan of his fellow expatriate resisters in Stockholm. How shocked he'd been to discover that the bitter American assessment of them as drug-users, traitors, misfits, dropouts, cowards and failures had not been far wrong. He'd gone to Uppsala to get away from them and to prove that assessment did not apply to him.

As he passed the strung-out Frisbee throwers and guitar players and dope smokers, it seemed a sign of his own aging that they were all so young. Once all bums seemed old. Here and at the Chelsea the night before, they seemed about seventeen.

Ancient history? In Sweden Dolan had been caught in one of time's folds. By 1979 there was an inbuilt nostalgia to his situation about which he could muster only a dry and sterile irony. For all Americans and Swedes the war in Vietnam was long ended and long forgotten, but for Dolan it was still the dominant fact of life. He had hated the war and, not without a sense of futility, opposed it. Yet, apparently for him alone, it remained a live issue because, just as it had made him for a time a reluctant celebrity, now the war made him a criminal on the run.

Dolan recognized the dreadful contradiction; only the war, endless and escalating, could have justified his permanent suffocating isolation from the real. The absurd hero in American fiction? Updike, Roth, Bellow and Salinger created characters whose pathos was a matter of their partiality, their refusal to live in more than one of life's dimensions. But Rabbit, Kapesh, Herzog and the Glass family had nothing on David Dolan. Resisters had referred to their situations in Sweden as "walking on water," perhaps initially because Stockholm was built on thirteen islands at the juncture of Lake Mälar and the Baltic Sea, but that phrase had come to embody exactly how Dolan felt. Even after going to Uppsala and long after the other resisters had dispersed, Dolan had no sensation of solid ground under his feet. At times he thought even the water on which he walked had long since evaporated.

He felt desolate. The bitterness, hurt and loneliness to which he'd been accustomed threatened to overwhelm him. His joy at having launched himself had been demolished first by Artie Rose and now by NYU. He could go to jail for not having been American enough, and now he had no career—lo and behold!—because he was not Swedish! What in hell had he crossed an ocean for? If he'd been a demonstrative person he'd have turned one of the park benches over or grabbed somebody's Frisbee and hurled it out of

Manhattan. The United States of America after more than seven years; what had he expected? Ticker tape?

The sun was already warming the city and pigeons skimmed above Washington Square's great marble arch. Dolan stopped to watch them, but he felt as little communion with the birds and the weather as he did with the junkies huddled in the arch's shadow. He'd intended to head uptown. Always in Sweden he'd carried in his mind pictures of himself walking up Fifth Avenue like a man walking across land he owned. Each mannequin, each green travel poster in airline office windows, each gargoyle of Saint Patrick's gawking down at the bright umbrellas of the café in Rockefeller Center, each luminous book jacket at Doubleday, each delivery boy's bicycle with its chain wrapped around its handlebars, each briefcase, each painted toenail and spike heel, each cop on horseback, each American cigarette, each glass mushroom at Steuben, emerald at Cartier, silver spoon at Tiffany, each drop of water in the Plaza fountain, each toy at F.A.O. Schwarz had a place of honor in the dream of his return. All that and, yes, ticker tape! Oceans of it! And a parade!

But Professor Littleton's sublime indifference, not only to him but to Lagerkvist and *Barabbas,* was what he got. What was the professor's word for exile? A disorientation. Dolan was not in exile anymore, but he was more disoriented than he'd ever been at Uppsala. He stood there facing uptown, but unable to walk, looking up at the arch, but unable to read what was inscribed on it.

At that moment a traffic helicopter passed over and reminded him of his other dream, his most common one, the dream he never willingly entertained. But the helicopter, as he watched it beat across the sky, hypnotized him. Dolan stood there, unable to move, at the mercy of the sight of that machine.

In his dream he hovers in a small brown chopper just above terrain illuminated by fooping white phosphorous marking rounds. In the distance can be heard booming large guns. He has the sensation that the gunship is sinking and sinking fast, so he presses the throttle to the floor and the machine shoots forward, gathering speed. His mission is to search for and rescue his kid brother, who is down on the gloom-shrouded battlefield.

But no sooner does the chopper clear a ridge than it drops into a valley. Dolan feels a terrible lurch in his stomach as the helicopter, suddenly impotent and spinning erratically, begins to fall toward a quilt of rice paddies. When the control stick comes off in his hands he realizes in the dream's logic that someone is clinging to the left skid underneath the machine's belly. He leans out of the cockpit so far into the wash of the rotor blades he thinks he is going to fall, but knows even in the dream that he can't fall out of what is falling.

And yes, he sees the form of a man stretched the length of the skid. The man's left leg is twisted wrong-side-up from the knee down, and Dolan begins to hit him with the control stick. But the man reaches up to the cockpit and starts to crawl into it. An M the color of blood is greased on his forehead. With an animal look of bewilderment, he sees Dolan's heel coming at this face. Dolan kicks him and kicks him again and the man whispers "David" once before rolling off the skid. Only then does Dolan recognize him as his brother, and immediately the helicopter rights itself and Dolan always darts out of his sleep.

He sat on a bench and took his coat off. He opened his folder and withdrew the letter that Brendan's wife had sent him. Its envelope still held also the uncashed government check for a thousand dollars. Brendan had taken out an army life insurance policy and had named him a beneficiary. Dolan had guessed at first that Eddie resented his getting the money, but he couldn't account for her accusing letter that way. She came from wealth; splitting insurance money wasn't the issue. To him the check was a heartbreaking symbol of his brother's love, even at the end, and he cherished it as such. But to Eddie the check had merely been the occasion to salt the misery he already felt. Dolan knew she'd written so spitefully out of her own grief and, for that matter, guilt. It had been her bad luck, after all, to be the instrument of Dolan's flight from the States; and, despite both their intentions, more.

In the upper left hand corner of the envelope was her address, 37 W. 70th St. It dawned on him suddenly that Eddie was only a few minutes away from the very spot where he was sitting. She was the one person to whom he could describe his dream.

He wondered if she still lived in New York.

He had to walk two blocks to find a phone booth that had a directory in it. There was no Edna Dolan. Under E. Brewster it said 37 W. 70th St., 273-4952. He thought of calling her, but he was so wary of being deflated once more that he decided despite the cost to take a cab to her place instead. He had the driver pull over at a deli, where he bought four bagels and

a pint of cream cheese and then, thinking of his
nephew, half a dozen doughnuts. He would say,
"Good morning, this is the breakfast we never had."
He hoped she would laugh. He remembered her as a
sardonic girl. It was his impression that she was
whimsical like Brendan, but ironic.

As the cab turned onto Seventieth Street he admitted that he had no real knowledge of the sort of person she had been then or was now. Their two days
together en route to and in Quebec had been a fantasy, an adventure, a dream. But it had ended badly
and led to nothing. They separated without even saying goodbye. Later Dolan's mother had passed along
news of her, but after the birth of Brendan's son, she
had stopped mentioning Eddie in her letters, an omis-
sion Dolan noted but never understood. It had been
more than four years since he'd had any news of her
at all.

At the door he stopped and lit one of his Danish
cigarettes. There were four buttons to push, but they
were identified only with apartment numbers. The
mail, apparently, was all pushed through the one slot
in the inner door. He peered through the glass and
saw a banister, oak-paneled walls, a red carpet going
up a flight.

He imagined her son barreling down those stairs to
meet him. Her son. Brendan's son. Dolan's own
nephew. He could never think of the boy without a
rush of guilt. Often he had intended to send him
something, a Scandinavian doll or carved pine auto
or reindeer antler. But he had never contacted him.
It was the image of his brother's child, not of a
woman, that would have belonged in Dolan's empty
locket, had he carried one. That he had no locket was

the perfect solution for the fact that he had no image of the child.

The thought of Giovanni's locket reminded him of Professor Littleton. What a humiliation to have been sympathized with and then rejected! It was not as easy to climb down from the Swedish shelf, or, better, onto dry land, as he had thought. He pushed Professor Littleton out of his mind, but then there was Artie Rose sidestepping him, warning him, calling him an arsonist.

He rang all four bells at once, with his fist.

And he waited.

No one came. There was not a sound of anyone coming. He rang all four bells again, this time in sequence. Nothing.

He went out to the stoop, turned and looked up at the building, originally a one-family town house. Two spider plants and a bright lamp in a window on the second floor were the only signs of life until the inner door opened. A weary looking middle-aged black woman stood at the threshold.

"How are you today?" Dolan said, approaching her.

She nodded noncommittally.

"I'm looking for Eddie Brewster."

"I just clean here, mister."

"For her?"

"For Mrs. Green. Don't know no Brewster."

"I'm pretty sure she lives here."

The woman shrugged.

"I'm her brother-in-law. Her son is my nephew."

"There is a boy lives upstairs."

"About six?"

She nodded.

"What floor?"

"Second."

"There's a light on up there."

"She was home before. I heard her." The woman looked up and shrugged. "I can't let you in."

"I know. Here." He handed her the bagels and the doughnuts.

That surprised her and she smiled at him, barely, but enough to relieve Dolan. She was the first person who'd smiled at him since he'd returned, and she rescued for him what little remained of his former high spirits.

He walked to the phone booth at the corner of Columbus Avenue. Was it his bright instinct or only his wish that told him she was still home? Suppose she didn't answer her door to unexpected callers. This was New York, wasn't it?

He found her in the phone book again, put his dime in and dialed, guessing on second thought that she was asleep.

The phone rang three times and then was answered and a woman's metallic voice said, "If that's you, Barney, I'm on my way to Mother's. I should make the ten o'clock shuttle to get to Boston in time for a noon flight to Bar Harbor. You can get me at Hunter's Island after, say, four. Call tonight, sweetie, I'm dying to know what happened. If that's not you, Barney, they got the wrong number because she hates these machines more even than they do. 'Bye."

Dolan stared at the phone after it went dead. He couldn't believe that having been received coldly by his old friend and indifferently by his mentor's best contact, he should now have been greeted only by that terrible cocky voice and its message for Barney.

He looked at his watch. What the hell! He had to go to Boston anyway. Why not now?

No excess of feeling, he told himself, no vivid, painful scenes of the past, no images and memories and dreams that only paralyzed. For once a clear and simple impulse on which to act.

He hung up the phone, went to the curb, hailed a cab and said, "The Chelsea Hotel, please, and then the shuttle at Kennedy."

"It's at La Guardia, Mac," the cabbie said, shoving the words at him through his raunchy cigar. "The shuttle's at La Guardia."

Dolan felt himself blushing. He would make mistakes at every turn. He felt as though he'd just been wakened from a nearly permanent sleep, and now had to do something, anything, to keep from drifting into it again. Feverish activity, he thought, motion, movement, whatever it takes to get his blood circulating. He felt as though he had only seconds in which to save himself.

CHAPTER 6

Bren was in his room on his knees before the two-foot-long model of the brontosaurus skeleton to which he was about to glue the last inch of bony tail. He had trouble keeping the hair out of his eyes when he leaned forward, so he was trying to work sitting straight up, and it hurt. He had to because the glue was fast-drying and permanent, and if he attached the tail piece at the wrong angle he was stuck with it. The building of that dinosaur, even with its dozens and dozens of pieces, was going to be perfect.

One part of him didn't want to finish putting the kit together. It was the only one he'd brought with him. He'd expected it to take a whole week. Now there would be nothing to do but draw the thing. That would take a couple of hours if he did it carefully, and he would. He had a large spiral book for the drawings he'd made of his models and in a way, he liked them more than the plastic creatures. Making a prehistoric model meant he had to follow someone else's instructions. Once you got the hang of it, it wasn't that hard and it was a lot of fun. But drawing the thing afterward was special because nobody at some factory had figured out ahead of time how you were supposed to do it.

Just as he secured the tail piece and sat back, some-body knocked on the door: Gram, of course. Bren thought it was weird how she was always knocking on doors. It was her house, wasn't it? At home he didn't knock on doors and neither did his mother.

"Come in," he said, and his voice echoed in the large, sparsely furnished room. He was kneeling on the hooked rug at the foot of the bed, which he loved because of its pillars.

"Hello, dear."

When he saw the basket crooked in her left arm and the fork in her right hand he knew what she wanted and, inside, he groaned.

"I'm going mushrooming."

"I was just finishing my brontosaurus." He expect-ed her to admire it, but she wasn't even looking at it. His mother would have admired it.

"Can you finish it later, dear? I was hoping you'd come with me."

"It *is* finished."

Mrs. Brewster looked at the model. "Oh." For a moment she was lost. She realized, too late, what he wanted. "It's nice."

"Thanks. Now I have to draw it."

"I could use your help."

Bren knew that wasn't true. He didn't like to go mushrooming with her because, even though he loved the woods, she moved so slowly through them, and she didn't like it when he ran ahead out of her sight. It irritated her when he made his usual kicking-through-leaves noises, as if mushrooms were animals you could scare off. He thought it was dumb, how she was always telling him to go quiet as an Indian. She expected him to think it was special to go with her just because she used to take his mother mushrooming when she was his age.

"But I was going to draw this."

"We have to get extra mushrooms. Do you know why?"

She would have waited a week for his answer, so he shook his head promptly.

"Because we'll need them for the salad. Your mother's coming."

"She is?" He said this cautiously, and then looked down at the brontosaurus. "How come?"

"Because she misses you."

Bren knew that wasn't why. He looked sharply up at his grandmother. "Is my dad coming too?"

Bren expected her to say, "He isn't your dad, dear," but instead she said, "No, just your mom." Then, putting the fork in the basket, she offered her hand. He had no choice.

He decided to make the most of it. "Tell me them again," he said, trailing her down the stairs.

"Boletus, coral, the oyster mushroom and chanterelle."

"And the poison ones."

"Poisonous, dear. The death cup and the destroying angel."

Such scary names. "And the deady nightshade, right?" It thrilled him just to hear them.

"That's a berry. You mustn't eat anything unless you show me first."

"Don't worry!" he said.

She tousled his hair, and that made them both feel better. In fact, though, the scary names made Bren feel it was all right to be a little afraid of the woods. Names like those meant they *were* dangerous.

Outside the midmorning air hit them twice, once as they left the house and again as they went into the woods where the wind blew the fir trees back and forth, staining the needle-carpeted floor with moving shadows. Bren took off as he always did on first entering the forest, running and dodging, but never cutting himself off, quite, from his grandmother.

On Saturday in L.A. there was a show called *Jamal the Jungle Boy.* Jamal was about fifteen, had been raised in the jungle by wolves, wore skins instead of shorts, and could run in his bare feet. Sometimes he ran up the trunk of a fallen tree and then grabbed a vine and swung across a ravine. He was like Tarzan, only he was just a kid, and that is who Bren pretended he was when he ran in the woods. He had tried running in his bare feet but couldn't and had decided that one of the differences between a jungle and a woods was that there were sharp sticks and rocks on the floor of the woods. It didn't matter if he wore sneakers as long as he ran fast. It seemed to him he could run faster in the woods than he could in the park in New York or on the beach at home, and that was one thing he liked about Maine. It was also possible in Maine to pretend that he was raised by animals, since his parents weren't around.

Jamal could defend himself because he knew how to fight. The jungle boy didn't call his way of fighting *kung fu,* but Bren knew that's what it was. After running he would stop in a clearing, making sure that his grandmother was well away, and go through the

slow motions of Jamal's fighting. At Masters some of
the boys did *kung fu* and karate and even aikido in
the playground, but not Bren. He only did it when
he was alone. He didn't like the boys who were mean
toward other children, especially when the second or
third graders picked on the girls or the first graders.
In the woods Bren pretended he was fighting off
older boys who pushed other kids around. He could
kick and chop with the best of them, and he knew it
was more important than ever for him to be able to
defend himself if he was going to a new school in
New York.

Another problem with New York was that the
shows on Saturday were lousy. They didn't even have
Jamal the Jungle Boy, for example. But in Maine
there was no t.v. anyway, and in Maine he could *be*
Jamal. He wished there were other children, though,
not that he minded being by himself, but because he
wanted to see if he actually was running in the woods
as fast as he thought he was. He wanted someone to
race. He was certain that he was speedy and elusive.
Even if he couldn't really do *kung fu*, he could always run. He doubted if anybody in that New York
school could run as fast, and since they never saw
Jamal on Saturdays, they wouldn't know all the tricks
Bren knew.

"Up here, Gram! Up here!"
Bren couldn't believe the waves. He was standing
on a cliff that overhung a heavy pounding surf. He
loved how the waves crashed into that cliff. The first
time he'd seen it he'd assumed that those waves had
cut that cliff over a million years, wearing away the

dirt, bashing through the granite grain by grain. But it hadn't happened that way. His grandmother said the whole south shore of Hunter's Island, which down at Seal Head was eighty feet above the sea, was a jagged cliff produced by a shift along the fault line, not by waves. A fault was a huge crack in the stone. It had scared him a little to think the cliff was created all at once when it rose up from below the water, like a sea monster. If a huge chunk of land like that could be moved up and down, then what couldn't be? But things like that had happened in those days. There were brontosaurus around then too. Nowadays only the waves remained, but they were scary enough.

What he wanted her to see was the lobster boat which was gliding out of the channel, heading for open water. "Look it!" he said, pointing, when she joined him. He had to hold his hair with one hand, against the wind, to keep it out of his eyes. The lobster boat drifted and slid and bounced across the water.

"That's Johnny Roche's boat," his grandmother said. "He lives in that trailer by the church."

"Oh yeah." Bren didn't like that trailer. It had tarpaper sticking out of the roof and there were growling dogs on chains in the back. He couldn't put the terrific sight of that boat fighting the sea together with the tumbledown shack of a trailer that even he knew was an unhappy place to live. "Does he keep going, Gram?"

Bren felt uneasy suddenly, watching that boat. It took him a minute to realize why. "It's going the wrong way."

She covered his head with her hand and helped keep his hair off his forehead. Her touch reassured him. She could be hard to put up with, but sometimes he wanted to be close to her, just to hang around, just to have her tell him things.

"She doesn't go too far, dear. Lobsters grow close in to shore. Only big boats can go out onto the ocean. You watch. Pretty soon she'll turn north or south and then go along the coast."

"Is Johnny Roche a girl?"

"No." Mrs. Brewster laughed, as he wanted her to. "Boats are girls, sort of. You call boats 'she.' "

"Why?"

His grandmother shrugged, but he knew she wouldn't say "I don't know." She always made something up. He was supposed to believe that she knew everything. She said, "Because boats take care of sailors at sea the way their wives do at home."

He stared at the boat, which was nosing into the swells, riding them well, but with a lot of spray. He thought the boat was worse off than his grandmother knew. He had a bad feeling for it that he couldn't shake. Maybe because it was a girl, he thought, but that was silly. The waves seemed to be getting bigger.

"He can swim, though. Right?"

"Sometimes fishermen don't know how to swim. They just take their chances."

"God."

"Don't say 'God,' Bren."

He looked up at her, shaking her hand off his head. He hated to be rebuked. His mother didn't care if he said "God." "I was saying a little prayer," he offered.

His grandmother looked away from him. He knew

he bothered her at times, but he didn't think it was his fault. A fault is a crack, he thought, in stone.

The boat was still going full blast out to sea. The horizon was so far away. Once his teacher had said the Milky Way contained billions of stars and that there were billions of other galaxies and that meant there were lots of Planet Earths in outer space, and on one of them somewhere was another kid exactly like him. Bren couldn't think of that without feeling weird in his stomach, and that was how the little boat heading out to sea made him feel.

Just when he was about to contradict his grandmother, the boat veered left, taking the waves at an angle and sloshing around like soap in a draining tub. It had changed direction and was not going out, and he felt a surge of relief. But as he watched the boat chug up the coast he realized that he was still nervous. Why had he worried about that boat? It looked small and fragile, but it was probably unbreakable.

His mind returned to the idea of that fault, that crack.

"If Mom's coming," he said, "I have to make my drawing." Before she could stop him he plunged with a yelp down the rise into the woods on the path toward the house. "The falcon," he called over his shoulder, "must fly! Jamal must run!"

He didn't want his grandmother to know what he was going to do. There was a crack in his family and it was having its own earthquake. His mother was coming to Maine because he had hurt her by talking to his dad. He would make it up to her by drawing a picture, yes, but not of an old brontosaurus. He would draw a terrific picture of the three of them, his mom, his dad and him. It would show how they used to be and how he wanted them to be again, and when his mom saw it she wouldn't think any more that the fault in their family was his.

CHAPTER 7

At the gate area which Bar Harbor Airlines shared with Downeast and Provincetown Airlines, passengers were arriving, some for the flight to Maine, which was due to leave in half an hour, but more for a flight to the Cape which was leaving sooner. An obese man took the seat next to Eddie. She tried to ignore him but his cologne assaulted her.

Cheney wore cologne like that. It would have embarrassed him to have recognized his own scent on such a fat person, and she wished momentarily that he was with her so she could arch an eyebrow at him.

Brendan had never worn cologne. Eddie forced herself to think of him again. She looked down at the yellow pad; her scrawl and scratches, the boxes and arrows, the cramped notes up and down the margins all seemed pointless to her. She'd been trying without success to describe the scene in which the girl arrives at Fort McClellan, Alabama, in her dusty sports car. She had driven through the night to get there before his unit left, but at the gate the MP refused to let her on the post. Eddie closed her eyes and tried to remember as much of it as she could.

"But please," she said, "I've come all the way from New York. I've been driving for three days."

"Sorry, ma'am. I got orders. No civilians on the post till further notice. We got an alert on."

The MP seemed too young to have finished high school. He made Eddie feel old. She was twenty-one. "An alert? Is that because they're leaving?"

"Don't rightly know, ma'am. We got folks leaving and coming all the time here. This is a jump-off base." The kid spoke with a self-importance that Eddie could have mocked, but his earnestness touched her. The sides of his head were shaved right to the rim of his hat. "You go back to town. Come out tomorrow. Maybe it'll be off. Then you can have a visitor's pass. Not today though."

"Do you know Brendan Dolan? Sergeant Brendan Dolan?"

"No ma'am. We got ten thousand GIs on this post. I'm going to have to ask you to put your vehicle in reverse now, ma'am."

"Can I ask somebody else? Can I call someone?"

"Yes, ma'am, you can. You can call the CO. You can call the Security Office. You can call the chaplain. But you can't from here. You'll have to do that from town. They got phones in town."

As Eddie backed her car away from the gate, the MP saluted her, so crisply and so sincerely it brought tears to her eyes. She was sure she'd missed Brendan. He'd called and asked her to come to see him before they shipped out, and she'd refused. But he'd told her he'd be looking for her anyway; it was just like him to have said that. For the year that he'd already been in the army, she'd tried a dozen times to end it with him. It was inconceivable to him that she would; his optimism was what seemed to keep it going.

But more than his expectation had brought her

down there. She had tried while they were apart to stifle her feelings, but she couldn't. He was wrong for her in a hundred ways—how could Eddie Brewster be a GI's girl?—but it didn't matter. Her dreams were always about him. And now that he was going to Vietnam her nightmare was about him too. She loved him. She'd come all this way one last time to tell him.

Tears blinded her as she roared away from the gate, and she nearly missed seeing the soldier standing by the road with his thumb out. His duffel bag was at his feet and crooked in his left arm was a huge bouquet of wild flowers.

The flowers told her it was him. When she stopped he grinned down at her and said, "Where you headed, lady?"

She lunged across the passenger seat and over the door to throw herself on him. "Nirvana, you bastard!" she said.

Of course the MP was in on it, and of course she was angry for an instant at their puerile trick, but then she let herself float free again of all her second thoughts, into his love, his simple, perfect love for her. In his presence she had no capacity to resist him. Her reservations evaporated, and the otherwise permanent brake on her emotions always failed. She crushed her face into his shoulder, so glad to have him after all, for however long, and she sobbed and sobbed and sobbed.

How could she write about that experience? Since they were her last ones with him, those hours were sacred to her; but even her bare memory of them seemed hokey. Could she do those hours justice? Could she tell this story without trivializing it?

During her apprenticeship at college and several summers at Breadloaf, Eddie Brewster had been called brilliant, a writer of infinite promise, an excellent poet, a superior stylist. Of course the tweedy men who were her teachers required less of women they found attractive. The fact that she could write sentences with appropriate modifiers and a proper verb tense had seemed enough to elicit great compliments. Unfortunately she was too young at the time to disbelieve them.

When *Quick Study* was published it was reviewed, naturally, by people who'd never laid eyes on her. Despite herself she thought that unfair. If she could only have had a few minutes in person with each reviewer, wouldn't things have been different? As it was, they killed her. She was called an exceptional storyteller, but one who sacrificed character to plot, meaning to narrative and, as one more exuberant critic said, everything to nothing. She wrote wittily and engagingly, but about stereotypes whose conflicts were obvious and whose inner lives remained as much a mystery to the reader as they obviously were to the author. *Time*'s faintly positive review was titled "Quick Sand," and *The New Yorker* ran a short paragraph which concluded, "*Quick Study* is a false start." The jibes came as a total surprise to Eddie, but even more surprising was how vulnerable she was to them. Each criticism, even the dullest, landed on her like a boulder because, after a lifetime of accolades from family and teachers, she had thought herself, not faultless precisely, but despite her faults destined to succeed greatly and quickly. She tried to protect herself from the hurt of the reviews by thinking of the critics as failed writers. But, as

Eliot said, so were most writers. In public she
shrugged off reviewers by saying they dismissed her
book because it sold well and was bought by Hollywood.

Unfortunately her treatment in the journals so undermined her confidence that when she did meet
movie people she was desperate for their praise, and
they lavished it on her. In doing so they prepared her
to commit what she now regarded as her set of great
mistakes. The first of those was to forget that Hollywood would flatter a dead tree back to life if it
needed the leaves.

One day, after the success of the film had made the
paperback a huge best-seller, after her move to L.A.
and marriage to Cheney, and after the pleasant tu-
mult of her own celebrity status had begun to seem
normal, she took all the old book reviews out of the
large manila envelope in which she'd stored them
and spread them on the floor. She read them again
one by one and decided they were right, especially
the rave in ladies' magazine which compared her fa-
vorably not to Françoise Sagan, but to Jacqueline
Susann. That was when she quit writing. Cheney, of
course, approved of her decision. He took her out to
dinner to celebrate it.

Now she was writing again. Her novel was going to
be sharp, funny and sexy, slightly sentimental, but not
serious, a World War II romance, but during
Vietnam. But to her surprise she'd found it difficult to
conceive the character based on Brendan. Brendan
had been boyish and ingenuous and affectionate and
honest, but in her book those qualities were coming
across as mere softness. This was not to be another

story about a man who domineered more by being
weak than by being strong. If Brendan had domineered her, it had been by being good.

In college Eddie was rebellious, intense, anxious
and competitive. She found the entire project of
courting and being courted tiresome when young
men were her inferiors, or nerveracking and bitter
when they weren't. Brendan was the first one with
whom it never occurred to her to feel either inferior
or superior. They used to meet in Manhattan and go
to movies in the afternoon.

Once, in winter, he'd thrown his parka in the trunk
of his car and only when he'd closed the lid did he realize his keys were in it. He laughed with embarrass-
ment, but Eddie didn't think it was funny because she
was going to have to take the bus up to Bronxville.

"So what are you complaining about? I have to go
to Fairfield for my other keys and get back here before dawn or I'll get towed. Come on." He took her
hand and started across Second Avenue. "Let's get a
cab to the Port Authority."

But halfway across the street he let out a great
roar, called the name "Julio!" and then was embracing a short Puerto Rican boy, twirling him about as if
they were long-lost brothers.

"Eddie, this is Julio Rivera. He was one of my
Neighborhood Youth Corps kids."

They stood and chatted awkwardly in the cold until Brendan told Julio the dumb thing he'd done with
the keys. Julio brightened. "Your trunk, man? Hey,
no sweat. I can get in it. I break into five, six trunks a
day."

Eddie thought, what a stroke of luck! But Brendan
refused his help and the boy left. Eddie was angry be-

cause she thought Brendan was afraid of the damage
Julio would do to the trunk, but his car was an ancient Ford beyond injury, and that didn't matter to
him either.

"Christ, Eddie," he said, "if he's ripping off cars it
means he's back on junk. Maybe I can't help the kid,
but I don't have to reinforce him either." Brendan
had made her feel apologetic without trying to.

Eddie wanted to make him a terrific character in
her book. But maybe in life he was too good. She was
unacquainted with his shadows, and that blocked her.
His brother had nicknamed him "Sunbeam" and often called him "Sunny." At the time Eddie'd thought
that cruel, but now it seemed appropriate. The
thought of his brother stopped her.

If she dealt with her feelings for Brendan honestly,
wouldn't she have to include in their story her ep-
isode with David in Quebec? The memory of it could
still make her feel guilty. She had taken to accusing
herself of having failed Brendan in death by offering
Bren to Cheney, but with David Dolan she had be-
trayed Brendan in life.

Even before they left for Quebec she'd felt am-
bushed by her attraction to David. She was cutting
his hair to make it look like Brendan's, and David
kept calling her his Delilah.

"If you're Samson," Brendan asked, "who does that
make me?"

As she leaned over him to clip the hair at his forehead Eddie and David exchanged a glance which
seemed to say, "Shall you tell him or shall I?"

Dolan laughed. "Who wants to be Samson? I'm trying to become you, remember?"

"That still leaves me with the problem, doesn't it? Who am I?"

"Hold still, David," Eddie said. She'd never understood before how like fondling the barber's touch could be.

"It's freezing without hair," David said with a mock shiver. "How do you make it through the winter like this, Sunny?"

Brendan came up behind Eddie and put his arm around her waist. She ignored him and kept trimming, but he said, "I've got my love to keep me warm."

"Not this weekend," David said.

An awkward silence fell over them.

"Right?" David pressed.

"I know we talked about it," Brendan said. He crossed back to his chair. "To tell you the truth, Doe, I didn't like the idea at first. It could be very risky. I don't much like the idea now."

"But it's up to Eddie, right?"

"Of course it is. I just wanted to say something about it. May I?" Brendan looked from one to the other solemnly.

"What?"

Eddie thought that Brendan was going to object to her going with David after all, and, to her shame, that excited her. She wanted him to be jealous. Despite herself, she wanted him to be possessive of her.

But Brendan looked at both of them with concern. He said, "It's just that you're the two people I love most in the world. Your going off to Canada like this, underground, illegally, makes me realize that if anything happened to either of you, I . . ." He stood.

His voice broke. ". . . couldn't stand it." He crossed to his brother and his girl.

When David stood, clumps of hair fell to the floor.

With a graceful authority that kept the gesture free of any mawkishness, Brendan put his arm around both of them, pulled them together and buried his face between their two bodies.

In returning Brendan's embrace Eddie and David were conscious of embracing each other. Their faces were almost touching. When their eyes met then, they had to avert them, but not before acknowledging what they both already knew.

She shook the memory off. She was not writing about Quebec. She was writing about Pardee, Alabama.

All the way into town Brendan sang what he said were songs of the Russian Revolution. His unit was full of educated draftees like himself who'd applied for NCO school in Georgia and then for advanced infantry training at McClellan, but only to delay being sent to Vietnam. However, their tactic had backfired. The war had not ended, and their training made their assignments inevitable. They were shipping out the next day.

Eddie was sure that when the others sang the songs of the Revolution, the effect was bitter and ironic, but Brendan made even that minor gesture of resistance seem, well, soldierly. He was a sergeant now and, as the ladder on his breast implied, a winner of commendations. Instead of bemoaning his fate or living with futile wishes, he had begun to prepare himself for war. He wanted to get through it alive, and he wanted to get his platoon through it alive, and he wanted to conduct himself honorably.

Brendan had made a reservation at the Holiday Inn. Eddie had assumed they would spend his pass in bed, and so did he, but he had something additional in mind first. Her inkling came while he was signing the motel register. The spaghetti board behind the clerk listed the names of the groups booked into various function rooms. Beneath "Pardee Lions—Jefferson Davis Room" the board read, "Sergeant and Mrs. Brendan Dolan—Jeb Stuart Room. Congratulations!"

Brendan turned from the desk with an impish smile on his face, but Eddie felt shock and anger.

"I don't get it," she said.

His smile faded quickly. "I didn't know how to ask you, I guess."

"You ask me by asking me. I didn't come all the way down here to be presumed upon."

"Eddie, let me explain. I thought your coming had to mean . . ."

"No, it doesn't. Don't say that." Brendan lowered his head boyishly.

The desk clerk was watching them, and a pair of other guests were approaching.

Brendan took Eddie's elbow and led her across the lobby. "The Jeb Stuart Room. I thought that was sort of romantic. Let me show it to you anyway." He ushered her in.

"You've been in the army too long."

The room was dominated by a bank of wild flowers like those in Eddie's bouquet. Brendan had spent hours collecting them all and arranging them. Before she could react, a short man in a black robe stepped out from behind the flowers.

"Oh," Brendan said. "Mr. Simms." He turned to Eddie. "The judge."

"Hello, miss. You made it, I see." Mr. Simms smiled nicely.

Eddie stared down at her bouquet.

"Not 'judge' actually," Mr. Simms went on. "J.P. I count it a high privilege to be of service to you young people at such a special time."

What struck Eddie most was his accent. She'd known few southerners. His syrupy manner put her off. "There's been a mistake," she said abruptly. She wanted to stop him before he sang his wedding song.

"*My* mistake, Mr. Simms," Brendan said. "I'm sorry." Brendan reached for his wallet.

"No, no, sergeant. That's all right. I wouldn't think of it." Mr. Simms bowed awkwardly at Eddie. "Nice to meet you anyway," he said and left.

Eddie and Brendan stood in miserable silence. She thought of a clever remark to make about Stonewall Jackson. It might have relaxed them, but she couldn't bring herself to say it.

"I'm sorry, Eddie."

"Will you quit saying that, please. Brendan, I simply never know how to respond to you, honest to God."

Her anger had drained away. She handed him the flowers, turned and walked back through the lobby to her bag, picked it up and went to their room alone. It had two double beds. She was overwhelmed with weariness and sadness. Though it was still daylight, she undressed and climbed into one of the beds. It was well after dark before she fell asleep.

When she woke up it was dawn. Brendan was sleeping in the other bed. She lay there for a long time listening to him breathe. In hindsight she had no sense of an explicitly made decision. In her novel she was going to insist that the heroine had a powerful intuition that he would be killed in the war, but as far as she could recall, that wasn't so. It was simply that she had changed her mind. She did love him. And he was a good man. And he wanted her to marry him. So what if he couldn't think of a more winning, sophisticated and, well, respectful way to ask her? Eddie frankly didn't want to get married no matter how he asked her, but she decided against herself. It wouldn't be the last time.

Before he woke up, she went out and found Mr. Simms and ensconced him in the Jeb Stuart Room again, and then she went across the street and bought a sport coat, slacks and shirt for Brendan.

"Here," she said, waking him. "Put these on. I'm not going to marry you in that uniform."

He squinted up at her for a moment, then threw the sheet back and leapt out of bed, singing, "Ahh-lay-*loo*-ya! Lay-*loo*-ya! Lay-loo-oo-*ya!*"

Eddie admired him while he dressed, his graceful body and the simplicity of his joyful response. It was a great relief to be acting on her impulse. Eddie loved to please him.

When Mr. Simms asked Brendan if he took Eddie to be his wife, he looked her in the eye and nodded, but he didn't speak because his emotion choked him. Eddie found it easy to make her vow, but she knew he was giving himself more fully than she was.

After the ceremony, Brendan apologized to the J.P. "I didn't say 'I do,' but I did."

"You sure did, son. That was obvious." Mr. Simms

turned to Eddie. "You're a lucky lady, I'd say, Mrs. Dolan."

That name shocked Eddie too much to respond. She wanted to say both "Yes! The luckiest in the world!" and "Wait a minute, what have I done?" But she didn't say anything. She held tightly to Brendan's hand.

He had his new clothes on for less than an hour. They went back to their room after the brief ceremony and made love without birth control for the first time. In her novel Eddie was going to describe her heroine's unspoken certainty that a baby was conceived at the very moment of her orgasm. In fact, Eddie had never had an orgasm with Brendan.

In her memory of that experience in Alabama, Eddie was a mystery to herself. She understood very little of what she'd done or felt. Surely the loss of Brendan afterward had short-circuited her ability to recall what had made their love compelling. Only when the army cable came with the news that he was missing did she realize that her insane impulse to marry him in Pardee could be justified only if he died. That plunged her into guilt again, and she crushed her feelings of having failed him once more beneath a load of grief and anger which, in turn, frightened her because she was certain it would infect the baby she was carrying. So she refused those feelings too and transformed all that chaos of emotion into love for her child.

Bren was still everything to Eddie and she still felt as possessive of him—despite the goddamned adoption—as if she'd had a virgin birth. How could Cheney have broken into that? What a fool she'd been to encourage him to try. Now she wanted him out. He was the only father Bren had known, but she didn't care. Bren had love enough from her.

But did Bren think so? Was it fair to make Bren choose between them? To make Bren eliminate Cheney from his affections? Does a good mother require such unequivocal fealty from a child? Eddie could not ask those questions. To fail a pair of husbands was one thing. But a child? Eddie was nothing to herself if she was not a responsible, generous and worthy mother.

How easily her train of thought had slid from Brendan to Cheney. She had to stop. Cheney could still undermine her.

Once, when they were both drunk, she'd accused him of having undermined her career as a writer, and he'd replied that she should be grateful to him for having rescued her from the pulp racks at drugstores. The next day he apologized for saying that and offered to get her a job doing script polish on his next movie. The son of a bitch.

She put her yellow pad in the accordion envelope with her manuscript and put it in her canvas satchel. It wasn't working anyway. Who can write in an airport? But she knew. Jacqueline Susann, that's who. She looked at her watch. Quarter to twelve. Another twenty minutes. She was impatient, but more with her own mood than with the airline. Cheney could undermine her, could still control her, only if she let him.

But a new idea occurred to her, a consequence of these reflections. If Cheney's special cruelty consisted in his willingness to exploit for his work what was secret and sacred between them, wasn't she doing the same thing in relation to Brendan? Who was she to feel superior? Who was she to pretend that writers exploited less crudely than actors?

Stop it, she told herself. She had to stop!

Once when Cheney, she and Bren were flying in the Cessna to their place in Idaho they'd begun to argue, but mildly, not nearly bitterly enough to justify his reaction. He stalled deliberately and dropped the plane into a kamikaze dive and she was sure he was going to slam them into a mountain. She feared she would vomit all over Bren, who was in her arms. Cheney didn't pull out of it until she began screaming hysterically. When they leveled off he was laughing. Bren was alarmed more by her reaction than by the dive, and she realized that Cheney's purpose had been to make a fool of her in front of her son. She forced herself to laugh too, and that soothed Bren, but Cheney had frightened her terribly. They had their good times after that, but she had lost her capacity to trust him, particularly in the air. She never flew with him again, or allowed her son to.

She took her manuscript out of her bag again, tucked it under her arm, stood and walked to the restroom, thinking she should work that scene into a book someday, herself screaming wildly in a falling airplane. It would be a comedy, with Cheney a stunting clown in a flying circus. But Eddie had no gift for slapstick writing, and anyway easy laughs undermine irony. Jokes short-circuit authentic humor. Sardonic cynicism may be the great failing of my kind, but it pays well, she said to herself, and the hours are good.

At the mirror she washed her hands until two other women left and she was alone. She leaned closer to the glass and stared at her face as if trying to decode it. Andy Warhol avoids mirrors for fear of looking in them and seeing no one, nothing. Eddie did not feel that way, but she was uneasy. She was acquainted with her face, but not a connoisseur of its reactions. Every time she looked closely at her eyes, brows, nose, cheeks, mouth, lips, chin and bones, her face seemed to be another's. When she thought seriously about what was happening in her life it seemed to be happening to someone else. Now, for example, someone else was flying to Maine to protect her child from her husband. By looking at her face she hoped to understand better what was happening. What was registered in her eyes, in the set of her mouth, her jaw? Eddie wanted a signal from outside herself to counterbalance the ominous inner dread she felt. What she saw, though, was the same dread, only now she recognized it, the dread of combat.

Eddie closed her hands over her face and eyes and made an effort to press her anxiety away. But could she press away the memory of nine thousand quarrels, two hundred jealousies, seventy betrayals, twenty outright lies, nine threatened beatings and one badly bruised face when he finally attacked her? That and her terror the next day when he'd left with Bren were all it took to dislodge her. She'd had an impulse to call the police, but instead she'd called his psychiatrist, who tried to calm her.

"Cheney's not going to harm that boy," he said.

"But he harmed me!"

Doctor Frazier hadn't an answer for that, and in the silence she saw what he meant. Cheney loved the boy, but her he could harm.

When the dreaded kidnapping turned out to have

been their day at Disneyland, that seemed the most violent blow of all.

Why weren't there scars? There should have been scars! She pressed and pressed. She told herself to stop it, and she did.

She did not know that he was in fact coming to Maine. Her mother didn't think so. Cheney was up to his ears in Shakespeare. What made her fear his coming? She knew. It was simple. Her fear made her fear it. Cheney always found a way to slide his blade into the one fold she tried to protect. If he had any idea how intensely she dreaded encountering him in Maine, he would—she could be certain of it—already be there.

She dropped her hands from her face and took half a step back from the sink and straightened her spine and looked again. She was a tall young woman with white skin—it should have been tan—smooth over good facial bones, set off by short black hair which framed her face, a fair-looking woman whose broad athletic shoulders suggested strength, not weight. Her red cotton shirt was too gay for traveling in, too frivolous, but that was why she'd chosen it. She hadn't thought to wear a bra, and she could see the outline of her nipples. Once she would have been pleased by it, but now it embarrassed her. Her mother would be displeased. She had only one remaining opinion about the standards of her daughters' generation, that they would be sorry when they sagged. Eddie was already sorry, though her breasts alone, of all the things she cared about, showed no sign of sagging. They were too small. That someone might think that she thought herself voluptuous mortified her.

Her foolishness made her smile and she was startled

to see unmistakable affection in her face. No one else was there. It had to be affection, despite everything, for herself. She brought her hands together once briskly. They made their noise and she recited a line from poor old Randall Jarrell. " 'Clap,' said the manager, 'the play is over.' "

Another woman came into the ladies' room. Eddie ran her brush through her hair, which was too short. For a decade she had worn her hair very long. The first thing she did in New York was get it cut, and only the week before, she'd had it cut again, even shorter. Her mother would not approve of that either, and Eddie wouldn't be able to disagree. She was like a teenager trying anything to find a look for herself.

The woman joined her at the next sink, but instead of washing she stared at Eddie, who turned to her finally and smiled. The woman was in her fifties and wearing a winter suit which, since it was August, was the tip-off. She handed Eddie a copy of the *Watchtower* and said, "Did it ever occur to you that the end of the world might be very near?"

"Yes, it did," Eddie said pleasantly, and left.

Back at the gate area she let her eyes play upon the passengers and tried to decide which were going to Maine and which to the Cape. But it was all too easy to guess: primary colors to Maine, pastels and madras to the Cape. She enjoyed her observations not because they gave her a feeling of superiority, although they did, but because she was pleased to have survived her bout of introspection.

It was pleasant simply to be noticing things about other people—their clothing, their hair styles, their good posture or lack of it—and that was how finally she achieved her relaxation. She dropped her guard a bit and let her gaze drift to the good-looking redheaded man by the Nantucket poster who, having just entered the waiting room, was looking at her openly. She was not used to that. Once she might have enjoyed it. She might have smiled at him.

Even then, for all her inhibition, she might at least have entertained a fantasy of sitting next to him on the airplane, but she suddenly had no idea whether he'd be flying to Maine or to the Cape, and that was especially curious since—it was as if an elastic she was stretching snapped back in her face—she recognized him.

CHAPTER 8

Dolan was looking for her, but the picture he had in mind, though of Eddie, was of no use to him. In it she had her back to him. She was standing in front of a Victorian floor-to-ceiling window. The first light of dawn made a silhouette of her figure, and even through the flannel nightgown he could make out the lines of her body.

He was studying the crowd of people at the gate area. A bald man with a carefully trimmed beard was arguing quietly with a younger man whose arm was in a sling the color of army fatigues. An overweight woman was softly swaying her baby to and fro. Three little girls were leaning over one comic book. They wore identical sunsuits with overall tops and no shirts. Behind Dolan people were still rushing into the corral-like area. A tall schoolboy bumped him as he went by. Dolan excused himself inappropriately and walked on, holding his suitcase in front of his knees. Another bearded man reminded him of someone from Sweden, but he couldn't think who. With his suitcase close-hauled he crossed the room slowly, eyeing the young women who misunderstood, if they noticed, his frank stare.

He saw her. She was standing by a pillar and she

was staring at him. Her eyes seemed huge to him, even from twenty or thirty feet, and he realized he'd forgotten how brown they were. He sensed her shock at once. When he saw her hand coming up he thought at first she was going to wave at him, but her hand went instead to her mouth, to cover it. He saw that hand's trembling and he was afraid suddenly of what it foreshadowed.

He continued to hold her eyes even while closing the distance between them.

"Hello, Eddie," he said.

"David!" she whispered, then looked away from him.

He let his eyes fall quickly down her body. He was surprised at how familiar it seemed to him, but it was far thinner than he remembered. When he looked at her face again he realized that she looked unwell. Her eyes had seemed huge to him not because they were beautiful, but because they were sunken. Her skin was pale and her hair was too short. He had always remembered her as a lovely woman, tall, bony, elegant. But now she seemed gaunt, weary and used. To his surprise he found himself feeling sorry for her.

"Forgive me," she said softly, "but not five minutes ago I thought of you, and for a second it seemed to me ..."

He smiled. "You'd made me up?"

"Yes, I felt quite crazy. Is it really you?"

He held his hand out to her. "Touch me and see."

She took his hand and as they shook she felt her own face breaking into a smile too. He was looking at her so fondly that it made her feel self-conscious. When she let go of his hand she fingered her buttons involuntarily, but when his eyes went to her throat she feared he would think it a coy gesture. She fastened the shirt at her neck, a deftly modest movement, but she was aware of his quick glance at her breasts.

"I thought of you five minutes ago too. You were standing against a floor-to-ceiling window at the Frontenac."

"I wasn't thinking of Quebec, David." But of course she was. She lightened her tone. "I remember you as shorter."

He laughed and looked down at himself. "I was. But only in comparison. It killed me when Brendan came home from Fairfield one June an inch taller than me. I've thought of myself as short ever since."

"You're six feet." Eddie was glad he'd mentioned Brendan. His name had been all too unspoken the time before.

"You're kind to notice." He looked around at the nearby people. "They think we're old school chums." He let the statement hang, and its implied question, "What are we?" After a moment he said, "And your hair is shorter."

She touched it. "Yes, I've become a nun."

A neat parry, he thought. Nuns have no futures with men and repent their pasts. He laughed. "Not you!"

Eddie wondered if he detected how unsettling he was to her. "Hair!" she said. "When we first met, yours was down to your shoulders!"

He smiled. "Do you remember who cut it?"

"Yes. I did." She lowered her eyes, but only for a moment. She grinned up at him. "There was hair all over the apartment. You and Brendan began to throw it at each other as if it was pillow-stuffing. Do you remember that?"

"You cut my hair to make me look like him. For my escape."

"Yes. His escape to Quebec. "I'd forgotten the resemblance. You could be him almost, even now."

One of Dolan's tricks in the classroom was to conceal his impatience with his students by unfolding and putting on his glasses. He did that now, but to conceal his unexpected sadness. His memory of the scene in Brendan's apartment was as bitter as Eddie's.

With his glasses on, he made a show of looking at her, as if he hadn't yet. "Eddie, it's good to see you. You look . . ."

Dolan saw immediately that he'd offended her by pausing. She knew how she looked. He shook his head, as if in admiration. ". . . Good. You look good."

"Thank you." She dropped her eyes again.

What had drained her of color and dampened her spark?

"You'll think this is foolish," he said, "but I've always pictured you in ski clothes."

She laughed.

"No, really. Because of Quebec."

She looked up sharply. "That was a long time ago."

"Eight years this winter. You and Brendan saved my life. I never thanked you."

"Please don't take offense at this, but I went with you that time because he asked me to."

Dolan was looking at her mouth. Her lips were dry, slightly cracked. One of the details he recalled from the other time was that her lips had glistened.

"I know that. You don't have to say that, Eddie."
She needn't establish her loyalty to Brendan. Hadn't
she written her letter?

Eddie clutched her brown envelope at her breast,
as if to shield herself from him. What she was feeling
would have disgraced an adolescent. She'd often been
shy with people she hadn't seen in a long time, but
this emotional incoherence was extreme. She remembered clearly how taken she'd been with his fast-talk-
ing good humor, his nearly physical wit. She'd
thought of him as a more complicated and more re-
flective and more ironic version of Brendan. And
there'd been that brief moment when she'd admitted
his was the version she preferred. That was what she
wanted to avoid admitting now.

"When did you come back?" she asked.

"From Quebec?"

"From Sweden."

"How did you know I was in Sweden?"

"It was in the papers. You were quite . . ." she
hesitated over the word that came to mind, then
thought what the hell ". . . notorious."

"When you wrote to me you sent your letter care of
my mother, as if you didn't know."

"How is your mother?"

"That's two questions too quickly." He smiled.
Smile wrinkles creased his face. Eddie found herself
mimicking his smile, as if they *were* school chums.

"I came back from Sweden yesterday. I haven't seen
my mother or my father since before the last time I
saw you."

"Yesterday! You were over there until yesterday!"

It was as if he'd claimed to have walked across the ocean.

Dolan shrugged and nodded, but managed to convey that he too found it incredible now that he was back. Eddie noticed his clothing suddenly. His corduroy jacket with its narrow lapels and chino pants with slightly pegged cuffs looked European. His hair was trimmed too closely above his ears. He was as pasty-faced as she was. They were two of a kind in a world of tanned summer deities, but he had an excuse. Eddie decided that she would spend every afternoon in Maine sunbathing without clothes on.

The thought of herself naked made her see him that way, but only for an instant.

"Are you catching a flight?" she asked.

"No. I've just come up from New York."

"Good lord, so have I! What coincidences!"

"I followed you." He let that sink in. "I went to your apartment this morning. I called you and listened to your message to Barney. I ran all the way from Eastern."

"To see me?"

"Eddie, coming back from Sweden means trying to pick up the pieces."

"Like me?"

He blushed, and slapped his forehead. "My English suffers. Please make to forgive me," he said with a self-mocking accent.

"But I don't understand. You came back from Sweden yesterday. You're looking for me today. Surely you've more important . . ."

"God, yes." He sighed and let his frame sag to show his weariness. "I'm off to a slow start. Do you remember Artie Rose?"

"No."

"Doesn't matter. A small time Kunstler."

"I remember Kunstler."

"You make it sound like he's dead. That's a long time ago for you, isn't it? For me it was this morning."

"I never expected to see you again. I haven't seen your parents in years."

"But you're my sister-in-law. We're relatives, right? It pleased me very much that you married Brendan."

Eddie stared across the room at the window through which the bright August sun poured its glare, as if that would cauterize her emotion. Since beginning her novel she'd been trying to remember her days with Brendan, and now here was Brendan's brother, his double, whose voice, hair, eyes, smile and ingenuous assertiveness were dragging her across a border she'd arrived at but dared to cross. He'd done that to her before. Outside the air shimmered off the pavement, airplanes coasted sluggishly in and out of their slots and the wash from the propellers and jets tore at the baggy trousers of the waving ground crew. She wished she was one of those union members whose job it was to park the huge machines. Eddie thought that just then she couldn't park a verb between nouns in a simple sentence.

"Where's my nephew?"

Eddie looked back at him sharply. His nephew! David Dolan was her son's uncle. The thought smashed over her mind like a breaker.

She stooped and got her wallet from her satchel and took out her photos, of which there were five, three of Bren, one of herself with Cheney and one of the three of them. She had an impulse to slide the pictures of Cheney out of the deck.

She handed David the five and he studied them. The most recent picture of the boy had him standing on a bench between Eddie and Cheney. The happiness in their faces was such a rebuke now, but Dolan could not know that. He was looking at that particular photo when he said, "He's beautiful, Eddie. He's a beautiful boy."

His statement moved her. She looked at the upside down photo in his hands.

"I would have recognized him," Dolan said. He looked up from the picture and waited for her to meet his eyes. "I'm so glad you named him Brendan."

Eddie made herself go rigid. She stiffened her ankles, knees, shoulders and jaw as if she were trying to control nausea, not tears. For months she had been able to conjure only the vaguest reminiscence of her attachment to Brendan, but now with what power could she feel it. Of course she'd driven straight through to Alabama! Of course she'd fetched the J.P. before breakfast! And of course, she thought with massive self-pity, they'd kept the war going just long enough to kill him.

Dolan handed her the pictures.

She said, "We call him Bren." She focused on the picture, hard.

"That's a nice form of it."

"He's such a little Irishman." She looked up quickly. "Would you like to keep one?" She offered him a picture of the boy posing with his teddy bear.

"I'd love it. Could you spare it? Thanks."

Eddie nodded, then looked down again at the family photo. Bren dominated it, standing on a bench with his head at the level of his parents' shoulders, which he draped with his arms as if he were a politician posing with two lackeys.

Dolan couldn't help asking, "Who's your friend?"

Eddie smiled gently.

"That's no friend. That's my husband." She put the pictures back in her wallet.

Dolan tried to conceal his surprise. "You got married, what, about five years ago?"

"Yes. You heard about it?"

"No. I didn't."

That surprised Eddie. Her marriage to Cheney McCoy had been a hot item.

"But I guessed because that's about when my mother stopped mentioning you in her letters. I think I get the picture. They wanted you to be a widow forever."

"I'm afraid they did." It soothed Eddie to have him say that. "I wanted Bren to get to know them and always think of them as his grandparents, but they quite thoroughly cut us off. I wrote a book they disapproved of and then I moved to California, so it was impossible to appease them and I so wanted to for Bren's sake. For a time I had him send them things, though, homemade valentines and popsicle-stick trivets. They never replied. Still he talks about visiting them someday. He never takes offense. He's not like me at all. Oh, David, it's so sad. It really makes me sad about your parents."

His conscience bucked. His parents obviously felt abandoned and rejected. And they were, and by whom more than him? He had a million thoughts about that catastrophe, but only one feeling. He fended it. "I didn't know about your book."

Once that would have insulted Eddie, but now she liked it that he knew nothing. She shrugged pleasantly. "I wrote a novel after Brendan died. It had its turn at bat."

"I'd have read it of course . . ." His mother should have sent him Eddie's book.

"You know what Andy Warhol says, in the new age everybody gets to be famous for fifteen minutes."

"Saki said be kind to tall men with moustaches because they invariably turn out to be the King of Sweden."

"You shaved."

He laughed and then she did. "What was your book called?"

"*Quick Study*. Your mother wrote to me. She said it was your father who objected, of course. To the sex. There was almost no sex at all, compared to what's common. I think *Quick Study* represented my new life to them. It did to me, I know. And they didn't want me to have it. I felt sorry for them. But they were cruel. And they failed their grandson, in my opinion. Bren especially needed a grandfather."

Eddie had showed more of her feelings than Dolan was prepared to acknowledge. "It's good you married again. I hope you don't think it presumptuous of me to say that."

Eddie shook her head sadly. Once she would have given anything for such a simple affirmation from the Dolan family. Now it could only seem ludicrous. If it hadn't been offered in such innocence it would have seemed spiteful.

"Your husband's a nice-looking fellow. What does he do?"

"You didn't recognize him? You don't know?" Eddie covered her mouth. "Forgive me, David, but you really don't know? Oh David, I love it!" She laughed a bit goofily.

"I really do not know." He didn't get the joke, but felt like the butt of it.

"Did you ever hear of Cheney McCoy?" She lowered her voice when she spoke his name.

"Cheney McCoy? You're kidding. You're married to Cheney McCoy?"

Eddie laughed delightedly, and as she did so she reached toward him, touching his sleeve. He thought that finally he was seeing her as she had been before.

"You look wonderful," he said, "laughing like that."

"I cherish your ignorance, David." She was still touching his sleeve. "Our life has been gossip-column copy. You're the first person I've met in years who doesn't know what I wear to bed."

"Flannel, right?"

Her smile disappeared and her hand shot back to her breast, but she continued to look at him. She shook her head slightly and said, "Only when it's very cold."

"Think of how I feel. Here my brother's wife is a celebrity and I don't know it. I've taught contemporary fiction for years and I missed your novel."

"You'd hate it. My readers are all women."

"You and Virginia Woolf. Hell. Cheney McCoy's movies even come to Sweden. I'd have seen them all if I'd known he and I were practically related. Talk about out to lunch!"

"That's an old expression. You never hear it anymore."

"How would you say it now?"

Eddie shrugged, charmingly he thought. "You know what? I don't know. I'm as out to lunch as you are."

"I can admit something too, something I just realized." Now Dolan touched her. "I set out to find you this morning because you are the mother of my brother's son. I want to establish ties, Eddie. My parents and Bren and you are still all I have. And they're too old, and he's too young. You're my first link; isn't that shocking?" He paused awkwardly. "But now I see that I unconsciously expected from you exactly what my mother required, a state of permanent widowhood, as if an engaging, bright, lovely woman like you had been suspended in time, like a figure on an urn." To himself Dolan completed the thought; an urn for ashes.

He waited for her to respond. She would not look at him. He took his hand back. "Eddie, I apologize for that."

The loudspeaker clunked on. The airline clerk picked up his telephone and announced the flight to Bar Harbor. Eddie responded automatically. She stooped, put her manuscript in her bag, which she then hoisted to her shoulder. The gate area came to life, like a creature stirring, with all the others doing the same thing.

"Eddie, I was hoping we might talk . . ."

"Oh, David, I'm so glad to have run into you."

"You didn't run into me. I told you. I deliberately caught up with you. I know this is unfair of me, but could you do me a great favor? Could you let me buy you lunch?"

"I have to catch that plane." She felt the surge not only in him, but in herself and she had to nip it. She was loath to go on fending off the emotions that clustered around the memories he evoked.

Dolan looked across the room at the line. The gate was not actually open yet. There were still a few minutes. He turned back to her. "Could you catch the next one?"

"No. I simply can't." She was going to Maine for Bren's sake. The next plane would get her there too late for the last ferry. Eddie stiffened. She had forgotten what it was like, except in relation to her child, to be the object of someone's urgent need. And not just someone's, but a man's. An unwilled, visceral responsiveness welled in her. "David?"

He pulled the blue airmail envelope from his pocket and, a protest against the pressure of time, very slowly opened it to withdraw her letter.

She looked at it as if it would burn. "What is it?" she asked, though she knew.

When the army sent her the two checks, she'd thought of burning them. Instead she sent hers to Nixon with a page full of curses. And she sent David's to him in care of his mother. She did not remember now what she'd said in her letter, but she knew what she'd felt in writing it. She remembered arguing at the Lincoln Center post office when they said there was no special delivery through a forwarding address.

"I never answered it," he said. "It's taken me a long time to know how."

"David, I don't remember what I said."

He looked away from her but managed to suggest how her statement hurt him.

"That was so long ago. You don't understand how different it is here. We remember nothing from those days."

He looked sharply at her. "I don't believe that."

"It's true and it's just as well."

He felt a blast of self-pity. He was not so thick-headed as to be surprised. Littleton had called it ancient history. Brendan had died in another era, the scars and divisions of which were long since proudly healed. Dolan was an anachronism. He sensed that she felt sorry for him. It had been her vulnerability which drew out his. Now he regretted exposing himself to her, but it was too late.

She said, "Whatever I wrote you, and I'm sure it was awful, I take it back. I was out of line."

"No. Don't tell me that. Don't say that to me. You were the only one who told me the truth. My father never spoke to me. My mother sent me nosegays. I learned a new language but could never explain myself. I was the self-appointed guardian of the conscience of the world. Then Brendan died. You were the only one who told me what I'd done."

"I said you killed him." She was barely breathing.

"Yes."

"I had no right to say that to you. I was insane then, and I was angry."

"At me?"

"You were the one with whom I'd . . ." She could not finish her statement. "I really must go."

After pressing his arm in a brief convulsive grip she turned and bolted for the gate. These were feelings she had been in search of. Now she fled them, but they swooped after her, grief, sorrow, guilt, mixed with her fear of Cheney and her love for her son and her ambivalence toward her mother and her resentment of the Dolans and her sense of failure as a writer and the futility of her effort to begin a new life and the sudden harsh discovery that David Dolan, to whom she'd written a cruel letter, nevertheless, apparently, thought well of her.

Instead of allowing the fact of his deflation—the third in twelve hours—to overwhelm him, he focused his attention on the details of her dismissal. He watched her fling herself through the door past the agent who had been about to close it behind the other passengers. He saw her as she dashed away from the window across the asphalt to the airplane. In the harsh noon glare her body was lit strangely, as if she were an apparition, a fleeting messenger. And of course she was.

What had he expected? Ticker tape again? He'd thought the decision to return to America was the hardest thing he'd ever done, but the decision was nothing compared to the deed of it. He'd simply wanted some reassurance that his coming home was welcome. Perhaps he'd wanted Eddie on behalf of everyone he'd offended to forgive him. She'd refused. He was diminished and he felt the weariness with which his travels and his thwarted efforts to touch ground were leaving him.

He was still holding her envelope. Without looking at it he recalled what he had written on it the night before, his agenda, his little list; jail, family, job. Artie Rose, NYU, Eddie Brewster. Three glimpses of the image that haunted his dream, a boot in the face. Most recently hers, in his.

In an oval window of the Beechcraft 99 he saw her. He had chastised himself before for thinking of her as a figure on an urn, but now she looked for all the world like a precious living cameo. The sun flashed off the glass. He could see the red collar of her shirt and he remembered how it had draped her breasts. In profile her short black hair framed her face and accentuated her long slim neck. Disembodied in that way and staring straight ahead, she had a timeless, uncontemporary quality.

The plane began to taxi in a grand burst of blue smoke through which he could see that she turned her face in his direction.

That was more than he'd gotten from her before and enough to make him realize that he did not regret his mad impulse to come and find her. She had touched his arm casually, but the warmth and affection even that touch conveyed had been enough to remind him that once he'd wanted all she had. The pain and vulnerability she communicated made him wish for a moment that he were the man whose place it was to care for her.

The plane was gone. Eddie was gone.

In his hands her letter was crushed into a ball. He had accused himself with it long enough. He dropped it in an ashtray, picked up his bag and left the airport for Cambridge.

CHAPTER 9

It took ten minutes to walk from the subway stop at Central Square to MacTernan Street. At Sacred Heart Church, where he'd been an altar boy, Dolan stopped, half-expecting the sight of the church to move him. Attached to the door at the top of a dozen stairs was a signboard with the schedule of masses and the names of the clergy. To see if any of the priests he knew were still there, he climbed the stairs slowly while donning his glasses. At the sixth stair he could read the sign well enough to know none of the names was familiar. He turned and from that vantage faced down the street toward his parents' house in the middle of the block.

It would never have occurred to him to look inside each automobile parked along the street, but when he noticed two men sitting in a car a third of the way down the block, he realized it should have.

Two thoughts hit him, one after the other. Artie Rose's phone was tapped. No, Artie Rose had called them.

Even worse than the prospect of being arrested was that of being arrested in his parents' house within minutes of his arrival home.

He was all too visible, and, with his suitcase, all too

obvious. He laughed briefly to think that in all their pictures of him he would have long hair and a beard. But what if they were using photographs of Brendan? He decided to leave his glasses on because they at least were new.

He climbed the rest of the stairs to the church, but the door was locked. He leaned against it and tried to think. Would the FBI be so blatant? Or was he simply being paranoid? If they wanted him why hadn't they arrested him at the airport in New York? But the answer was obvious; Artie Rose hadn't fingered him yet.

The thought of Artie Rose made Dolan realize what he was feeling, a dose of resister's adrenaline. Hadn't we made fools of the FBI in the old days, he thought. How he had loved to tease at rallies by introducing the agent who'd infiltrated. "Come on, G-man!" he would chant, "Take a bow. You in the new chamois shirt, take a bow!" Dolan realized that a contest of wits with the FBI right now was almost a relief.

He left his bag by the church door and slipped along the side of the building between the granite wall and a line of shrubs and came out on Pearl Street. He walked quickly to the next corner and went into Jack's, the neighborhood grocery, in which he'd bought his jawbreakers and sugar daddies. A girl at the register looked up from her magazine, but otherwise did not acknowledge him until he asked her for change. He went to the pay phone behind the first aisle of groceries. It reassured him that the phone was there; he'd called girlfriends from it as a teenager.

He was exhilarated by the threat that the FBI was after him, but it made him angry too. His anger fueled his sense of mastery. He called the Boston Field Office.

He was going to tell them to get the fuck off his street and leave his mother and father the hell out of it! They were in their seventies and had lost a son in Vietnam, for Christ's sake! But when they said politely, "What street? Whose mother and father?" what was he going to answer? When a woman's voice said, "Federal Bureau of Investigation," he hung up. This was real and no game. It was important not to underestimate them. He had to get hold of himself.

And do what?

He could not deal with the government until he knew what they were charging him with. He could not learn that without a lawyer. Artie had someone in his firm that could help. But what firm? And not Artie. Dolan was not that desperate.

He looked up Legal Aid. No such thing. He looked up Public Defenders, and there it was, an office even in Cambridge. He dialed it.

"Listen," he told the woman who answered, "I have a problem. I think I'm what you call wanted, and the FBI, I think it's the FBI, is sitting on my parents' doorstep. I have to talk to a lawyer."

"Are you in Middlesex County? Or did your offense take place in Middlesex County?"

"Is this a lawyer I'm speaking to?" Dolan had to press against the adjacent stainless refrigerator to vent his anxiety and frustration.

"I'll be glad to refer you to an attorney, but I have to establish that you're in contact with the right office."

"I'm in Cambridge, and so is my trouble. Does that qualify me?"

"Yes. Your name, please."

"What do you need that for? Listen, I just want to

ask a couple of questions. How the hell do I find out what I'm charged with and what they plan to do? It's been eight goddamn years and I forget how this shit works."

"I'm sorry, sir, but we can't give counsel over the telephone. I could make an appointment for you for tomorrow morning."

"Who pays you?"

"I'm sorry?"

"Who pays the Public Defenders?"

"The Commonwealth does."

"The government. Right. Thanks very much," he said and hung up. Be careful, he told himself. How would he have proceeded before? Were there agents at his parents' house? How could he be sure?

At that moment someone came into the store and he froze. A wall of soap cartons stood between him and the cash register, which rang then. The customer left.

He dialed his parents' number. He was not so agitated that it didn't please him to have remembered it.

His mother answered.

"Mom, it's Dave. How are you?"

"Dave?"

"Yes. It's Dave."

"Where are you?" There was caution, even suspicion, in her voice. It tagged his. Everyone's first question: where are you?

"Mom, are you alone there?"

"Alone here? Who is this?"

"Mom, it's me, Dave."

There was a long silence, followed by an even more tentative "David?"

"Yes, Mom."

"I don't believe you."

"Mom, listen to me. Can't you hear my voice?"

"My son lives overseas."

"In Sweden, right?"

"Yes."

"Well, I've come home."

"No, you haven't."

Dolan understood he was simply not going to be able to lay her confusion to rest until she saw him. "Listen," he ordered, "I want you to do as I say."

"I'll call the police."

"Are you standing in the living room?"

"Yes."

"Do you still have your Royal Doulton on the windowsill?"

"Yes."

"Move to the window for me." He waited. "Are you at the window now?"

"Yes."

"Do you see that brown car across the street?"

"Yes."

"Are there two men in it?"

"Is this really you, David?"

"Yes, Mom. Are there?"

"Two. That's right."

"Do you know them?"

"No. They've been sitting there. I noticed them before."

"Before today?"

"No. Where are you?"

"Is Dad there?"

"Should I get him? He's asleep upstairs."

"Let him sleep. I want you to do as I tell you. OK?"

"Yes, dear." His authority relieved her.

"Get your laundry basket. You still have that basket on wheels? Do you still wash the clothes on Pearl Street?"

"At the laundromat, sure."

"OK. Fill up your basket and go to the laundromat. I'll wait for you there."

"You're here? David, you're here?"

And why shouldn't the joy in her voice have made him weep? "Yes, Mom. I can't come in the house because I think those are FBI men waiting for me there. Come to the laundromat and we'll talk. Be careful. You have to fool them."

"I understand. Don't worry."

Outside Dolan went up the block toward the laundromat. Even in his state he could not walk that street without memories of those affectionate times, but he deflected them. He had to pay attention to what he was doing.

He slipped into the laundromat. From its window he could see down Pearl to the corner of MacTernan. He quickly checked out the room. There were no people, but three machines chugged away. He took up a position by the window and waited. He had spotted the Feds and, so far, duped them. For the first time since his return he was feeling sure of himself.

Soon his mother came around the corner pulling her basket. He wanted to watch the street behind her to see if anyone appeared to be following her, but he could not keep his eyes off her. He found himself assessing her appearance as a way of keeping his feelings at bay. She'd always had the best hair in the neighborhood. It was now silver and pulled back in a tight bun like a Quaker lady's. Even across the distance she appeared thinner. Her wrists were bony and her shoulders were at hard angles to her neck. She was walking slowly, but her posture was still strong. She believed in posture: his slouch was how he'd first disappointed her.

No one seemed to be following her.

When she approached the laundromat Dolan left the window for an alcove between machines in the back of the room. He was not visible from the door. He listened to her enter and come halfway back, then stop. He stepped out of the alcove. She came to him, and he enfolded her in his arms.

Finally she pulled back. "Is it really you?" she asked, but not emotionally.

"I'm sorry I didn't let you know, Mom. And I'm sorry about this." He let his eyes indicate the dingy room.

"That's all right. I love this old place. It's where I come to be alone." She hugged him again. "And none of this sorry business. We're all sorry, a sorry lot."

"I wanted all my trouble with the government to be cleared up before I got home, but . . ." He stopped. His feelings threatened to overtake him. He had to keep himself steady.

"Are you going back to Sweden?"

"No. I'm home. But apparently the FBI is one step ahead of me. Come in here." He led her back out of sight of the door. "I have to get a lawyer before I can . . ." He paused before his next word. It suggested an aspect to his situation that frightened him. ". . . Surrender." He squeezed her arms. "But that's enough about me. How are you? Golly, you look great! How's Dad?"

"Dad?"

"Yes, how is he?"

"All right, I guess. I mean, I'm confused. How could you be back? Should I have known you were coming?"

"No, Mom. It's my fault."

"He wouldn't understand." She turned slightly away. "He's not ..."

"Not what, Mom?"

"He only wears carpet slippers now," she said. "He never leaves the house. I shave him every third day."

"How long has he been like that?"

She looked down. "He hasn't been himself since Brendan."

Dolan hugged her and they didn't speak for a minute. But then she pulled back again and said, "He doesn't believe it."

"What? He doesn't believe what?"

"That Brendan died. There was no body, you know. He just stepped on something and disappeared."

"A mine."

"Your father thinks he's just missing. He writes letters to Washington all the time."

"Is he ... ?"

But she cut his question off by heading for her basket. "I should be doing some laundry, don't you think?" She loaded clothes into a washer, an old ritual to establish that she wasn't dreaming. She smiled at him and said, "I just washed these yesterday. For once, everything was clean." For as long as it took her to stuff the machine she held her composure. But when it was going she leaned over it and put her head on her forearm. Her shoulders shook.

He wanted to go to her and touch her and say, "I'll

take care of you now, Mom." But he knew it wasn't that simple. From where he was, he watched her weeping.

Finally she collected herself. She came back to him, dabbing at her face with her handkerchief. He pulled a pair of creaky old folding chairs together and they sat.

"I called you from the corner store. It hasn't changed a bit."

"Jack and Marie moved to the Cape."

"Who runs it, then?"

"Marie's nephew. Was there a girl at the counter?"

"Yes."

"That's his daughter. I forget her name." Mrs. Dolan smiled suddenly. "She's too young for you."

"Oh, you're going to fix me up, are you?" Dolan noticed a tear stain on her cheek and reached across to wipe it for her. They sat looking at each other for a moment. The chugging sound of the washing machine reinforced the silence.

"I saw Eddie today."

"Eddie?"

"Brendan's Eddie."

She shook her head firmly. "She lives in California. It couldn't have been her."

"I talked to her. At the airport. It was a coincidence."

Mrs. Dolan shook her head again, but said nothing.

"She told me she never sees you."

"It's been hard, Mom, hasn't it? You've missed your grandchild, haven't you?"

"Your father says it isn't."

"What?"

"Our grandchild."

"Why do you say that, Mom?"

"Before your brother was dead, she took up with this other man. Your father thinks she was glad when Brendan died so that she could be free to marry him."

"Is that what you think?"

She met his eyes. "At first they said Brendan was missing. Missing In Action. They didn't say he was dead for a long time. And before that it was in the papers that she was with this Cheney McCoy."

"But the Army called Brendan missing because he stepped on a mine, right? Not because they thought he was alive. There were no remains. You told me yourself there were no remains."

"Your father says Cheney McCoy wants the boy because he thinks it's his child."

"What do you mean?"

"In the divorce."

"What divorce?"

"It's in the papers."

"Eddie's divorced?"

"Not yet. They're fighting over the boy. If it was Brendan's would her husband fight for him?"

Dolan was shocked by what he was hearing, but now he understood why Eddie had seemed distracted and unhappy. How callous of him to have expected her to assume his agenda, as if nothing of consequence could have been happening in her life.

"Mom," he said, handing her the picture Eddie'd given him, "do you think he could be anybody's but Brendan's?"

Mrs. Dolan's eyes filled as she studied the photo. She covered her mouth with the corner of her apron.

Dolan could see what blows she'd taken. Her behavior toward Eddie was cruel only if considered apart from them.

"Your father calls her a slut of the first water."

"He's wrong."

"The priest says the divorce is a scandal. We shouldn't seem to condone, Father said."

"Who's asking you to condone?"

"Her lawyer is."

His mother's statement surprised him. "Tell me."

"Her lawyer wrote to us. We were supposed to sign a letter he enclosed saying she was a good mother. The 'paternal grandparents,' he called us."

"When was this?"

"Last month."

"Eddie didn't mention it."

"We didn't do it."

Dolan could feel himself stalking again, as if his mother now was quarry. "Why not, Mom?"

Mrs. Dolan was staring at the photo of Bren and slowly shaking her head. "I asked the priest in confession. He said I couldn't do it, either. Your father forbid me even to keep the letter."

"But you kept it."

"It's in my sewing. My heart goes out to the little boy."

"It should. He's yours. Eddie told me that he misses you." Dolan was as seized by emotion as she was. "And so do I, Mom. I've missed you a lot." He put his hands on her bony shoulders.

Relief agitated her face, and the old bright eyes came back, hers at last, if full of water.

A woman came into the laundromat just then. Mrs. Dolan whipped around and called, "Helen Mac-

Ready, it's about time you came back. That cycle's been over ten minutes now."

Helen MacReady hardly looked up from the laundry she was hauling out of the machine. "Thanks for keeping an eye out, Peg," she said with friendly sarcasm. "What would I do without you?" She loaded up her gray sack and left.

"If she asked, I was going to say you were my nephew."

"You're as slippery as I am."

She looked toward the window. "Do you really think it's the FBI?"

"Yes," he said. He was sure of it. "And that's a problem because I want you to go back to the house and get the letter. I want you to sign it."

"But what . . . ?"

"It's not condoning divorce, Mom. It's helping Brendan's son stay with his mother."

"The lawyer said it has to be notarized."

Dolan figured that too; his mind was working quickly. "Is Mr. O'Meara still at the pharmacy?"

She nodded.

"He's a notary. Or he was. He stamped an application of mine once. Do you remember what the affidavit says?"

"I've read it a hundred times. 'We attest of our own knowledge that she is a dutiful, capable and loving parent.' "

"You can sign that, can't you?"

"Is she?"

"Yes."

"I want to sign it, David."

"Good. Now here's what you do. Pretend you're out of soap. OK?"

She nodded.

"And to get some more you go home. You get the soap, but you also get the letter. Right? When you come out don't look at the car with the men in it. You don't notice them at all. And then, on the way back here, you stop in the drugstore. They'll think you're just going in there for change. You need more quarters, right?"

"And dimes."

"Right."

"While you're in there you sign the letter in front of Mr. O'Meara."

"But he might tell the priest. He might tell your father."

"He doesn't need to know what it says. He just needs to watch you sign it. Fold it back from the top. If he asks you, tell him it's to Social Security and you don't want him to know how old you are."

"And then I come back here?" She had never looked at him with such subservience. That more than anything made her seem old.

"Right. You're good at this. You should have been a spy."

"Or a crook." She smiled. "Don't worry about a thing. Watch my laundry."

From the window he watched her cross the street, and it made him nervous suddenly that there wasn't a crosswalk there. Once she made it to the curb he relaxed. She had her spunk still. He watched her walk to MacTernan Street, and he waited to see if anyone followed her. No one did. Both agents must have remained at the house. He hoped his mother could pass them without giving herself away. When she disappeared around the corner he tried to picture her. It made him angry that the FBI had laid their trap at his parents' house.

Dolan was not a criminal, and by God he would not be treated like one. He was going to report to the government, but on his own schedule, Goddamnit! He felt the rush of his old resistance. The FBI was not going to arrest him; he swore it to himself. He was going to walk freely into the U.S. Attorney's Office with his own attorney at his side. After eight years, Dolan was going to control the events of his return himself.

He wanted to watch his mother coming back, but he knew it was foolish to loiter at the window. He returned to the alcove in the back of the laundromat and waited. His mother found him there.

"Mr. O'Meara didn't even ask me," she said. She gave him the affidavit.

"Everybody knows you're forty-five." Dolan saw that she'd signed the statement and O'Meara'd stamped it. "Were the men still there?"

"Yes. They didn't follow me. They're just sitting there."

"They won't bother you. They'll go away when I don't show up." Would they, though, he wondered? Would they try to intimidate his parents? "Listen, Mom, if they ask you . . ."

"Don't worry." She smiled. "If I can fool your father, I can fool them."

He smiled too. She was all right.

She indicated the affidavit. "Thank you. I just needed a little encouragement. Can I keep this?" She held up the photo of Bren.

"Sure. Eddie asked me to give it to you." He started to hand the affidavit back to her, but thought better of it. "I'll take care of this, though." He put it in his coat. He wondered if Eddie's divorce meant something for him.

"There's my wash." The machine clanged to a stop. She looked nervously about the laundromat. "I usually hang it on the line in the yard. Do they know that? I never use the dryers in good weather."

"Why don't you get your clothes then, Mom, and take them home. I wanted to see you, was all. And tell you that pretty soon it'll be like it used to be."

"I hope not." She grinned. Then, a quick change of mood, she said, "Your father won't believe me."

"Why don't you just tell him that I called from New York and that I'll be home real soon. Would he believe that?"

She said tentatively, "I told you that he pretends Brendan is still alive?"

"Yes?"

She lowered her eyes. "He pretends about you too."

Dolan saw it. "That I'm dead?" he asked softly.

She nodded once, briskly.

He put his hand on her shoulder. "I put him through the wringer back then. I'll make it up to him."

She looked at him, tears in her eyes again.

"I'll make it up to both of you."

And then they hugged each other.

Something nagged at Dolan, then he remembered. His bag. He had to get his mother to deal with it, but casually. "Listen, Mom, will you say a prayer for me? Stop at church, OK? And put in a word for me?"

"The church is locked."

He'd forgotten.

"But I can go through the rectory."

"I left my bag by the door. Do you think you could . . . ?"

"I'll take care of it. My nephew's." She winked. "This is like t.v."

"Can you stow it in the church somewhere? We don't want them to see you with it."

"There's a confessional they never use."

"Perfect." He made the three-ring sign. "You're terrific at this, Aunt Peg. One more thing. Do you still have a car?"

She opened her purse. "Sure. It's at the lot next to the trolley barn. We never use it." She took a key off a ring and handed it to him. "They let us park it there for free. Do you remember where the barn is?"

"Are you kidding?"

"All the fellows are retired, but the new ones are nice to your dad. It's the only place he ever goes, but he hasn't been over there all summer."

"What kind of car is it?"

"Oh. A Duster. It's brown."

"A what?"

"Plymouth Duster. You'll recognize it. It looks like me. Old and beat up."

He kissed her. "Thanks, Mom. Be careful now, OK?"

She made a show of composing herself, collected her wet laundry, then trailed her basket out of the laundromat without looking back at him.

Dolan waited for ten minutes, then slipped out onto Pearl Street, cut through an alley to Walnut and headed for the river and the old trolley yard.

On the way he stopped at the Mobil station that Marty Ryan's father ran. Mr. Ryan was still there, but he didn't recognize him even when Dolan spoke to him. Dolan asked for a map of Maine.

CHAPTER 10

"Nobody gives a rat's fart for morality in this play except me and you, Cliff; and you're the hired killer." Cheney laughed weirdly, then downed his beer and concluded with his arm around the actor. "The assassin has his doubts, but I never do."

Cheney and half a dozen others were sitting at a large round table in the rear of Joe Allen's, the bistro around the corner from the Studio. It was after dinner but before the shows let out, so there were only a few other patrons at the bar and at four or five tables. As the actors drifted in from the rehearsal they joined Cheney. Peter Garvey had been giving them notes one by one and most were obviously deflated. But where Garvey was not pleased with their work, Cheney was encouraging. He had been expostulating nonstop for an hour, loudly and dramatically. The actors knew he was still performing. The fact that nearly everything he was saying contradicted what Garvey had said heightened their interest. Not only was he stroking them—he told each new arrival how splendid he or she had been—but his comments about the play itself were astute and unusual. If there was something disturbing in his carrying on, it was his emphasis on the extreme cruelty of the action as its definitive note, and he was insisting at great length that each actor had the responsibility to uncover and flaunt the sadistic quality that prepared his or her character to be—literally—the devil's own accomplice.

"Christ, Cheney," an actress said, "Garvey called it moral collapse. You make it sound like triumph."

"It *is* triumph!" He slammed his fist on the table and glasses bounced. "Triumph exactly! I'm not talking about Richard. I'm talking about us! If we make it live, that evil of his, then it isn't evil anymore. Don't you see?"

He looked around the table. The others found his energy and conviction irresistible, but they couldn't look at him. Whatever they thought about the implicit philosophical dispute, Cheney, not Garvey, was already the lightning rod of the production. They sat with him, drinking, wanting to be as close to him as possible, but without touching him.

"The transformation of life into art, eh?" the actor who played the First Murderer offered.

Cheney ignored him because another girl joined them then. He stood up, his chair scraped loudly. He felt dizzy for an instant. It wasn't drink. The work that day had left Cheney feeling physically shaky, and his success in discovering in himself what he needed to play Richard had left him in a state of overcharged emotion, unrooted, unspecific and barely controlled.

When he sat again he surprised Cliff by turning and replying, "Or the transformation of art into life. Isn't that the real danger?"

"I don't follow. You mean what happens if I actually become the assassin?"

"No! No! No! Don't be silly. What is this, *House of Wax*? Mad actors? I want to know what happens to all that free-floating venom you pump up. An actor lives by loosely linking an emotion from his own life to that of his character. All right. But what happens if the link breaks?"

No one spoke for a moment. Cheney looked at them each in turn.

"At which end?" a girl asked.

"Huh?" Cheney said. He wasn't sure suddenly what they were talking about.

"Broken at which end?" she repeated. "From the past real event or the present stage event?"

"Either one," Cheney said. "And that's the triumph."

When no one replied now, Cheney realized they were uneasy with what he was saying. He felt like a tightrope walker with an audience; he could tell how close to falling he was by how still they were.

He was like two people to himself. In addition to the engaged, wildly manic declaimer, he was also loitering above himself in slow circles. No one lifted their heads far enough to see that part of him, flagging, dispirited, inanimate, only watching. In addition to watching himself, he was watching Eddie as, in his mind, he pictured her. He was acutely aware that she was only blocks away, getting ready for bed probably, taking her clothes off, sleeping in the nude, sleeping alone. How he longed to be with her. The cruelty and anger required of him to play Richard were nothing compared to the tenderness she could elicit, simply by curling her body into a question mark inside his. With Eddie his worst feelings had almost always been sheathed safely inside his best ones. If he was now at the mercy of feelings he could not control—however splendidly he used them on stage—wasn't it because she had left him?

Still no one spoke. They wouldn't as long as he sat there dominating them with his mood. It would have helped him to talk about his clash of feelings. The brilliant glimpses of his past with Eddie left him in the darkness more than ever. The flashes of feeling for Richard's sake had revealed for the first time to Cheney how desolate he felt. It was too simple to hate Eddie for what she'd done; Eddie was what could save him from chaos. He called it chaos because he did not understand it. He did not know precisely where his cruelty and cockiness and under it, just, his fear were coming from. Or going. But these punk actors were glib and superficial. They thought that there was nothing to the high wire but a genius for fancy footwork. Everyone safely on the ground thought that. Cheney knew that work of the kind he'd begun that day required only a genius for not falling, and he suddenly wasn't sure that he had it.

The postcurtain crowd arrived, as it always did, in a bunch shortly after ten. They were breathless and dazzled, determinedly so, as befitted the ticket prices they had paid, if not the staged hash-with-music they had sunk their gums into. Joe Allen's at the moment of the show-goers' arrival was transformed from the actors' common room into another Broadway saloon where before going home one went to see, with luck, a movie star or two. Cheney realized he was being stared at, not openly, and pointed out. He excused himself from the table. He went to the bar and asked Red Thomas for the *Times*. He took it into the employees' toilet in back and turned it to page C-17, on which the weather map was printed.

The weather in New York that day had been hot and dry, but Cheney was interested in the weather elsewhere. The map located the fronts, the highs and lows across the continent, and it indicated a northwest airflow over the Midwest with strong winds coming from Canada. That meant that the weather up and down the entire East Coast should have been excellent that day, with fair weather cumuli and good visibility everywhere. But in the upper right-hand corner, just showing on the map, were the blips of a crescent across Nova Scotia which located an occluded front, on the northeast of which was the faint shading of precipitation. An occluded front blocks weather and for as long as it holds nothing moves through it. Cheney studied it as if a longer look would tell him more, because a front like that can act like a cork on carbonation. It can pop under pressure and the weather unleashed then can be fierce, especially in that quarter, coming from the northeast. New England's worst summer storms are generated beyond just such crescent lines in systems high above the North Atlantic.

Cheney was not familiar with off-ocean patterns. He knew everything about winds bouncing off the Rockies and the convergence of weather when the mountain swirls in Idaho are overswept by cold Alberta air. But the Maine coast, with its warm backwash from the Gulf Stream, the prevailing march of fronts from the continent and the cold drift down from the Maritimes, was strange territory. He'd need more information to be certain, but it looked good. Occluded fronts most often hold for several days at least, guaranteeing perfect weather in the lee. It was possible this one had already eased southwest into Maine, but that would mean in all likelihood moderate winds and rain, and it could be spent already. It was also possible that behind the front, pressure was continually mounting. If the front held against that instead of letting it seep through, it would break all at once before an August nor'easter within a day or two.

But the crescent of blips was the minor feature of a map which otherwise showed perfect weather where he wanted it. The average dewpoint was forty degrees below temperature, and that meant no fog. Fog was the problem a lone pilot flying the coast of Maine for the first time should worry most about. Better hard rain and robust wind than fog. If you make your landings without air control to help, you'd better be able to see.

Had he decided that? Was he flying to Maine? He closed the paper and insisted to himself that he had made no such decision. He put it out of his mind. If he was thinking about weather he was doing so in the abstract, because he loved to contemplate it.

At the bar again, he slid onto a stool and called to the bartender, waving the paper at him.

"Keep it, Cheney," Red Thomas said. "I read it."

"No, no. I got one for you. Come here. You'll never get it."

He waited for Red to serve a pair of drinks. When he came over, Cheney recited with pompous expansiveness, ". . . 'the good and the bad, the ecstasy, the remorse and the sorrow, the people and places and how the weather was.' OK, where's it from?"

Red Thomas smiled at Cheney. He was a large, overweight man with wild, pitch-black hair and an elaborate moustache. He leaned over the bar and showed his pleasure as he said, "Papa. *Death in the Afternoon.*"

Cheney looked at him impassively. "You son of a bitch."

"That's fifty," Red said, and went down the bar laughing.

Cheney mugged for the couple on the stools next to him. They'd made no effort to disguise their interest. He slapped the newspaper. "Weather," he announced to them, 'is the perfect daily rendition of the only matter, in Chekhov's phrase, for art; the contrast between what is and what ought to be. Don't you agree?"

The couple laughed, embarrassed.

Cheney tapped the polished wood rhythmically with eight fingers and whistled the first bars of "Stormy Weather" while nodding at Red, who'd put a beer in front of him.

The young man on the next stool said, "Can we buy that for you?"

Cheney stopped. "That's damn nice of you, you know it?" He raised the glass. They did likewise, and the three of them clinked. Cheney thought he recognized the girl. She had fantastic cheekbones, but her nose was narrow. "I know you two, right?"

The girl said, "I was in *Quick Study*. I played Miranda." She paused, then added, "Tammy's roommate."

"I remember. You were terrific. *Quick Study* was a piece of shit, though. Name this tune." He drummed and whistled dramatically.

"Stormy Weather," the man said.

"Right! A prize for you!" Cheney twirled around. He was himself the prize. "Stormy weather with its thunder and its howling winds and pelting rain or cold whipping snows is not the work of nature's enemy, as we like to think, but of nature herself! Do you like storms? I love storms!"

The couple exchanged a glance with each other, but Cheney was oblivious to them.

"Storms show us what we are! Which is why Shakespeare always ends his tragedies with them. Did you know that?" He leaned rudely across the man to the woman. "Did you?"

"No," she said.

"We should hit the road, actually," the man said, and he offered a weak smile.

"I thought you were buying me a drink."

"We are."

"I've hardly touched it. You have to stay until I've finished. Where were we?"

"Shakespeare."

"Of course! Shakespeare believed that the truth could be revealed only by distortion. Do you believe that? Of course you do. The tree is never more itself, in other words, than when it has been struck by lightning. Or when it holds the naked body of Christ, whose death looses the real storm, the worst one."

Cheney took a deep draught then. If he'd been asked he could have explained what he was doing; he was trying to vent the pressure inside him. If Joe Allen himself came over and told him he was acting foolishly, he'd have told him that he was superficial. What is foolishness, he'd have said, but inner grandeur in conflict with the way things are? Some kinds of foolishness are better than others; those, for example, which, while amusing, don't hurt anyone.

The act of drinking deeply from his beer calmed him. He had the attention, he suddenly realized, of the dozen people within earshot. He knew instinctively that they were observing him with admiration. They, like his colleagues at the Studio, had no idea what inner seething boiled beneath the surface of his manic creativity. He turned to the couple, like a teacher trying one more time to make his point. "Fair weather in Shakespeare is always ominous because it implies its opposite in a way that its opposite never does. Fair weather has never saved anyone. Bad weather has ruined armies and therefore whole nations. Weather, my friends, weather." Cheney draped an arm over the man. "More than one of life's mysteries is tied in its knot. And Shakespeare, like an expert pilot, had an innate distrust of it only when it was good."

"That's terrific," the man said. "You should publish that." He reached for his wallet and turned to his girl. "Isn't he terrific?"

"You know who I am, don't you?"

"Of course."

Cheney winked. "I'm the weatherman on the nightly news." He slapped the man's shoulder and blew a kiss to the actress. "Hey, Red," he called, "you got a dime?"

Red shot him the coin along the bar's lip. Cheney caught it, went to the phone booth and called Frazier collect.

"I wanted to give you a chance to flash a red light. I've been thinking of going to Maine."

"Is there a problem with that?" Frazier was accustomed to Cheney's enigmatic openings. They were at the service, usually, of evasion, but Frazier's strategy was always the simple one of asking and asking again that Cheney explain himself. If Cheney wanted to obfuscate, he would, regardless of Frazier's strategy. If he wanted to confide and find support, on the other hand, he would do that too. Frazier had long since left such choices to his patient. It was unusual for Cheney to call like this. He had done so only twice in the eight years of their relationship. Obviously something was bothering him.

"To see Bren," he explained.

Frazier did not react.

"He's at Eddie's mother's."

"What does Eddie say?"

"She doesn't know. She's not there. I'd just show up. Take him for a ride maybe. For the afternoon."

"That sounds plain enough. I don't see the problem."

"I'm not saying there is one."

"But you called asking me to flash a red light. Why is that?"

The silence that fell between them was, on the telephone, like the silence of a grotto, full of a meaning both obscure and ominous.

Frazier said finally, "It's your nickel." He would of course bill Cheney for the phone charges, as well as for the time. Any fraction of an hour counted as an hour.

"Josh Kann tells me I'm within my rights."

"I should think so. Why not let Eddie know?"

"Within my rights to take him, I mean."

"I don't follow. You said for the afternoon."

*   *   *

He saw himself and Bren one afternoon whirling in
the cup-and-saucer ride at Disneyland. The more the
cup spun the more Bren was pressed back against
him, and Cheney remembered feeling that the child
and he had become in that centrifuge the same person. It was not erotic, but only sex in his experience
approached it for intensity and delight and, indeed,
communion. Cheney had never heard anyone laugh
the way Bren did. They rode it three times in a row,
and when they got out they were both so dizzy they
had to hold on to each other to keep from falling. In
fact, of course, they were both taking advantage of
their dizziness to keep hugging each other. At the end
of that afternoon, they each bought a box of Crackerjacks for Eddie. Cheney and Bren had never felt
closer. When she saw how much her son loved him,
how could she not forgive him? How was he to know
that she would assume he'd kidnapped Bren?

Cheney was indifferent neither to Eddie's feelings
nor to her rights. She was indifferent to his, however,
and that galled. Having been dismissed he was now
expected to fade from the scene; exit with the body,
the corpse of their marriage.

"Look, I've been having some trouble with this
part."

"What, with Richard?"

"We've talked about that disconnectedness of mine
. . ." Cheney leaned his forehead against the cold
metal of the phone box. He waited for Frazier to say
something, but he wouldn't. "To tell you the truth I
wish I was lying on that fucking couch of yours."

"You could come out, couldn't you?"

"No." If he was flying anywhere it wasn't to L.A.

"This play is too important. I did fantastic work to-day. Even the fag director thinks so."

"But it makes you feel . . .?"

"Lonely for them. I hate her because I love her. You know?"

"So you're feeling your anger again?"

"Not like before. Worse. Everybody here thinks I'm a fantastic actor because I can create this hate-ridden, chaotic, impulsive genius. What they don't know is that I, meanwhile, am floating above it all, taking aim."

"I'm not sure I follow that."

Cheney fell silent. He pushed open the door of the phone booth to get some air, even though the noise of the restaurant made it harder to hear and harder to think.

"If he was with me, then Eddie would have to deal with me, wouldn't she?"

"Are you talking about her son?"

Cheney slammed his fist down on the small shelf. "Goddamnit, I'm not paying you to tell me he's her son!"

"Why are you paying me, Cheney?"

"He's *my* son!"

"You didn't phone to tell me the boy is your son. You phoned because you wanted me to tell you not to go up there."

"Oh, come on."

"I don't think you're leveling with yourself. What are you afraid of?"

"Nothing."

"What are you afraid of doing?"

" 'What! do I fear myself? There's none else by. Richard loves Richard; that is, I am I. Then fly.' "

He paused. "I've been thinking of renting a plane."

"Why did you call me, to recite Shakespeare?"

" 'Throng to the bar, crying all, Guilty! guilty! I shall despair. There is no creature loves me, And if I die no soul shall pity me.' "

Frazier said nothing.

"Look, I'm sorry I bothered you. Let not our babbling dreams affright your soul."

"They don't."

"Mine either."

"Good."

Cheney waited, as if to give Frazier a last chance to warn him or forbid him or—unlikely thought!—encourage him. But Frazier responded, for it was a response, only with more of his damnable silence.

"Thanks," Cheney said. How he wished he hadn't called.

"You're welcome."

They hung up.

Cheney sat holding the phone on its hook. He wanted it to ring. When it didn't, he shrugged and thronged to the bar.

Reah Whitson was sitting there sipping gin and tonic. Peter Garvey was standing next to her with his back to the room, his hand around a bottle of Perrier. Other patrons at the bar made a point to sit or stand at an angle to see who had come in, but not Garvey. The position he'd taken up said he didn't care who else was there and he probably didn't. He never came into Joe Allen's. He didn't drink, for one thing, though as far as anyone knew he wasn't an alcoholic, and he didn't believe, for another, in socializing with actors. Once he left the stage apron in the half-light of which he exercised absolute authority he looked pretty much like everybody else, only shorter. When Cheney saw him, he knew Garvey had come into the saloon looking for him.

He slapped him on the back. "Peter, how nice to see you." Cheney ignored Reah. "Word is Joe Papp had a stroke when he heard you're directing an all-white cast in *Richard Three*. He was going to do it himself, but he didn't think New York was ready."

"You took off before I had a chance to talk to you."

"You wanted to give me notes?" Cheney signaled Red Thomas for a beer.

"No." Peter Garvey did not give Cheney McCoy notes, and both knew it. "I thought the three of us might sit for a minute where we can talk." As he said this he looked at Cheney but nodded at Reah.

Cheney turned to Reah. "About what?"

She didn't raise her eyes from the drink.

"You were pretty rough on each other today."

Cheney realized Reah had been crying. Her wrecked face touched him, and for the first time that evening someone else's misery took precedence over his. He put his hand on her shoulder. "You were great today, sweetheart. You pushed me right to the edge."

"I can't play out at the edge with you." She could barely be heard. "I . . ." And then she stopped.

Cheney looked at Garvey, who said, "She wants out."

"Do you?"

She nodded.

Cheney took his hand from her shoulder, snapping

off his sympathy. He reached for his beer. "OK, babe. Whatever you want. Who was that bimbo, Peter, your first choice, the one you were going to cast before I forced Reah on you?" He sipped.

Garvey looked at the floor.

Reah raised her head and turned on the stool. Tears had filled her eyes again. "You bastard."

"No," Cheney said harshly, "you punk! You're doing the best work of your career. A door is opening in front of you onto the best room in the house and you want to slam it shut. You surprise me, Reah. You're gutless."

"You never told me you forced me on the show."

"Of course I didn't tell you, but you knew it. You've never darkened a stage in your life. You thought Shakespeare was a bookstore in Paris. Why the hell should they have given you the role? But you took it and you're making it yours. You scared the piss out of me today, all day. Out of Richard the fucking third, for Christ's sake! You can be the best Lady Anne of the decade. Ask Garvey here. He didn't want you before, but he'd give his teeth to keep you."

She looked at the director, who said, "You're good, Reah. I want you."

"I'm afraid of what happened. I tried to stab you."

"Of course you did. You were supposed to."

"The script says 'drop the knife.' "

"Fuck the script."

"I can't agree with that," Garvey said, smiling. It would reflect badly on him if he couldn't keep his cast together, even this one. He thought McCoy was handling her just right, and he was beginning to relax.

"I never thought it would be so intense," she said, and shuddered. "So crazy."

"But we're playing the most intense characters of all," Cheney explained. "They're demonic people, Reah."

"But does that mean *we* have to be?"

He smiled and looked at his beer, shaking his head. How would Strasberg explain it to her? "It's not overidentifying with the characters that sends us around the bend. It's that the characters require from us stuff from our own lives that might . . ." Cheney paused because he realized that, despite himself, he was telling her the truth ". . . better be left alone."

"I wish we were doing *Romeo and Juliet*."

"Anybody can do swooning teenagers, Reah." Cheney raised his beer to her. "It takes a real man and a real woman to do Richard and Anne."

"If you say so yourself," Garvey put in, but affectionately.

Before Cheney could toast him, they were interrupted. A decked-out middle-aged couple, the man in a velvet jacket, the woman in a long dress and too much jewelry, apologized grandly while asking for Cheney's autograph. Sometimes Cheney refused such requests. He didn't then because it underscored the difference between him and Garvey. After signing his name he introduced them to Reah, whom they claimed to have recognized. She signed for them too. Before going off they eyed Garvey and decided he was nobody. After they'd left, the bartender leaned toward Cheney and apologized.

Cheney put his arm around Reah's waist and slid

his two fingers into her jeans under her vest and silk shirt. He whispered, "You thought I was mad at you?"

She nodded.

He shook his head. "I've been distracted because of my son," he whispered.

She had forgotten that his son was sick. She had read Cheney's mood—he was aloof, cruelly cutting her off all day—but she had assumed he was furious at her for spitting twice in their scene that morning, for taking him by surprise and, in her opinion, showing him up, if only for a minute. Now she saw that it was worry for his little boy that burdened him. She covered his hand with hers.

Cheney said to Garvey, "I think Reah could use a day off, Peter." He paused, trying to read the director's reaction. "And, for that matter, so could I."

Garvey finished off his Perrier and put it down. "Good idea. I've been wanting to work the others anyway. With you two out of the way maybe they won't be looking over their shoulders."

"Don't kid yourself, Peter. That's you they're looking at. They think you're God, which is your problem . . ." Cheney gave it two beats ". . . since all actors are atheists."

"That they think I'm God is not my problem." Garvey laughed abruptly. He was relieved. He even touched McCoy as if he liked him. "It's my solution."

An exit line. He kissed Reah on the cheek. "Take the day off, kid. Go to the zoo." He patted Cheney's forearm. "Both of you. But don't tell Lee I let you off." He smiled slyly. "Whatever they think, we know that he's God." Another one. He left.

Cheney and Reah were silent for a few minutes, and that was their mistake. Reah had demolished her manicure. It would take weeks for her nails to recover. She stared at them surreptitiously. She didn't want Cheney to notice how she'd chewed and chewed during her fit in Garvey's office.

But Cheney had noticed and now couldn't avoid fixing on what he didn't like about her, that core of desolation that prevented her from believing in what she had done. It was as if Reah stood outside Lady Anne's lunging passion, helpless, gazing on it while its heat blasted her. But from where Cheney stood, all was cold. To him Reah was a weak woman whose brains, talent and skill enabled her on occasion, particularly in public, to seem strong. She had a gift for simulation.

But it wasn't her fault. This was the stage, not movies. For the first time in her life Reah was having to insert her body, her own body, and not some director's, producer's or editor's image of it, into a scene, a role, a catastrophe. No wonder she was feeling hung by her heels. She had not faked the swoon for Garvey. If she were only trying to keep her claim on his and Cheney's attention, on their worship, they could have responded without breaking stride. Directors and male stars have to know how to wrap their leading ladies in warm looks when they are chilled. But Reah was showing something else, something devastated and, to a fellow actor, devastating. Cheney was ashamed that he had not noticed how hurt she was.

He moved his glass next to hers so that they quite gently touched. "I apologize for not explaining better."

"It comes out of nowhere, doesn't it?"

"Not nowhere."

"What scared me wasn't what I was putting into Lady Anne, but what she put into me."

He raised a finger. "Life creates art." And then a second one. "Art creates life."

"Doesn't it scare you?"

Cheney could feel himself tense up. He wanted to avoid this conversation, but he knew he owed it to this woman to try to let her see that his capacity to be undone by their work and its reverberations matched hers.

He gestured with his beer toward the crowded restaurant, the after-theater people at their dinners. "Do you know what Groucho said about them?"

She looked at the boisterous diners.

"When they go to the theater, they want a real old lady to come crashing down a steep hill in her wheelchair, and they want her to slam face-first full-speed into a real cement wall at the bottom." He turned his back on them and drank. "And then they want her to get up, dance a little jig, and walk away unharmed."

"It doesn't quite work like that, does it?"

He shook his head. "Did I ever tell you about my first role? The first time, I mean, I had the lead in a real show? It was here, at the Cherry Lane, a piece of fluff called *Fog People*, an update on the Tyrones. I played the older son, but I was only eighteen. He was supposed to be about thirty, a tall good-looking guy who was getting married in the first act. But he knew that his fiancée had gotten it on with his kid brother once. My guy was convinced she really loved the brother, she was marrying him as a second choice, et cetera. His craziness about that led him to set it up so she and his brother, in the second act after their mother's funeral, of course, get it on again. The play was unbearably shallow, but that character just bowled me over. I wasn't ready to walk around on knees that shook like his did. He was too fucking scared. He couldn't stand the fact that nobody's anybody's first choice, and so he ruined everything. The guy moved me enormously."

Reah watched him as if she were watching a man free-fall end over end; what struck her was how slowly he moved.

"Opening night I did something terrible and ridiculous." He grinned at her. "I played the guy with a speech impediment, like this." His voice went up in pitch and, with a lisp, he squeaked out several lines that began, "Dave? Dave? You there?"

Reah laughed.

"The author ran from the theater screeching. The audience took the play as parody of O'Neill, a farce. They were supposed to weep uncontrollably, but they had a laughfest. At intermission the director was afraid to talk to me, but I heard him ask an actress how she felt. She said, 'How would you feel, playing Donald Duck's mother?' The show closed that night. That was when I changed my name to Cheney McCoy. That character freaked me out because his feelings were just like mine. What the playwright never understood was that they were pathetic feelings and absurd. My shrink told me that sabotaging the play was probably a very sane way of handling the conflict it set off in me. Anyway, what they don't know or care about—" he gestured over his shoulder

to the diners "—is that when the wheelchair slams
into the wall, we don't get up unharmed." He put his
arm around her. "Do we?"

She shook her head.

"That's why we have to help each other."

Cheney had forgotten by then that *Fog People* had
not been performed in the Village, but in the barn of
the summer theater in Williamstown. He was conscious, though, of his other lie. He'd used it on Frazier too. The lead in that play had flipped and done
the show like Donald Duck, but it wasn't Cheney.
He'd played the kid brother, practically a walk-on
with a total of seven lines. But it had been his first
speaking part in stock, and he couldn't forgive the actor who'd ruined the play until he started claiming to
have done it himself.

It was a lie, perhaps, but that was less important to
Cheney than the two kindnesses it made possible.
First, over the years, the kindness toward himself implied in the lie's admission of vulnerability and
weakness. And second, the kindness right then to
Reah, his friend and colleague. When the artists continually push emotions and experiences to the limit
for the sake of their art, then it is banal in the extreme to regard the fictions they create in their own
defense as dishonest. The business of theater is not
facticity but truth, and the business of friendship is to
help each other any way you can.

"I didn't know you'd changed your name."

Cheney realized that the new generation of actors
rarely changed their names. Reah hadn't, but he
guessed that was because her immigrant grandparents
had done it for her. That he'd changed his name

would probably make him seem old to her. He smiled and said, "I wanted a name that was unusual."

"What was your name before?"

"Anson Ennis."

As Cheney watched Reah's face break into its sprinkle of laughter, she seemed young to him and he felt responsible for her. But also he felt free of her, now that she was radiant again. He was beholden to her only as long as she showed him her suffering.

He did not know what to do next, could have used a playwright's intervention in the scene, a phone ringing, say, with news of a nuclear plant disaster in the next county, his editor ordering him to get the story. Or perhaps a gunshot with which to bring the curtain down. Only blanks, after all. Pistols on stage, like the leather-bound books, have nothing in them. Cheney's mind did not want to settle on what it knew; he had to take her home now and fuck her, and then stay the night. Why not? A phone that rings but doesn't connect. A gun that fires but doesn't shoot.

"Shall I take you home?"

She nodded, then lowered her eyes. She was embarrassed, it seemed to him, genuinely embarrassed, and that touched him.

They walked from midtown to the Village. On the way Cheney stopped and bought the next day's *Times*.

At Reah's place they did not turn on the lights. They could see clearly because the street-lamp flooded the loft with its eerie glow. Cheney began lovemaking by going through the motions, pretending, while undressing her, that he was as moved by their reconciliation as she seemed to be. But the sight

of her naked in the shadows, not quite exposed, interested him, stirred him, finally excited him. She was
exquisitely made. Her body never failed to arouse
him. They stood under the skylight handling each
other carefully, going slowly, brushing lips together,
forgetting everything of that day, forgetting in a way,
each of them, who the other was.

Cheney moved her toward the bed.

She turned and took a step away, toward the
bathroom. He stopped her, and, when she looked at
him, he shook his head.

"I have to get ready."

He shook his head again.

"My diaphragm," she whispered.

"No. Not tonight. Let's give each other everything." He said that, in part, for the effect he knew it
would have. It shocked her, and then made tears
come to her eyes. Reah Whitson was a cool cookie.
She had never had sex unprotected before, and when
she realized, at his suggestion, how much she wanted
to, she thought for the first time that she loved
Cheney.

That was why she was crying when she took him
into her body. She had assumed she would not love
anybody ever again.

When Cheney came, he was thinking quite deliberately of Eddie. It was Eddie he longed to be with. It
was Eddie he wanted to fuck. It was Eddie with
whom he wanted to make dozens of babies. Reah's
weeping irritated him. Eddie never wept except when
they fought, and he found it impossible to pretend
for long that his wife was under him, giving him everything he wanted at last.

*   *   *

When he went to the bathroom afterward, he took the *Times* with him. He turned to the weather map. The occluded front over Nova Scotia had not moved, and that decided him.

CHAPTER 11

In the strange instant between sleep and wakefulness it seemed to Eddie that her infant son was at her breast. She felt the pleasant suction of his mouth and the flow of her milk. The oldest intimacy there is came back to her and sent one delicious shudder through her body.

When she realized she was alone in bed in her childhood room on the second floor of the house on Hunter's Island, she was not disappointed exactly, but it took her a moment to locate herself, not in space, but time. She had been a cuddled infant in these rooms herself, and they had only warm, friendly associations for her. When she opened her eyes they went directly to the cracks in the ceiling that formed the outline of a face which had been to her at various times the face of a fairy queen, of a beautiful actress, of a triumphant horsewoman, of a ballerina, of a beloved teacher. Now it appeared as the fairy queen, smiling benignly down on Eddie, who felt, to her great surprise, wonderfully happy to be there.

She tossed back the comforter and leapt from bed. Two steps brought her to the window automatically. The sun was only inches off the horizon and it washed a line of clouds and the sea itself in orange.

The sight held her for a moment, until she shuddered again, but now with the dawn chill. She donned an ancient flannel nightgown, faced a mirror over the bureau and smoothed her short hair. She remembered standing before mirrors the day before and, to her relief, saw no sign now of the turmoil of those hours. Beginning with the mugger in the park and ending with her emotional arrival in Maine, but including her grotesque self-doubts about writing and her paranoia about Cheney and that particularly upsetting encounter with David Dolan, the previous day now seemed a remote, grueling marathon to her.

She thought with excitement of the magic place to which she'd always gone when, as a child, she'd been the first to awaken, so she left her room and made for it. She went as quietly as she could, although the floors of the house, cold underfoot, creaked like ship boards. Her grandfather had bragged to her that he'd hired shipwrights to build the house. "An island!" he loved to say, slamming his hand on the porch railing, "It's like a ship, only you don't have to caulk it!"

The "ark with windows" was what her grandmother had dubbed the place. She claimed to hate it for its red shingles and barnlike aspect. Her husband railed that gambrel houses were supposed to look like barns, but to appease her he installed a white banister around the edges of the roof and an enclosed cupola on its peak from which the children could watch the sea. That generation of children named the cupola Noah.

It was to Noah that Eddie was headed now. She climbed to the third floor, paused at Bren's door, thought of going in just to hug him, but then realized, for all her renewed maternal fondness, she really did want the first moments of this day for herself.

The cupola was a brash appurtenance more suited to a sea captain's stately Georgian than to that oafish summer house. Seen from the ground, back from the house a bit, the cupola with its graceful onion dome capped by the rooster weathervane, its twelve-over-twelve window sashes, lacelike in light which poured both in and out, and its spare classical columns at the corners, did not mesh either with the tacked-on balcony that bordered the roof edge or with the unornamented lines of the rest of the house. It seemed overly flamboyant, but more eccentric than whimsical, and attracting altogether too much attention to itself, like a silk cravat at the throat of a farmer. But that was why Eddie had always loved the cupola from the outside; it looked as a man named Noah should look.

But the cupola from within, that was her real love. It was like the inside of an egg, but with a view. The windows didn't open—her grandfather hadn't wanted the children climbing out—so there was a particular odor to the space too, partly of the stale salt air, partly of flaking old glazier's putty, partly of the remains of spider webs that had to be cleaned out each June. It was a smell not pleasant, not unpleasant, permanently fixed in her mind. Involuntarily her nose called up faint suggestions of it whenever she felt especially secure, snug, content.

During the seasons of her childhood she had had the cupola to herself—her sister Susannah already avoided heights and cramped places. There was room only for two to stand abreast and she was up there often. She learned to daydream there and later to render her daydreams as drawings and poems. She loved to climb the ladder in the closet at the end of the long third-floor hallway and emerge with a flap-bang of the trapdoor from dark to light. The sight of the world from that peak always snagged her eyes with delicious pain—when she learned that the shock to her pupils of the bright light did that, she still thought of it as magic—and made her dizzy for an instant. She grew to look forward to that dizziness because her recovery from it always reassured her.

In the cupola, "with Noah," one could be completely alone yet not cut off from the active crowded household down below. Eddie liked to watch her sister, her parents, her cousins, aunts and uncles, all in summer clothing, playing on the lawn, croquet or badminton, or in swimming suits at the dock and float past the rocks in the cove three hundred yards across the island. It thrilled her to be able to see them and yet not be seen. That was the meaning she gave to her mother's Bible phrase: being in the world, but not of it. Later she would take that experience of watching her family carry on happily without her as an image of the detached, observing eye, cursed and blessed at once, that made her a writer.

But in summer her childhood hours in the cupola were only blessed. The options one had! With the barest movement of the head she could direct her attention from the mundane recreations of her family to the sea, that great field of the infinite, that first image of what she wanted and of what limitless stimulations life promised. The sea made her feel that nothing was forbidden her, no place too far, no experience too dangerous, no ambitions too bold. Her fantasies took her everywhere.

*　　*　　*

The morning haze hung on the firs, which on the island were relatively stunted because of the thin soil and harsh wind. From her tower on top of the three-story house she could look across their jagged, tooth-like points, and, despite the haze, take in the rough shape of the entire island. The steeple of the Congregational church in Barrett's Cove also stuck up above the trees a mile and a half away, and it still looked, as it had when she was a girl, like the top of something buried. She had taken it, solitary, white against green, finished angles against snaggled branches, as an image then of the refined and perfect loneliness of God, a notion she remembered now and was amused by. Beyond the steeple the fir world of the mainland was more blue than green, function of distance. The hills across Frenchman Bay glinted in sunlight, but differently because, higher, they took more of it and, removed from the sea, they were not wrapped in the faint cloud of morning mist. Beyond the near hills, Eddie knew, was majestic Cadillac Mountain, fifteen hundred feet of it, but that morning it was not visible, a sign, her father'd always claimed, of coming bad weather. "The mountain's out, rise and shine!" he would exclaim up and down the hallway outside their rooms. If the mountain couldn't be seen in the morning he was more subdued and more likely to let them sleep. When they woke up on their own, they knew already to be slightly disappointed in the day.

She was standing in her cupola, her Noah, with her back to the sea and its melonball, the sun. She couldn't yet face the immensity of water and light, so indefinite, so devoid of detail on which to fix the mind, until she had satisfied her need to notice things. She focused on sights and sounds, an osprey's

nest in the tallest tree, dew glistening on pine
needles, the caw-caw of gulls, which was sharp even
through the shut glass, and down below the gravel
path, dazzled with wet, which led from the kitchen ell
to the weed-ridden modest orchard just short of the
woods. Everywhere else the lawn was cut and tidy,
but her mother never allowed the caretaker to run
his mower through the orchard until after harvesting
in September, not that she was ever still there to take
the apples, but that that was how her father had run
the place. Eddie traced the uneven contour of the
land itself along the edge of the yard where her
grandfather's once-crisp terraces now folded on themselves, softly, showing a loss of definition the way a
man's stomach does once the muscles go.

Her husband's firm, lean torso came to her, but she
snapped her mind down on the thought of Cheney.

She turned to face the sea, but her eyes went immediately down to the rocks which, like a rotten mouth,
sucked the tide through their gaps. The water rushed
in, kicking up spray flamboyantly, but it was the gray
stone, each worn tooth of it, that caught her eye by
defying the boisterous surf. Solidity and resolve like
that, despite time's cavities, were what was needed.
Old gray rock, reproof to everything else which had
changed not just since her grandfather's day, but
since Noah's. The image reminded her of the
strength she longed for but was sure she didn't have.
Eddie wanted to be what waves crashed over and
didn't touch. She wanted to withstand Cheney and
herself. She wanted to withstand everything for the
sake of her son.

The open sea, when she looked, surprised her by
being so rough. Frenchman Bay behind her in the lee

of the island was tranquil by comparison, and that
had deceived her. The wind, now that she noticed it,
softly rattled the cupola's glass, as if after all these
years it was still out to break those panes. It made her
shiver. How desolate Noah must be in the barren
time of the year! On the coast of Maine, she remembered, the year becomes barren every night, even in
August, and only slowly each morning does it ease its
way back into summer. But in August a peculiar light
makes itself evident, a mood of expectancy settles, of
anticipation, something coming, a change in the
wind, which though it seems dry enough when it
blows, will leave the cushions on the rattan furniture
damp. That wind tells you when to leave; then you
leave or turn to stone.

That's it, she thought, we'll stay. We'll stay here
with the weather and the cold people, and Cheney
when he comes will find us stone pillars. We will have
become Bren's statues after all.

As if the thought of her son called his name, Bren
walked from under the eaves of the house at that very
moment, and Eddie at the sight of him caught her
breath. Her creaking of the shipboards must have
wakened him. He danced onto the boulders amid the
spray. She began rapping on the window at him, not
with alarm—it never occurred to her that he was in
danger on those rocks—but with joy, the unfettered
joy of seeing him, her agile, swift, beautiful son. His
appearance punctured her wish for solitude, which
gunned away, leaving her without a reverie, memory
or thought, leaving her with only a desire to yell
down to her boy against the ocean itself, "I love my
kiddo!" And so she did, with her hands cupping her
mouth. The sound of her shout filled the cupola, but

did not budge it. Bren remained standing on a far rock with his back to her. She tried slamming the glass with her open hands. She would have tapped on it with her wedding ring if she still wore it. She had nothing metal, so she cupped her hands again and repeated with her loudest voice—to herself suddenly she reeked of happiness—"I love my kiddo!"

Bren did not hear her, but he turned around just then and looked up.

She didn't look like his mother. With her hair short like that and in the long white nightgown and with her hands outstretched against the glass panes, she looked to him like a crazy lady in a haunted-house movie. He would not have wanted her to know that's what he thought, of course, and he waved hard at her.

It was still amazing to him that his mother, who seemed so powerful, so able to do anything, could not read his mind. The knowledge that he could have secrets from her—though there were still moments when he wondered—made him feel powerful himself and, sometimes, like a traitor.

He waved and waved and he was sure she did not know that he imagined her as the lady with a lantern creeping down the hallway, feeling with the fingertips of one hand against the wall, inching along, with her eyeballs rolled back into her head so that she seemed blind but wasn't, or else why would she have had that lantern? Her child is crying and she wants to reach him, but he is dead, he died of fever in the hold of the great sailing ship that brought them to the New World. But she refuses to believe it and goes about the eerie old house at night looking for her child while her husband is out at sea. Who wouldn't go crazy in a house where the noises of the wind coming through cracks sounded like a baby bawling? It wasn't her fault. It was her husband's fault for leaving her in that unfriendly village where jealous old ladies had made her cut off all her pretty hair. It was because of him that she climbed up to that tower every morning to look across the ocean hoping to see on the horizon his great four-masted schooner, which hauled along in its wake the carcasses of all the whales he'd killed.

Bren shook off his dream, but not the sadness he felt for her, the sadness he did not understand. As soon as she had got here the day before, he could feel how sad she was, and even in her arms at the airport he had wanted to hide like a mouse where that feeling couldn't find him. But instead after the ferry ride back to Hunter's Island he had led her by the hand into the house and up to his room to show her the finished brontosaurus, which so cheered her that, for a minute, he thought of showing her his drawing too. But he hadn't. He'd given her a peach, which she took as if it were a ruby ring with her initials. He showed her the cozy box with his snail shells, which, when she scooped up a handful, looked like petals to him. He told her so because usually she liked it when he told her what things looked like, but she said shells don't die like flowers do. Even though he was just a kid, he knew what a sad thought that was, and he nearly said maybe so, but what about the snails? He had to be careful, though, because he knew her sadness was already his fault; it was because he had talked to his father the day before. That was why she'd come to Maine, Bren knew that much. And he knew she hadn't wanted to come. She was, in other words, sad to be there. And he was sad—what kid wouldn't be?—because she was. Here was Bren's question: why didn't she like being with him as much as he liked being with her?

She waved at him to come on up, and he took off like a shot, racing back over the boulders he'd scaled and up the rickety stairs to tufts of soil and across the lawn into the house. Inside he ran on his tiptoes because he didn't want to wake his grandmother. This was going to be his moment with his mom, and in the tower where his grandmother forbade him to go alone. He took the stairs two at a time all the way to the third floor, practically without a sound. At the end of the long hallway the closet door was open. Before he climbed the ladder he looked up at the trapdoor, a square in the ceiling; it was down. Suddenly he wondered if he'd dreamed it, her signal to him, her wave. His mother hated it when he interrupted her. She never yelled at him or hit him, but he could tell when he barged in before she was ready, how angry it made her. In New York it wasn't his fault, since there was so little room in that apartment and where else could he go? Not like the house in California—home—where there were lots of rooms. But it had been only in New York that she was always getting mad at him, and that was what he feared now, barging in without meaning to. But it was stupid, that panic. If she was typing up there, he'd have heard. And how could she have carried her typewriter up there anyway? He hated the sound of her typewriter. But there was no sound. His mom was up there waiting for him. She was quiet as a mouse. She had waved at him to come. Hadn't she?

With the ceiling trapdoor down, the closet was dark, but he wasn't going to call up to her just because he couldn't quite see clearly to the top of the ladder. He could climb ladders with the best of them. He was the falcon. He was Jamal. He grabbed the slats and swung his weight onto them. He liked the feel of the smooth wood in his hands and under his sneaks. It was a sturdy ladder and he took it jauntily and noisily.

Before he reached the top, the trapdoor swung up as he hoped it would and sunlight spilled down so brightly it took him a minute to see her. But then she looked not like a crazy lady, a whaler's wife, but—with that halo of sun behind her and her translucent white gown next to the blue sky and that smile and those arms open and hands reaching down—like an angel whom God had sent to sing for him.

"Hi ya, Mom!"

She pulled him up. He had to press against her so she could close the trapdoor underneath them, and he took advantage of that to hug her extra hard.

"Where's your sweater?"

He squinted up at her. "You know what a sweater is?"

"What?"

"What a kid wears when his mother is cold."

She laughed and held him, swiveling with fondness. It was true.

"I came up here looking for you," she lied.

"I was on the rocks. I always start my day on the rocks."

"When I was your age I wasn't as brave as you are. I liked it up here because it was so safe."

Bren looked out at the sea. "But it's pretty high."

"That's true." Bren had absolutely panicked when she'd taken him to the top of the World Trade Center.

"Anyway, Gram doesn't want me up here."

"Sit with me." Eddie lowered herself onto an old blue boat cushion. It was damp and cold; the cork stuffing had crumbled into lumps. She took Bren onto her lap, something she could never do lately without a pang at his weight. "Tell me what else you've been doing."

"Gram said we could put fingernail polish on the lippets."

"The what?"

"To see if they come back to the right place."

"The limpets."

"I've been trying to see when the tide changes. It's hard to tell here, with the rocks. Not like home. I can always tell at home."

"I doubt it." Eddie knew his comparison and his use of the word *home* were far from innocent, and she had to admire him for scoring so quickly.

"I can too."

"What else?"

"I've been making a study of the gulls."

"And?"

He faced her and grinned. "They're cleaner in California."

She nodded sagely. "And the water's warmer."

"Right."

"I wonder what a person is driving at?"

He fiddled with the lace border of her gown at her throat. Strategic silence.

"Aren't you glad that Sadie and Jason are going to be here with you?"

He shrugged. "I don't care."

"You like Jason. He likes you."

"He stole my ball."

"Nonsense."

"Last year."

"When?"

"At Disneyland. The man at the Ping-Pong pool gave me a ball and he took it."

"Do you think you could be nice to Jason anyway?"

Bren nodded, then abruptly changed the subject. "Know what I saw two of already? Seals!"

"Seals! Fantastic! Two of them?"

Bren nodded.

"Can you show me what they did? What they looked like?"

Bren stretched up and swiveled his head and clapped his forearms as if they were flippers.

Eddie laughed. "What'd they sound like?"

"Arf! Arf! Arf!" He collapsed into her lap.

Eddie hugged him as hard as she could. "You know what?"

"What?" he said, but the sound was muffled in her lap.

"I'm so proud of you sometimes I could cry."

"Because I made you sad?" He angled his head to watch her eyes. He saw no sign of tears.

"You know the difference between sad crying and happy crying, don't you?"

"Yes."

"You never make me sad."

He didn't respond to that, and she wanted him to. "You know that, don't you?"

He shook his head.

"Well, you don't."

"But you are sad."

"Sometimes I am, but not because of you. You're the one thing I have that makes me happy."

Bren wanted to argue about that; something else must make her happy, but he couldn't think of it. It made him feel very good, what she was saying.

She could feel him relax against her. She remembered that the moments after feeding him at her breast were the best of all. She'd loved how he rested against her then, sated, worshipful. A full dose of that bliss was what she felt then, and she guessed he felt it too.

After a long time she said, "Penny for your thoughts."

When he didn't respond she thought he might have fallen asleep and that doubled her happiness.

She wasn't ready for it when he said, "Dad's going to take me to a ball game."

She had to stifle an urge to rebuke him for calling Cheney "Dad." Instead she squeezed him fondly.

"And you know what?" he pressed.

"What?"

"You'd like baseball if you gave it a chance."

She shook her head. "When you get to be my age you know what you like and what you don't like."

"I'll bet he could get an extra ticket."

"He probably could, but I wouldn't enjoy it. And you know what? Maybe you better not count on it yourself."

"What if it's the World Series?"

"The World Series is special, I admit. We'll just have to wait and see."

"Promise?" He brightened.

She looked at him askance. "What did I say?"

"You said we'd see."

"That's not a promise."

"But you might?"

"No. *You* might." The kid was clever. "We'll wait and see if you can go. Not me. Thought you had me, didn't you?"

Bren grinned. That she seemed happy made him go on. "Let's go back with Dad, Mom." He felt her stiffen and immediately he was defensive. "You asked me for my thoughts."

"I offered you a penny. That's about what that one's worth."

"He said he loves you."

"Cheney says a lot of things."

"You mean he lies?"

Eddie had to admire his moves. "I think it's time I taught you chess."

"I know how to play chess."

"Who taught you?"

"Dad did. But does he?"

"What?"

"Lie."

"Cheney's an actor. His job is to pretend."

"Does he pretend with me?"

That stopped Eddie. She saw that the kid was better at it than she was. If she said yes, he'd be heartbroken. If she said no, he'd demand to know why he couldn't see him. "Look, it's too early in the morning. We didn't come up to Maine to talk about Cheney."

Bren pulled back from her. "We came up here," he accused, "to get away from him!"

She refused to get perturbed. She had to deflect

what he said without denying it. He was on the lookout for lies. She shook her head. "We came to have a nice time together. And we will." She started to hug him, but he tensed up. "What?" she asked.

"What about me?" His voice was cold. "Now I don't have a dad."

"Cheney isn't your dad, sweetheart."

"Yes, he is." He stood up. "Would you let me out, please?"

She ignored him for a moment to watch the tide, the rocking waters. Was there a lullaby in the waves? If there was she didn't hear it. She felt for an instant that old harmony, that intimacy that had made her and her child one person. She felt it, but as something gone.

She stood to open the trapdoor.

Bren climbed down onto the ladder, but paused. "You see, I do too."

"What?"

"Make you sad." And then he dropped out of sight.

Eddie stared at the hole, thinking it was possible her son got his wit from her, but certain that he did his self-pity.

Bren took the ladder carefully and walked quietly through the house and out the kitchen door into the yard. At the forest's edge he broke into a run, not Brendan Dolan McCoy anymore, but Jamal the Jungle Boy, who'd been raised by animals.

"Good morning, Mother," Eddie said, and liked saying it. There were only reassuring connotations in those words. Eddie and her mother had always had their best moments over the day's first coffee.

Mrs. Brewster turned from the stove with the old

agateware pot and poured for both of them. "Good morning, dear. What can I fix you? Your son and I had waffles yesterday."

Eddie was distracted. The long wooden table was bare. The night before, she had made a futile effort to rework her chapter after her mother and Bren were asleep, and she had left her papers stacked on one end of it. "I left my work there last night."

"I know you did. I put it on the desk in the parlor. I hope you don't mind. I tried not to disrupt your pages."

But Eddie went into the living room to check. When she returned, her mother said defensively, "I didn't read any of it."

"I know. If you had, you'd be complaining about my foul language."

They sat opposite each other over their coffee.

"Is the book going all right?"

Eddie shrugged. She couldn't discuss it with her mother. "How does Bren seem to you? He loves it here."

"I spoil him, of course. What he loves is being pampered."

Was there a rebuke in that? "But really, how does he seem to you?"

"He's wonderful. I always forget what an exceptional child he is. He's the 'Prince of Whales.'" She laughed and purposely displayed her admiration. "The prince of *all* the whales!" Mrs. Brewster thought that if Eddie wrote the way she bore, she'd be Dostoevsky. But if she said that, of course, her daughter would take it as an insult. Her generation so grotesquely devalued its own offspring, as if anything else were as important as well-raised children.

But Mrs. Brewster sensed her daughter's need for encouragement. "He's growing, Edna, and not just physically. Children are better than the rest of us at that, you know. They cope quite well with the most extraordinary difficulties."

"I know. I'm the one who can't cope. He laid me waste this morning."

Mrs. Brewster reached across the table and touched her daughter's hand. "Tell me."

Eddie withdrew her hand and pressed both her temples to corral her stampeding emotions. "He wants me to go back with Cheney."

"That's only natural, dear."

"But he was there. He saw it. He saw it."

"What?"

Eddie had never told her mother about the beating. "Cheney flipped out in May. It was why I left him."

Eddie saw his fists coming at her, one after the other.

"He could have done me real damage. He was quite mad."

"He hit you?" Mrs. Brewster could hardly breathe. The sight of her daughter across from her with her cropped hair and pale cheeks and thin wrists, looking very modern, but also suddenly quite lost and vulnerable, made her want to take her into her arms.

Eddie raised and lowered her head slowly. Tears filled her eyes, then overflowed them. "He terrifies me."

"I had no idea."

"I thought he was going to kill me. I'm certain he would have . . ." she was sobbing now and it was difficult to talk ". . . but Bren came down. He saved me."

Mrs. Brewster finally crossed to Eddie, who turned and threw herself on her mother. "And now he wants me to go back." And then she began to weep uncontrollably.

While Mrs. Brewster poured fresh coffee she said, "If your father was alive he'd have handled the case himself instead of that young lawyer the firm gave you."

"Dad?" Eddie laughed. "A divorce case?" She was relieved both to have spilled over to her mother and to have collected herself again. "I don't have any complaints about the lawyer. Divorce is like a merger, only in reverse." The fact was that Eddie felt enormous gratitude to have her father's firm representing her, not because it was prominent, but because it was her father's.

Mrs. Brewster thought that by now the lawyers should have had a court order forbidding Cheney to take the child. It was absurd that he should have as much legal right to him, even temporarily, as Eddie did. Mrs. Brewster resolved to make a call or two herself.

"It's hard to stay unhappy here for long," Eddie said. "I didn't know how much I've missed the place."

"You love it because you're seeing it again with your child. Just when the charm of Hunter's fades, some innocent comes along to rescue it for us."

Eddie agreed. "I like being a mother here, but you know what?" She paused, wanting *her* mother to hear her statement as an admission and as thanks. She was about to say, "I like being a child here better," when the telephone rang.

They stared at each other.

Mrs. Brewster shifted toward the living room, but Eddie stood. "No, I should take it."

Eddie went into the living room feeling calm and, to her surprise, well prepared. At the desk, while letting the phone ring once more for measure, she touched the pile of pages of her manuscript and felt the infection of what she'd been unable to do. She had not yet written her way remotely near the lode of her feelings. Maybe she should be writing about Cheney, not Brendan, after all. But what would be his last defeat of her, if not that? Eddie insisted to herself that there was more to her life than him.

The phone rang for the fourth time.

Eddie knew that she had done the right thing in coming to Hunter's, if only to take this phone call. Cheney was never again to have free, unsupervised access to her son.

Mrs. Brewster was standing behind her. "It was this time yesterday that he called."

At that time the day before, too, Eddie had whipped the stiletto antenna in the face of that mugger, and he had fled. She had felt invincible. She could do anything.

She snatched the phone before it rang again and, conscious of the blade in her voice, said, "Hello."

"What are you doing there?" It was Susannah.

Her sister's voice habitually plunged and bobbed like a kite. It cheered Eddie at once. "Hi, Suebee," she said, and turned to wink at her mother, who rolled her eyes in relief.

"I thought you were staying in New York."

"I wanted to see you," Eddie lied. Susannah worshipped her and felt neglected by her, and Eddie knew it. They hadn't seen each other in a year.

"Oh, God, that's why I'm calling. Now I'm really crushed. We can't come. We've had a disaster."

"What?" Eddie couldn't tell from her sister's voice whether something serious had happened. The last thing she wanted to hear was that Bren's cousins wouldn't be coming to Hunter's.

"Mumps," Susannah announced with a perverse triumph. "And you'll never guess whose. It's unbelievable. The doctor just left. They all have mumps but me."

"Both of them?"

"The kids *and* Bob."

"Bob! You can't be serious!"

"He never had them as a kid."

"But mumps are dangerous for a grown man. Jesus, Sue, it sterilizes them."

"Bob had a vasectomy last spring. The mumps, as the doctor put it, have lost their sting. Except that he aches all over and is swollen like a beach ball. You should see him. The whole place shakes with his groaning. He resents having to share my ministrations with the children. He hasn't been sick in years and wants the full treatment. I'm under orders not to tell anyone it's mumps, of course. Including you."

"Mum's the word."

"No, 'Mom' is. I was hoping she could get free to come over and help out for a few days. I'm going nuts."

"I can imagine. She's right here." Eddie started to hand the phone to her mother while trying to pinch off the resentment she felt. Not only was Bren to be deprived of his cousins' companionship, but also of his grandmother's. Susannah assumed their mother would drop everything and go to Blue Hill. She took the phone back. "What did you have in mind for Bren?"

"I thought if he'd had mumps already, Mother could bring him along."

"He hasn't."

"Oh. Well, you're there." Susannah paused, then lobbed, "You can take care of him, I suppose."

"But, as you know, I hadn't planned to be."

"Is there a problem?"

"I just wondered what you had in mind for my son?"

"Oh, really, Eddie, we've got illness here. Could I speak to Mother, please?"

Eddie handed the phone to her mother and stepped toward the window to stare out while she listened. The haze had lifted, but there were clouds far out on the ocean. Eddie knew, for a change, exactly what she was feeling. She didn't want her mother to go to Blue Hill, partly because she resented her sister's usurping her mother's attention, but more because she very much wanted not to confront Cheney by herself.

But she didn't know even that Cheney was coming, only that her mother regarded her intuition about that as irrational if not downright paranoid. She considered taking Bren back to the city. Her mother could drop them off at the airport on her way to Blue Hill. But the flights would be booked. Bren would be crushed to go back to the city. Eddie would have acted out of panic again, and Cheney would thereby have defeated her without even showing up. She had to stay put. She had to be there with and for Bren alone, and she had to like it.

Mrs. Brewster hooked the phone at her collar and turned to Eddie with acute indecision showing in her face.

"You must go, of course," Eddie whispered emphatically, sliding her arm around her mother's waist. "You *can* help them a lot. Don't worry about us." Eddie thought of taking the phone back and apologizing to Susannah. Who wants to nursemaid a trio with mumps?

Mrs. Brewster put the phone to her face again. Eddie moved back to the window to look for Bren on the rocks, but he wasn't there.

Her mother finished the call, then joined her. "Just a couple of days. Do you mind terribly?"

"We'll have a grand time."

"I so wanted the two of you to myself. I wish that had been Cheney calling."

"So do I."

"You see, there are worse things than he."

"Mumps in men, for one. If Cheney does show up I'll bring him over and he won't tell him what it is when his neck starts to swell."

"Is Cheney sterile?"

Eddie looked sharply up at her mother. The question was unlike her. "Who knows? We tried the whole time. He wouldn't go to a doctor about it."

"Did you?"

"No. Obviously I can have children."

Eddie had never used her certainty as a weapon against Cheney, but only, she had to admit, because he'd never given her the opening. She wasn't sure it bothered him that they hadn't conceived, and that was another blow.

Her mother said, "I didn't know until now about Bob's vasectomy. I'm not sure I approve."

"Approve?" Eddie marveled occasionally at the prerogatives her mother's generation took for granted. It would never have occurred to her to approve or disapprove of her brother-in-law's vasectomy. It was enough to know that, were she a man, she would never submit to one herself. "She should take the pill and get cancer?"

Mrs. Brewster shrugged. The mention of cancer always reminded her of Harold, who would have insisted there were other choices besides mutilation and disease. Susannah and Bob could have more children, for example. "Well, it's only mumps, fortunately. Your sister sounds quite at her wit's end."

"When are you going?" Eddie, like her mother, would display now only her woman strength.

She looked at her watch. "I can make the noon ferry."

"I'll help you pack."

A short while later Bren was loading his grandmother's bag into the trunk of her Volvo. When he succeeded, his mother and grandmother clapped.

He knew their praise for what it was, a false cheer that was intended to cover the disappointment everybody felt. Bren didn't mind having his mother to himself for a couple of days, but she had brought her papers from New York, and since he had hurt her feelings that morning, he was sure she was going to lock herself up and write. He wondered what mumps were. It surprised him to have discovered that he had looked forward after all to Jason's visit and even Sadie's.

Mrs. Brewster stooped to grasp Bren's shoulders. "Now you take care of your mother and be good. Promise?"

Bren nodded.

"I'll bring you something."

Bren took a pair of shells out of his pocket and he offered them to his grandmother. "These are my best ones. One for each. Say I said to get better."

"I sure will, dear." She kissed him and then kissed Eddie, promised to call, got in the car and drove off.

Eddie held Bren's hand while watching the green car disappear into the woods, but she wasn't thinking about him and he knew it. He decided, despite their earlier fight, it was up to him to cheer her up. He tugged on her hand.

Eddie allowed herself to be pulled toward the house, but she let her eyes linger on the road. Perhaps she was feeling bereft because, with her mother gone, she and Bren had no car. How would they leave in an emergency? But that was ridiculous. There wouldn't be an emergency. It was not the car she missed; it was her mother. *Sometimes, I feel,* she sang to herself, *like an autoless child.* The time alone with Bren at Hunter's was going to be precious and they would both cherish the memory of it. *A long way—from home.* Besides if they had to get out there was always the Whaler at the float. She should have asked her mother if it was gassed.

No sooner had the slam of the kitchen door behind them faded than it happened again, the telephone.

They both stopped walking and stared at it. Bren knew as well as she did who it was.

Eddie looked away from it. Why wouldn't the bastard leave her alone? She looked through the window at the benign sea and it suddenly seemed like an enemy to her, surrounding them, imprisoning them. How he terrified her! She had never quite admitted it until that morning, never quite felt the full blast of her fear, and not only for her son.

The phone rang and rang while that monster dread rolled over in her. She felt nauseated. She simply could not answer it. Why had her mother abandoned her to this? Finally, under the weight of despair she'd never felt before, she admitted that she had nothing left with which to fight him.

"I'll get it!" Bren cried suddenly.

"No!"

The boy froze. His mother had screamed the word at him. An instant later he bolted toward the stairway and ran up noisily.

Eddie approached the phone only when it stopped ringing; she approached it gingerly as if it might explode. She stood in its silence.

After a minute it rang again.

She snatched it up, cutting the bell in half, and pressed it to her face.

"Eddie?" a voice said. "Sweetheart?"

"Barney? Is that you, Barney?"

"Of course, it's me. Who else would be calling you at the crack of dawn?"

"It's nearly noon."

"Not here, it isn't."

"You're in L.A. I forgot." Eddie couldn't be sure that her voice wasn't trembling. Her hands were.

"You forgot? You told me you wouldn't leave the

telephone. Now you're in Maine. I thought you wanted to be clued in."

"I do."

"I'm calling so early because I have a breakfast meeting with Shapiro. You're not going to like what I have to tell you."

"He wants Cheney."

"No. He doesn't see Cheney for the role anyway. He's too old."

"So what won't I like?"

"Well, he just can't put a clause like that in the contract. Shapiro just can't."

"Like what?"

"Cutting Cheney out."

"Why not?"

"It's just not done, love. You can't ask Shapiro to slit his throat with someone like Cheney McCoy. Not to mention what it would do to you."

"Oh? What?"

"Well, Shapiro says people would be amused by it. I mean amused at you."

"You mean they'll laugh at me."

"Look, Eddie, you can't put the studio in the position of choosing between Cheney and you."

"Because they'll choose him." Eddie waited, but Barney didn't respond. "Right? Right?"

"Of course."

"Fine. That settles it."

"Eddie . . ."

"Forget the option, Barney. Let me write the book. Leave me alone, OK?"

"Think about it before you . . . Shapiro's very interested. The film connection could do the book a lot of good."

"And then Cheney could do the film a lot of good."

"Don't be paranoid, Eddie."

"Why the hell not?" She hung up.

She stood over the phone, leaning on it. Paranoid, she repeated to herself. Damn right she was.

Bren, whose return she had not noticed, touched her hip and said, "Mom, this is for you."

She took the drawing he offered and was stunned by it, a picture of the three of them holding hands, she and Cheney on either side of Bren, whose great red smile dominated the chaos of lines and colors which rendered perfectly the image of his hope.

It devastated her, and made her see for an instant how she too longed for such recovery; she too wished desperately that the three of them had survived as one. She was not so far from loving Cheney as she thought.

The drawing was the most finished he'd ever brought her, technically complex, but in what it portrayed, so simple. The integrity with which he'd drawn it and offered it—his loyalty to the truth of his own need—was what moved her, despite that despair, to say, "It's a miracle, Bren."

"It is?" He craned and looked again. "I was trying for a family." Then he scrunched his nose at her.

And Eddie melted, stooped, hugged him gratefully and for his strength.

CHAPTER 12

Dolan was standing on the deck of the car ferry, which was better than halfway down Frenchman Bay on its way to Hunter's Island, a journey altogether of about three miles. The boat rattled along, a converted Navy landing craft with room in its open hold for perhaps a dozen vehicles and on the balcony deck for stacks of green-wire lobster traps, cartons of produce and canned foods and cases of soda pop. It was a battered mean-looking boat, not a graceful sleek ferry like those that plied the Baltic waters to and from the countless islands around Stockholm. Obviously Hunter's Island traffic was modest even by comparison to other resort islands off Mt. Desert. Dolan's fellow passengers were mainly working fishermen. There were only a couple of other "people from away," and Dolan found himself thinking for the first time since he'd set out from the motel in Rockport that morning that perhaps it was a mistake for him to have come. Despite the beautiful bay and the curious balmy weather, he was jolted by an insecurity.

What right did he have to intrude on Eddie? What would her family make of his arrival? What would she? He could offer his mother's affidavit as an excuse, and he could say that he'd come to meet his nephew. But how actually would he present himself?

That question vexed him while the boat made its way toward the solitary island at the mouth of the bay, an island which, unlike most others, took no shelter in the sound, but stood exposed to the full blast of the Atlantic. As they approached it, Hunter's assumed the shape of a flattened dome, a dark green against the gray-blue sky. It seemed to bob in the swells of the ocean. Dolan held on to the rail and studied the heavy bank of clouds on the horizon as if he could read them. The car ferry creaked down the bay under the squealing gulls and diving fish hawks and over waves blazing like bits of mirror in the sun.

He had just begun to feel the weather in his stomach when the boat pulled into the lee of the island and the sea grew calmer. The wind fell and he took his jacket off. He watched the single church steeple emerge in pristine clarity, white cone out of black fir. The harbor village grew around that steeple just the way the founding preacher intended it should, and as the boat cut into its cove the water flattened utterly. Dolan was charmed first by the village, its weathered shacks along the shore with wood-stove chimneys at odd angles and, up the hill, small white houses. The ferry tooted once and a pair of figures appeared on the single wharf, which balanced precariously on spindly pilings, half-exposed in the ebb tide. Apart from the two men who sauntered out on the pier, there was no discernible movement in the village. After the bustle of Bar Harbor, the quiet seemed errie to Dolan, and it underscored the difference between this island and the others. Dolan's stomach was not right yet.

The two men watched the ferry approach. They did not wave or call a greeting, or did anyone on board. They wore heavy boots and rubber aprons. One held a curved blade, the other a long rag. Dolan guessed they had been gutting fish in their shed. Indeed, the smell of fish hung over the scene, the harbor, the village and certainly the men. The closer the ferry drew to the wharf the more primitive it seemed. The charm of the place faded. The sheds were dilapidated and the houses neglected. Still, the steeple and church on the hill seemed majestic and alone immune from the forces of slow collapse below it. Forest encircled the cove settlement, not enchantingly but ominously, as if waiting to reclaim its purloined acres.

When Dolan could make out the features of the two on the pier, however, it wasn't nature that threatened, as the French would say, but man. The fishermen were twins and had the unmistakable idiot look of the inbred. Neither seemed able to focus his eyes. They watched the boat pull in, but only approximately, their stares missing its progress by whole degrees. Dolan turned to see if the man next to him was as shocked by the appearance of the islanders as he was, but his shock doubled when he saw that his near companion was a third version of the polluted two.

"Pretty village," he said, stifling his unease.

The man nodded. He was a crewman. He wore dungarees and several shirts. His indefinite eyes belied the brisk coordination that showed in his stance. He was watching the angle of the ferry's approach.

"Are you a ferryman?"

The ferryman smiled at Dolan, showing terrible teeth, but also the hint of a generous welcome. He

seemed suddenly not at all retarded. He turned and
walked to the pilot house and, to Dolan's surprise,
took over the wheel from a lad. He was the captain,
and he proceeded to land the boat with great skill,
coaxing it into its slip at the crotch of the wharf.

While the boy secured ropes to the ramps, the passengers climbed into their cars and started their engines. Dolan prepared to ease his mother's Duster off
the boat. The roadway up from the ramp was narrow,
rutted and steep. Only by gunning the weary sedan,
which spewed out a black cloud of exhaust, was he
able to negotiate the hill. On its crest, in a lane to the
side, was a row of autos waiting to board the ferry for
its return to the mainland. He noticed one in particular because it was a Volvo, and it reminded him of
Sweden. As he pulled abreast of the Volvo he recognized the feeling: an arrival again, but as an alien.
He hadn't been on Hunter's a full minute, and already he seemed disembarked on yet more neutral
ground. He was abroad again.

And then he saw the Volvo's driver, a white-haired
lady alone, resting her chin on the back of her hand,
yet staring at him with such open curiosity that he
nearly stopped his car. He knew she was Eddie's
mother, but he was past her and the rattling pickup
truck behind him was still hurtling from the run up
the hill, and so he pressed on along the access road
until it widened out. He pulled over and got out of
the car and started back on foot. They had never
met. He recognized her because her face was a perfect
version of Eddie's. He hadn't a clue what he would
say to her.

The line of autos, eight of them, was already snak-
ing onto the ferry. The green Volvo crossed onto the

ramp as Dolan jogged over the hill, and he stopped. He had missed her and he was not sorry. Perhaps Eddie and Bren would be alone. It was just as well her mother should leave the island. No, it was better.

When Eddie heard the car approaching the house she assumed that it was Cheney and she thought, miserably, how like him to arrive on the boat that took away her mother. But by the time the driver pulled the car to a halt between the orchard and the house, Eddie had steeled herself against him and had decided she was glad in a way to be getting the awful moment over with. She crossed the living room, and when her sandals hit the linoleum of the kitchen floor she was conscious of their brisk slap-slap as she walked confidently toward the door. If she could force authority into her step, couldn't she also force it into her voice and her eye and her manner? She would say, "We have nothing to discuss. Now leave." And then she would point toward the road and Cheney, because he sensed that she was deadly serious and that it was useless to argue, would put his car in gear and drive away.

But what car? That brown clunker? She saw it as she approached the screen door, and it threw her because Cheney would no more drive a car like that than he would wear a leisure suit. She stopped at the door, just inside it.

David Dolan got out of the car and stared at the house. Eddie knew he couldn't see her. She wanted to watch him for a minute, to collect herself, to recover from the surprise of seeing him again. In a way, she'd have preferred it to have been Cheney—as with the phone call from Susannah—because Cheney's threat, no matter how acute, was familiar to her. David Dolan was like a ghost, and it almost didn't matter whether his coming was benign or not. She stepped through the screen door and deliberately let it slam behind her.

She startled him, as she'd intended. He took half a step back, which reminded her of the mugger in the park the day before. "What are you doing here?"

Instead of flinching, Dolan grinned at her. "Didn't you order . . ." he stopped talking to lean into the car and pull out a brown paper sack. He held it up. ". . . lobsters, lady?"

"What?"

It was Eddie who backed up now as he walked toward her, rhyming, "I have three two-pound lobsters fresh from the sea / ready to cook for the kid, you and me." He pulled one of the lobsters out of the bag and held it out to her. "I drove all this way to ask you to see / that while I have the lock, you have the key."

Eddie blushed. "I don't get it."

Dolan looked around and shrugged dramatically. "Would you believe I was in the neighborhood?"

"Really, David . . ." Eddie shook her head. She couldn't believe that he thought it was still possible to take her by storm. Yet his flair disarmed her. She smiled at him despite herself, and remembered that she'd found him irresistible years before because his choices seemed extreme. Politically and emotionally David Dolan had seemed dangerous to her. He'd made her feel that anything could happen, and too much had. But she wasn't a schoolgirl now. She was a protector of turf. She'd had enough charm to last a lifetime.

When she stopped smiling, it was to display her will. "Things are going on here, David, that don't involve you. It's frankly irritating for you to show up like this."

He looked at the lobster in his hand and then up at her, appearing suddenly every bit as foolish as he felt.

Eddie pressed her advantage. "I quite deliberately did not invite you to come up here. Can you explain yourself without rhyming it?"

Dolan put the lobster back in the bag. "When I showed up at your place in New York I had bagels." He rolled the bag shut and looked at her helplessly. "The truth?" he asked.

"Please."

"When I left you yesterday I went to Cambridge. The FBI had my parents' house staked out. I *think* it was the FBI. I wasn't ready to deal with them, so I took off. I had to think, to get an angle on my situation. I don't even have a lawyer. I drove up here because . . ." He paused. He had not explained it even to himself yet. ". . . I couldn't think of any-place else to go." He looked at the bag in his hands and felt more foolish than ever. He felt, in a way, pathetic. "Actually, now that I've had the driving time to think about it, I don't even know for sure that it was the FBI, or that they were after me at all. There were two of them. They could have been meter readers. I don't even know if I'm a fugitive exactly. But I can't find out until I have a lawyer." He laughed at himself. "I'm afraid I've been feeling fairly paranoid."

His use of the word that she had only moments be-fore applied to herself moved her, but she couldn't acknowledge that. Her situation still seemed more complex than his. "I can hardly believe you're still dealing with the same old thing," she said, softening slightly.

"Imagine how I feel! I arrived in the States day before yesterday with the illusion that I could quickly launch a new life, me who left Sweden because it's the land of illusions. It serves me right that everything I touch is more complicated than I thought." He paused. "Including you." He reached into his pocket for the envelope and as he did he saw her draw back from him. He realized why. "This is not the letter you sent me."

The thought of being faced again with that letter repulsed her. "You're a regular mailman." She smiled awkwardly.

"Special Delivery." He handed her his mother's affidavit.

"What is it?"

"Why don't you read it?"

They stared at each other. Dolan remembered that as her plane pulled away the day before, she had seemed to him in her oval of glass a priceless cameo. She was glaring at him unpleasantly, and he had to strain to remember how beautiful she had seemed. "Read it," he repeated. "Please."

She opened the envelope, withdrew the affidavit and read it. When she looked up at him, she had not melted. "You expect me to be grateful for this."

"No. I don't. If anything, the Dolan family owes you an apology, quite a large one, I gather." He paused long enough to fend off the sadness he felt about his mother and father. "My folks aren't themselves, Eddie. They never recovered from losing Brendan."

"Maybe no one did," Eddie said quietly. "Your brother was the best man I've ever known. I regret everything I did to hurt him." She looked at the paper. "Even what he didn't know about."

"Me too," Dolan said, thinking she was referring to Quebec. But for the pull he felt toward her—he did not regret it at all.

"How are they?" Eddie asked dutifully. She looked up. "Your folks."

"Not themselves," he repeated. He nodded at the affidavit. "Can you use that?"

"Yes, I can. It may not mean much, but not having it would have meant a lot more."

Then what was wrong? He sensed that this meeting was going to be even briefer than the first. Despite the ludicrous extremity of his behavior and the obvious intensity of his feelings, she was about to brush him off, as if he were a flea, a gnat. But then he saw it was not in spite of his behavior and his feelings, but because of them. "Look," he offered, "I've made a mistake maybe in . . ."

Eddie cut him off with her hand. She didn't want him asking to be forgiven again. She could already taste the guilt that would depress her later for having treated him cruelly, but she genuinely felt she had no choice. However much she might have wished once to be an accepting, complying, welcoming female, that was simply not an option for her now. She had become as bony, angular and edgy inside as she was physically, but for a purpose. The opposite of softness was not bitchiness. It was survival. She was prepared for Cheney, for an assault. She had made herself

ready for combat, and so, even with this man whose
regard for her was tangible and could have been
soothing, she could only focus on what threatened,
on, for example, his transparent earnestness, that old
male ploy. I'm only thinking of you, baby. Right,
buster.

Eddie had the capacity to shield herself behind a
numbness. She could keep at arm's length what
threatened her until she was ready to take it on. She
was not proud of that capacity, but she was grateful
for it.

Dolan surprised her by offering his hand. "If
there's any way I can help with that . . ." He indicated the affidavit again. Eddie gave him her hand to
shake. ". . . get in touch, OK?"

He handed her the bag of lobsters, turned around
and walked back to the car.

"But I don't know where to find you," Eddie
called, to her own surprise. Suddenly she wanted to
resist that numbness because it shielded her from
more than threats.

He had the door open. "Get in touch with my
folks. They'll know. My mother'd love to hear from
you. She'd love to see Bren."

"Oh, Bren! But you haven't seen him either! He's
your nephew!" Eddie said that as if it had just occurred to her. "You have a right to see him."

Dolan smiled, but slid behind the wheel.

Eddie ran toward the car, awkwardly, with the affidavit in one hand and the lobsters in the other. "I
mean, I'd like you to see him. Really, David, I'm
sorry. What's wrong with me? How can I be sending
you off like this? With the FBI after you, and with
Bren here. Don't you want to meet him?"

He looked at her sharply. "I'd love to meet him. He's one of the reasons I came home."

His simple statement shocked Eddie. "Well then, stay for lunch. I have these terrific lobsters."

He shook his head. He did not want to be received politely now for decorum's sake. "You could get in trouble, for harboring a fugitive."

She stared at him and said, dead seriously, "I could have gotten in trouble for helping him escape."

"Funny, I thought you did."

She held his eyes. He was the one to look away.

He started the car engine. "I'll meet Bren another time. It'll be better. If I leave now I can get back to Boston tonight."

"This is an island, remember?"

He looked at his watch. "When's the next boat?"

"Three. Please stay."

He thought about it, then shut the engine off. "Thanks."

"You're welcome, Doe."

"Eddie, nobody's called me that in years." Nobody but Artie Rose.

" 'Doe, a deer.' Right?"

Dolan nodded. He wanted to talk about the past with her because the past was what connected them. "He used to sing it at me. 'A female deer.' It drove me nuts, but the name stuck."

"It was his way of getting back at you for calling him 'Sunbeam.' " Eddie wished she could smile as she said that, but talking about Brendan with David made her feel uneasy.

" 'Sunbeam Electric,' actually." He got out of the car and took the lobsters back.

"I never called him 'Sunny.'" Eddie said. "I resented it when you did."

"You thought I looked down on him." Dolan stopped. They both knew that he had, but how could he admit it?

"He loved you, David. He told me that once he crawled after you into a sewer pipe because he thought you'd gotten stuck. But you'd climbed out a manhole a block away and hadn't come back to tell him. He thought you were dead."

"When he found me later he started hitting me. I never understood why. Brothers! Christ, Eddie, we didn't have a chance."

"Some people say the same thing about husbands and wives."

"I've heard."

"Are you married?"

"No. Never."

She looked away from him.

He said, "I didn't mean I wouldn't. Just that I never have."

When she raised her eyes they wore an expression of pain that stunned him and he remembered how vulnerable she'd seemed to him the day before at the airport. He felt attracted to her again in exactly the same way he had then; he wanted to protect her. He wanted—this thought unsettled him—to care for her the way Brendan would have.

"You've been smart," she said.

He shook his head. "No. Just alone."

They stared at each other until she said, "Let's have some lobster, eh?"

She turned toward the house, took a few steps, saw her son and then stopped again.

The boy was staring at them from behind the screen door. He was draped from the shoulders by an oversized beach towel, a cape, which, together with the soft-focus gray mesh of the door and his rigid face behind it, would have been enough to give him an otherworldly air. But for Dolan his exact resemblance to his own younger brother was what made the sight of him startling.

He remembered the time to which Eddie'd referred, when Brendan came at him swinging. Dolan had been unable to pin his arms. The kid was like a tiger. It was one of the few times they'd fought physically and it ended with Brendan getting a tooth chipped when he fell against the curbstone. That memory, together with Dolan's sense of having neglected his nephew all these years, brought his guilt forward again.

Bren's likeness to his father fell away when Dolan saw signs of a great suspicion. Brendan had never been suspicious enough, never cautious enough.

He walked slowly forward. "Hello. I know who you are."

Bren drew a wooden sword from his belt, but absently, and he held it at his side. "Who?"

"Superman."

Bren shook his head.

Dolan snapped his fingers. "What a dummy I am. You have a sword. He doesn't." He stepped closer. "I'll try again, OK?"

Bren looked at Eddie, then at Dolan again and nodded.

"Captain Marvel."

Bren shook his head again. "Who's he?"

"Batman?"

"He wears a mask."

Dolan slapped his forehead. "I forgot." He stooped and balanced on his haunches, squinting through the screen door. "You know what? I give up. Will you tell me?"

Bren shook his head.

"Do you know who I am?" Dolan stood and opened the door.

Bren looked uncertainly toward his mother. She nodded, but she sensed the importance of their doing this on their own.

Bren said, "Yes."

"Who?"

"My mother's friend."

Dolan looked quickly at Eddie. He was amused by Bren's answer, but Eddie was horrified by it. In the argot of the divorce capital of the world, "friend" meant "lover," and out there even the children knew it. "No, he's not, dear," Eddie said. "He's your uncle."

"My what?"

"What do you say when you give up?" Dolan asked lamely. "You say 'uncle,' right? I gave up, and I'm your uncle."

"Don't, David," Eddie said, approaching them. She saw how confused Bren was and how alarmed. The child's poise was all too fragile. "This is your Uncle David. Your real uncle."

Bren ignored his mother. "What's your name?" He stepped outside to see him more clearly. He could feel the ginger ale in his legs.

"David. Or Dave, if you want."

"I mean your whole name."

"David Dolan."

Bren looked at his mother. "Is he?"

Eddie reached toward him. "Sweetie, he's your father's brother."

Before she touched him, Bren bolted and made for the woods, his cape flying behind.

Dolan was too surprised to move at first, but when he saw the expression on Eddie's face he realized that he had to undo what had just happened. He started after Bren, but Eddie stopped him by yelling, much too loudly, "No!"

Dolan faced her. She was desolate. "Let him go," she said. "We have to let him go."

"Tell me what's wrong, Eddie. What can I do to help?"

"Nothing," she said, but without bitterness. Only defeat informed her voice. "I'm losing him. I'm losing my son. Don't you see?"

Frankly, he didn't. Perhaps that ignorance was what kept him from moving toward her.

CHAPTER 13

The ground under Bren's feet fell away as he went over the crest of the hill and down the western slope of the Brewsters' point of land, weaving an expert trail through the thin trees across the occasional splotches of sunlight. He tore past small boulders and stunted scrub and he crashed through light brush with an abandon utterly unlike him. Despite his customary woodsman's swagger he always checked for poison ivy before allowing any leafy plant the slightest contact with his skin or even clothes, but he did not care about poison ivy now, or spiders or lizards or bobcats or bears. He had heard that all kinds of animals were in those woods and believed it, but only a snake could have stopped his flight then. He was surging and swerving with a wild eye toward the island's other shore, the barrier of it, the limit.

He was angry at his mother, but he knew it wasn't for a good reason. He had made a mistake in his mind about the stranger at first, thinking him her boyfriend. As far as he knew, his mother didn't have a boyfriend, but who could say? His father had girlfriends, he knew that much, and not because his mother said so. When he was coming home in the school van one day he saw his father in a convertible with a pretty woman whom he was touching on the leg as he drove along. Once they left California, Bren expected that at some point his mother would get a new man to be with. That was how it worked, and that was who he guessed the stranger was that morning, even though when he'd heard the car he'd hoped it was his father.

When somebody adopts you they become almost your real father, and Bren planned to think of Cheney that way no matter what, because in his opinion he needed a father. He and his father had made promises to each other. Once when his mother got angry at him for going to the movies without permission, his father took him aside and promised to take him every Saturday, and he would have, except that Bren's mother made them move to New York. He and Dad had gone to only four movies by then, the best of which was *The Bad News Bears*. Dad was also going to take Bren to Little League, which was another entire reason he had to get back to California, even though it was too late for this year, plus he wasn't old enough yet anyway. In New York, though, there wasn't any Little League, and even if there was, who'd want to be taken by his mother?

But an uncle. Why not an uncle?

Jason and Sadie's father was someone everyone said was his uncle; he even called him Uncle Bob, but he hardly knew the guy, since he lived in Cleveland and wasn't usually around even when Jason and Sadie were. His mother had talked about his other uncle once, but only when he'd asked her right out how many relatives he had and who were they? What surprised Bren now was that this uncle was an American. What his mother said had made him think that he was a foreigner. Bren did not like the feeling that his mother wasn't leveling with him.

Maybe he could have thought of the man as his uncle and been pleased to meet him, but she ruined it by calling him his father's brother. Which father? He didn't know why it panicked him to think about his other father, his first one, but it did. If he was dead, where was the grave? Maybe she made it up about his father being a soldier who got killed, so that he wouldn't know the truth, which was, of course, that Cheney was his real father after all. But that didn't make sense either. It all confused him, but he knew one thing, that the adults, including his grandmother, hadn't hesitated to tell him lies.

When the stranger arrived, therefore, Bren had hidden behind the screen door listening to him and his mother because he knew he would only get the truth if he overheard it. Even if the guy was his uncle there was more to it than that, obviously, because his mother had been upset to see him like she used to be with his father when he came home and surprised them. Bren was an infallible reader of his mother's emotions, which alone could not deceive him.

Maybe he'd panicked and fled because of the other hunch he had, the wild one. He'd tried to make it go away but couldn't. Maybe the stranger wasn't his uncle but his first father, who his mother would have grown tired of and left, even though he asked her not to, just like she left his second father.

There was one moral principle in Bren's universe which was this: do not fail Mom. He had just failed her by being rude. Unfortunately for the clarity of his feelings and thought, a second principle had begun to impinge upon him: love desperately what is going to die. Bren feared that Cheney, rejected and alone, was going to die, and he felt responsible. Here were the two thoughts he found it nearly impossible to consider directly, but also impossible more and more to keep from his mind: he was the cause of his mother's break-up with Cheney, and he was, despite his ignorance of the circumstances, the cause of his first father's disappearance from their lives, the cause even, maybe, of his death. If his first father was dead without them, wasn't it logical that his second one would be too?

And why shouldn't a boy with such a set of honed intuitions, a fox in his shirt, have been tearing through the woods away from his mother and her mystery man as if not one life but three depended on his escape?

He stopped at the cliff, but a little close to the edge of it, and he had to swing his arms in circles to keep from going over, yet he wasn't afraid of that. He had his cape and not for nothing. He was sure-footed. The cliff was twenty feet above the water and it reminded him of the cliffs in Topanga Canyon. Right behind their house in California the cliff fell off a hundred feet, so what was twenty? And here if one fell it was into the water and he could swim. The water was smooth, relatively, because this was the back of the island and the sea couldn't get at it.

To Bren's right at a distance of fifty yards was the Brewsters' pier and float, on which the Sunfish was dismantled and to which the Boston Whaler was tied. He thought of going over there and sitting in the boat, but didn't. He stayed where he was for a long time staring off at the misty green of Mt. Desert. The sun had peaked already and was bright enough to

make it hard to keep looking at the sky, but he did,
as if it could answer the absorbing mysteries of his
morning. Is there something behind the great sky, the
hills, the smell of pine, behind the birds and limpets,
behind the soft dirt, behind his mother's unhappiness, behind his feelings? A primitive impulse, an
unfamiliar one, made him want to speak. Another
child with different training might have spoken to
God. Bren stood there mute and frustrated, staring at
the sky, aware of the tears in his eyes which blocked
his vision and, eventually, made it difficult for him to
watch carefully an airplane come swooping down
over the hills across Frenchman Bay.

The chart told Cheney that Hunter's was the right
kind of island. It had steep shoreline with no outly-
ing shoals. Since the land fell off abruptly under
water, the incoming ocean waves would break on the
windward side without slowing down and without
therefore refracting a wave-train farther out which
would cause swells to encircle the island and meet on
the inland side of it in a choppy sea. But Hunter's
was the peak of an underwater mountain and the
swells would pass by with a minimum of distortion,
guaranteeing, all other things being equal, a calm surface in the lee. And so it seemed on first glance from
his vantage at a thousand feet. He edged out the flaps
a notch, adjusted the pitch of the propeller, dropped
the nose slightly and pushed the wheel over to
descend. Unless the wind was wrong, he would take
her in parallel to the shore because that would put
him parallel also to any swells he couldn't read.

He made a first pass at two hundred feet over his
landing area, his eyes smart on the surface, checking

for obstructions and wave patterns. The trim of a
sailboat, a flag, smoke from a chimney, a craft at anchor would have told him exactly what he needed to
know about wind direction, but there were none of
those at the southwestern corner of the island. He
watched a pair of gulls land, though, and that told
him, because gulls, like planes, land into the wind.
The one thing about seaplane landings that could
cause trouble was the divergence of wind direction
and water flow. But on that day wind and water were
congruent. The Bangor Flight Watch had told him to
expect a coastal wind velocity of up to fifteen knots,
but he guessed it was less, perhaps twelve. Good conditions, in sum, but there should have been sailboats
out. He thought of calling Bangor again for a new
check, but what could they have learned in fifteen
minutes? He glanced downeast for the tenth time.
The clouds had built up considerably, but they were
still cumulus. The front was still holding.

He eased back on the stick and throttled down to
pull the plane in a thirty-degree bank up and around
to reverse direction, and then he immediately pitched
down into a shallow dive to cover the same path
again, only now leveling off a few dozen feet above
the water for one last survey, a standard procedure. A
seaplane pilot has to make his own airport and be his
own controller. McCoy was thorough and careful, but
when he roared by what he knew was the Brewsters'
pier and raft at the end of the island, he saw Bren
standing on it and waving wildly, and that was why
on the instant he decided, though his round-trip fuel
margin was slim and though the Cessna Skywagon
with floats wasn't stressed for stunts, to take her up to

altitude again and do an inside loop to show the kid
how much he loved him.

He pulled the plane through the maneuver with a
deft series of adjustments on throttle and stick
pressure, always alert to keep rpm's below red. Even
an uncertified plane, handled correctly, can be made
to defy G-forces, but Cheney longed for his own Aero-
bat, in which he could feel in his backside every nuance of the machine's performance. In this plane he
flew with his eyes open and by the steps. Through the
loop he focused first on the artificial horizon, then on
his wing tip as it went over, then on the point of
Hunter's as a ground reference, but the field of his attention was actually taken up by an image of the boy
whom he pictured on that raft with his head back,
mouth agape, eyes sparkling up at him with admiration.

Cheney liked a good entrance. He liked an audience. He liked the feel of his own competence. If he
did all things as well as he did loops, Cuban-8's and
snap-rolls, then, among other things, every child in
the world would be his instead of none. At least some
creature besides the dog Pronto would know his
smell. Pronto fell all over himself to welcome Cheney
when he arrived, but no one else did.

The kid was hailing him, though. Cheney saw him
as the plane shot by the raft. Bren was waving his
arms over his head and leaping with an improvised
cape at his shoulders, dancing about on that plat-
form, rocking it; hailing him as if he were a miracle,
which was exactly how Cheney felt. He was so glad
he had decided to come.

The runout took him a hundred feet down the
shore. He came about and taxied toward the pier as

slowly as possible, and cut the engine while well out so that by the time his son, with his usual instinct for the right move, began to fend the aircraft off, the propeller, which could have chopped him to pieces, was dead.

Cheney climbed out of the cockpit onto one of the two catamaran floats. He tossed a line to Bren and knotted it to the cleat at the base of the N-strut. Bren hauled him in. For a minute they were both all business, then Cheney hopped to the raft and swept the kid up in a hug which, when Bren returned it fiercely, moved him too much to speak.

Cheney began to turn him in circles as if they were in that cup-and-saucer ride at Disneyland. As Bren's legs swung out Cheney reached down and grabbed an ankle and continued swinging him, but by the leg and an arm. "Airplane!" Cheney cried over Bren's squealing laughter. "Fly! Fly!" And fly the boy did, giving himself completely to Cheney, soaring around and around with his free arm and leg out like wings. He was not frightened that the arc took him over the water for a third of each circuit, or that his head repeatedly came within a foot of the upright four-by-four that supported the railing of the float-ramp.

Cheney didn't notice that post at first or how close Bren's head was coming to it, but when he did his mind fixed for an instant on a quite detailed vision of that head striking that post, not once but again and again as he was unable to stop himself turning even while his son's head was being smashed like a cabbage.

He stopped himself, too abruptly, and Bren hit the deck with a thud.

"Hey!" the boy protested.

"Crash landing," Cheney said. "Bail out! Bail out!" And he picked up the kid again like a bundle, but this time to crush him against his chest. Cheney buried his face in Bren's body and breathed deeply, as if he were oxygen. For several moments he held him like that, swaying gently, and he could feel himself coming down.

"Hello, ace," he said at last.

"Why do you call me, 'ace'?" Bren wanted Cheney to call him "son."

"Ace is what they call crack pilots like you."

"And you?"

"You bet."

"Can I call you 'ace' too?" Bren thought that would solve his problem. He knew how it bothered his mother to have him call Cheney "Dad."

"You call me whatever the blazes you want." Cheney hugged Bren again before putting him down.

Even though he was so happy to see his father Bren was surprised how hard he squeezed him, and when, once on his feet, he tried to look Cheney in the eye, he couldn't because too many feelings were showing there.

Cheney hadn't a clue what to say. It was as if he had to build his next statement a word, no, a letter at a time. He had vaguely planned to offer to take Bren up for a ride, but that was out of the question now because of fuel.

Like the front over Nova Scotia holding back the weather, there was in Cheney's mind a barrier holding back the impulse he had bared to Frazier on the phone the night before, the impulse he'd hoped Frazier would interdict. Why not just bundle the kid into the copilot's seat right now and go?

"How's Pronto? I miss him."

"Pronto's fine, except he misses you too."

"How do you know?"

"He told me." Cheney winked. He claimed to be able to converse with Pronto, a pretense Bren enjoyed, but not now.

"Help me secure the plane?"

"Sure."

They tied the line to a cleat on the dock and Cheney fetched a second line from the cockpit which they attached aft.

They sat on the raft's edge to admire the airplane.

"How come you're not home?" Bren asked.

"Because I'm here." Cheney leaned into him, but Bren wasn't playing. He had to figure out what was going on.

"I mean L.A. You're not in L.A. You were in New York."

"Yep. I'm in a play. I hope you can . . ." Cheney stopped himself from saying what he didn't mean.

"You have to do it tonight?"

"No. I took the day off to come up here. Big shots can do that. Did you know I was a big shot?"

"What's the play about?"

The word that came unbidden to mind was *murder*. Cheney looked at Bren, then put his arm around him and tried to fend off this definition: the play is about the deed which changed a well-loved king into an evil crouchback, the murder of his brother's heir, a child, the Prince of Wales.

"About kings," he said. "On my pointed red shield above the royal lion is my motto, and you know what it is? 'Loyalty Binds Me.' It does too. To you."

"Are you a king?"

Cheney closed his eyes and saw himself hunch-backed, two-thirds of the way up the great staircase.

Bren wondered if Cheney had heard him, or if he should repeat his question. He watched Cheney closely. Something was wrong. He ducked out from under Cheney's arm and stood up. "How do like my cape?"

Cheney turned around. "I noticed it from the air." He took a corner of the terry-cloth towel between his fingers and rubbed it.

"Real silk," Bren said.

"So I see."

Bren was trying to decide whether to tell Cheney who he was when Cheney asked, "But does it fly?"

"Watch!" Bren flew up the ramp and over the pier to shore, Cheney thought the boy was right to run away from him, and he didn't know whether to give chase or not. Something told him that he should climb back into his cockpit and fly away. What? He knew; what had dogged him for days, an inability to shepherd concentration, to control the images his mind was flashing before him. What more warning did he need? But also dogging him was the boy himself. Why was he running away? Cheney felt suddenly angry. Didn't loyalty bind him too? The child should not have run off like that. For one thing, Cheney did not want to deal with Eddie's mother. For another, Cheney McCoy hadn't canceled rehearsal and flown all this way to be teased, toyed with and run from.

Clumsily for him, perhaps because the water rose under the float just then, Cheney got up and gave chase. He loped across the ramp, up the rocks and into the woods. He hadn't been to Maine since a visit with Eddie in happier times, and the woods struck him now as they had then, as eerie and corrupt. A permanent dampness in the ground and in the knuckled bark of the pine gave off the odor of rot. As the forest closed around him, Cheney wasn't sure whether he was following a footpath or not. He ran on, unable to glimpse the boy. Branches slapped at him, but he ignored them and ran faster. Suddenly he didn't know where he was, as if he'd lost himself in a sense exercise before doing a scene. What forest was this, pray tell? Birnham Wood? Nottingham? And who was chasing him and why?

Strange things were bound to happen in Richard's life. There had been omens after all; it was said he was two years in his mother's womb, that his body issued from it backward and with a twisted spine and withered arm. It was said he ate live frogs as a baby. It was said he was bewitched and would lead his army into any place but woods, which alone terrified him.

Bren caught a glimpse of the house and he almost stopped. What was his mother going to say when he showed up with his father? Would she think he knew that Cheney was coming? Would she think him disloyal? Maybe at the sight of Cheney she would change her mind.

He broke out of the woods, no longer playfully fleeing his father, but now running to his mother with the good news. Maybe she would think it was good news too if he thought so hard enough. "Mom! Mom! Guess who's here! Guess!"

Eddie opened the door with a smile. "What, sweetie?"

"Guess!" Bren halted a dozen yards short of her. "Guess who's here!"

Eddie knew.

And the knowledge immobilized her. She could only stare at the woods and wait for him to come out, a flushed grizzly for its dinner.

When he appeared his eyes went right to her and he stopped as if he'd been slugged. She sensed his surprise and his vulnerability, but didn't understand either. What right did *he* have to be surprised? To feel exposed?

"Eddie!" Cheney cried from where he stood. "Eddie!" He wanted to fling his arms out toward her, but instinctively he checked himself. Inwardly he was overwhelmed by longing for her. It didn't occur to him that Bren had arranged an ambush or that she was going to screech at him now and throw him out. He didn't see Bren, who was rigid between them, waiting for them to react. All he saw was the woman, the one whose affection, like a battened sail, would enable him to ride through the new and awful turmoil that had swooped down on him. "Oh, Eddie," he repeated, but now calmly, more cautiously.

"Hello, Cheney," she said gently, as if she too believed that the kindly speaking of names would settle everything.

CHAPTER 14

On the east side of the island the wind was far brisker and it, together with the way the air felt in his ears, registered with Cheney enough to distract him even from Eddie. He looked at the sky. The huge red house blocked the horizon. He tried to look through the door and the windows on the far side. He saw a shadow, a person's shadow, moving in the kitchen.

Crossing toward Eddie, he said, "I didn't expect to find you here. Bren said you weren't here."

"She wasn't, Ace! She came after you called." Bren looked at his mother furtively.

"It's OK, kiddo," Cheney said. "I'm grateful." He stopped in front of her. "I'm very glad to see you, Eddie. But I didn't come to make trouble. I only wanted to pay a short visit and split. That's still what I'd like, if you'd allow it." He looked so earnestly at her and had spoken so courteously that she instinctively distrusted him. She wanted to tell him not to come an inch closer, but instead she said, "I expected you," as if it were the most reasonable thing in the world for him to have arrived.

"You look swell," he said.

"No, I don't."

"Your hair looks great, but, well, you could use some sun."

"And you know where I can get it, right?" She smiled.

He squinted up at the sky. "Not here. Not for much longer anyway."

"How's the play going?"

He looked at her carefully, trying to decide if she really wanted to know. But then he realized it didn't matter. He could use the truth to disarm her. "I'm having my troubles, since you ask. I had to get away from it. That's why I came."

Eddie had to suppress an impulse to ask him what troubles. Cheney never admitted to difficulties, or confided them.

When she didn't pick up on it he added, "I hope I make it."

She had to look away from him. "Oh, Cheney, you'll make it."

"Will you come and see it? I could use the luck."

Eddie didn't answer at first. After all that she'd been feeling, how could she possibly commit herself even to be a member of his audience? But she sensed how he hung on her reply. What the hell, she thought. "Sure. I wouldn't miss it."

Bren almost yelped with pleasure. "Can I come?"

Eddie was about to say sure to him too when Cheney stooped and grabbed Bren by both shoulders. "Listen, ace, I'll take you to every goddamn game of the World Series on both coasts, but I can't let you come to my play. It's for grownups."

"You're hurting my Goddamn arms," Bren said.

Cheney let him go, but said, "No, I'm not. I'm hardly touching you."

Bren sidled to his mother.

Cheney looked at her helplessly. "I hardly touched him."

His stricken face made her feel, despite herself, sorry for him. "It's OK," she said, covering Bren's shoulder with her arm.

"Or I hardly meant to. I can't have him coming to the play. Richard is nuts."

"Look, why don't you stay for lunch? We're having lobster and you have to wait for the ferry anyway."

He laughed. "I flew, sweetheart." Cheney looked into the kitchen, after that shadow again.

"You flew!"

"A seaplane, Mom! You should see it!"

That stopped Eddie. Had she forgotten whom she was dealing with? How could she have sympathy for him? The world was his playground. His flying here, there and everywhere epitomized Cheney's privilege. His flying was what had attracted her to him in the first place and what, later, terrified her about him. Whenever she had a falling dream she woke up thinking she was in that kamikaze dive of his.

"Flew!" Cheney repeated, snapping his fingers at her eyes. Then he opened his arms like wings and flapped toward Bren. "Right, ace?"

Bren nodded and made a thumbs-up sign. "Roger."

Cheney straightened and grinned at Eddie. "I'd love to stay for lunch. Thanks. Especially if it's lobster, which is, aside from your mother, Maine's only charm."

Eddie led the way into the kitchen. "My mother's not here," she said over her shoulder.

"Oh," Cheney said, following, "I'm sorry to miss

her." But his thought was about that shadow. If it wasn't Mrs. Brewster, who was it?

Bren took up the rear. "Who's Richard?" he asked.

Inside Cheney turned back to him. "The King."

"The king is nuts?"

"Well . . ." Cheney leaned over with his hands on his knees. "He does some awful things."

"Like what?"

He murders a child like you, Cheney thought. He touched Bren's head and said solemnly, "War, ace. He starts a war. War is bad, you know that."

"Not in those days, it wasn't."

Cheney stood up, tossing Bren's hair goodnaturedly. He knew better than to engage the boy's logic.

When Cheney turned, it was toward Eddie at the stove, but the sight of a man in a white shirt with the sleeves rolled, framed by the archway that led into the living room, stopped him.

"You're the shadow," Cheney said abruptly. When no one understood, he laughed. "I'm sorry. I saw a shadow from outside. Yours, I guess." Cheney crossed toward him with a host's kindly authority. "I'm Cheney McCoy." Like many celebrities, Cheney loved to introduce himself. He liked it that he was taller than the stranger.

"My name is David Dolan."

Cheney flinched, but recovered instantly. "David Dolan?" They shook hands. "Are you related to Brendan?"

"I'm his brother."

When Cheney faced Eddie, she seemed both guarded and sad to him. He felt especially drawn to her then, and he knew both that he had to have her and that he could. Richard's line cued him; was ever woman in this humour wooed? Ha! In this humour won! He faced Dolan again. "I didn't know Brendan had a brother. I'm honored to meet you. I admire him enormously."

"You do?" Dolan was put off by Cheney's kindliness. "Why is that?"

"Because of how he died. For his country. For our country."

Dolan walked casually to the stove to hold a platter while Eddie fished the bright red lobsters out of the pot.

"Your brother was a hero."

Dolan did not want to have this conversation. He concentrated on the lobsters. He said, "Perhaps so." Dolan thought it would be callous to talk about it in front of Bren.

Eddie looked at Bren, who was studiously examining the edge of his wooden sword. "Sweetie, you can have peanut butter and jelly if you like."

He brightened. "Can I make it?"

"I'll help you," Dolan offered.

"I like to make it by myself." Bren ignored Dolan and climbed onto a stool for the bread.

Dolan put the platter of lobsters on the long table while Eddie poured melted butter into cups.

"I wish I'd brought my camera," Cheney announced. "This is beautiful."

Eddie and Bren sat on one side of the table, Dolan and Cheney on the other. Once they were launched into their separate attacks on their shellfish, Dolan said to Cheney, "I saw a film of yours once, about a shopkeeper who takes on a neighborhood gang." By acknowledging Cheney's celebrity status with an off-hand remark, he hoped to defuse it. If he was ill at ease, wasn't it because Eddie's estranged husband was by far the most famous man he'd ever met?

Cheney said, "I remember that flick, but for the life of me I can't think of its title."

Eddie said, "*Streetfight*."

"That's it," Cheney said. "George Manilla."

"I liked it," Dolan said.

"Thank you. I enjoy acting. What do you do?"

"I teach."

"That's nice." Cheney turned to Eddie. "How's the writing going?"

Eddie shrugged and then cracked open the large claw of her lobster. "It's going all right."

"Good. I think it's magnificent that you're writing again."

Eddie wanted to steer the talk away from her book. She knew Cheney did not feel that way at all. "You said you're having trouble with Richard."

"Richard the Third," Cheney explained to Dolan. "You know the play?"

"I've heard of it." Dolan smiled.

Cheney pushed his chair back on its two legs and wiped his mouth. "Shakespeare begins his histories by bringing home from exile a prince who personifies the hope of a new order and who challenges the villain who has usurped the throne."

Eddie and Dolan exchanged a look. Both wondered if Cheney knew Dolan's history; Eddie wondered how he could.

"And he ends his histories with the returned prince taking the villain's place as the usurper. One play's hero is the next play's blackguard." Cheney paused to look intently at Eddie. "In Shakespeare the better you are, the worse you are. You know what I mean?"

Eddie stared back at Cheney and realized as she did that she was stronger than the last time. She was keeping up with him.

"For the king," he went on, "a second banishment would be worse than death."

Eddie stopped working her lobster.

"The trouble I'm having, love, is in the way Richard's plight keeps reminding me of my own." Cheney turned to Dolan. "Excuse the personal note. You've probably gathered that I've been banished."

"Cheney, really." Eddie could not rebuke him when she saw that, in fact, his face was bent with emotion. Even the subtlest display of hurt was utterly unlike Cheney. It both touched her and angered her. She did not want to involve Bren or David Dolan in a scene with Cheney, and something told her that their presence was stimulating him. He was acting.

She got up and dumped the bowl of discarded lobster shells. She thought she could use a crust like a lobster's. When she sat again she said, "David's just returned from Sweden."

"Oh, really? What's Sweden like?" Cheney's ability to shift moods served him well. His interest seemed not at all studied.

Dolan shrugged. "Like any place. Only colder, darker."

"Sweden's neutral, isn't it? They're always neutral." Cheney watched Dolan over the rim of his water glass. "They didn't even oppose Hitler, as I recall."

"That's true. And much is made of it. Especially by the Swedes themselves. They're not like us. They tend to be aloof and indifferent. God help you if your car breaks down in the middle of the night. Once I stood by the side of the road from midnight to after dawn trying to get someone to stop. That was the night I decided I could never live there." Dolan stopped. He hadn't intended to say that much. "Nevertheless, Sweden was good to me and I'm grateful to it."

"You say aloof? I thought Swedes were spontaneous and free, sexually at least, right?"

"Swedish men and women expect from each other approximately what they expect from nature. Nothing."

"Oh, come on."

Dolan raised his eyebrows. "Seen any Bergman lately? Any Strindberg?"

Cheney turned to Eddie. "He sounds like Woody Allen." To Dolan he said, "You probably haven't heard of him. Woody Allen, our foremost expert on Ingmar Bergman and Gus Strindberg."

Dolan didn't respond.

Cheney went on cheerfully, "I envy you the experience of another culture. What brought you there in the first place?"

"I was a draft-dodger."

Dolan and Cheney stared at each other.

Finally Cheney said, "I'll be damned. You say it right out, don't you?"

Bren asked timidly, "What's a draft-dodger?"

Eddie said, "Your Uncle David was a famous leader against the Vietnam War."

"David Dolan!" Cheney sat forward. "I remember you." He turned to Eddie. "Why didn't you tell me?" And then back to Dolan. "I admire your guts. I don't think it's cowardly at all, what you did."

"Thanks," Dolan said, reining his own sarcasm. He

thought it ironic that Cheney McCoy had heard of him. Once, despite himself, he'd have been flattered.

"Quite the contrary. Conscience is the most important thing there is. That's what *Richard the Third* is all about, conscience. And what happens when we fail it. Or when it fails us. I think Richard is tragic, quite genuinely tragic." He turned to Eddie. "Don't you?"

"I don't remember the play that well."

"Don't you think it's tragic when somebody loses hold of one dream while reaching for another, then loses both?"

Eddie could not look at him. She was not familiar with his undefined intensity. Usually Cheney was cool, snappy, fast. "I don't know what that means," she said quietly. But she had clasped her fingers tightly together, as if to display her tension.

"Richard only wanted to be an honorable man, a pride to his family. He had a son of his own, and he knew what it was to love a boy and harbor great hopes for him. But then something immortalizing was put within his own reach, cruelly put. He took the crown. Who wouldn't have? As much for his line as for himself. But then his son died, and then, of her grief, his beloved wife died, and his trusted friend Buckingham led a revolt against him which he had no choice but to put down ruthlessly. In a civil war like that violence goes unchecked. For the sake of England's good order, he had to eliminate pretenders. Including . . ." He checked himself. He looked at Bren, who was staring up at him, mouth agape. Only then did Cheney realize that he had tears on his own cheeks. He did not wipe them.

"I see what you mean," Eddie said. "That's very sad."

Dolan didn't accept it for a minute, either Cheney's version of Richard's plight or the swoon with which it was offered. He was embarrassed, not for Cheney, but for Eddie. To Dolan, Cheney's morose sentimentality seemed a blatant and ineffectual effort to seduce her. He couldn't believe she would be taken in by it.

But Eddie saw more than Dolan did. She saw the hole in Cheney's armor, his wound. Eddie saw quite clearly that Cheney was afflicted with her absence. She had indeed cut him, and it surprised her to have drawn blood. She had expected him to shrug off whatever bruise his pride took when she left. Obviously he had been unable to, and that hit her like a jolt. She could feel her defenses against him crumbling. If he were to turn and repeat what he had just said obliquely about Richard, but in simple language about himself, she would not resist him. She was tired of resisting him. She wanted to love him again. If he was hurting, couldn't she perhaps help him? "You said that Richard's plight touches yours." She spoke softly, leading him.

Dolan was alarmed that she should willingly make herself vulnerable to Cheney again. He wanted to stop her, but he sat still and watched.

Cheney's head snapped, as if he'd dozed off. "Thank you," he said. "Did you like it?"

Dolan didn't understand, but Eddie did. She slumped in her chair. He'd been acting. He'd been watching his rushes. Now he expected kudos. He'd consider it an achievement that he had moved her.

"Not particularly," she said. "I don't like it when

you do an exercise with me." All behavior was a kind of acting with Cheney.

"That was no exercise!" Cheney's voice rose, but he controlled himself. "Or not merely," he added forcefully.

"I'm not making a moral judgment, Cheney. Relax. I know what it's like to have personal material all enmeshed with the imaginary, or if you like, the professional. I always know the difference, though. I don't think you do." When she said that, Eddie realized it was the perfect summary of why she'd left him. She never knew for sure with Cheney what was real and what was made up, because he didn't.

"Ah, yes," he said, but so condescendingly. "My wife, the artist." He turned to Dolan. "Her new book. Do you know what it's about?"

"No."

"It's about your brother."

Eddie dropped her knife. "How do you know that?"

"You told me, didn't you?"

"I did not."

"I must have read it. Rex Reed or someone." Cheney gripped the edge of the table and stared at her. She stared back. She always stared back, the bitch. He remembered hitting her, and for once the memory gave him pleasure.

Dolan wanted to soothe her. "It's splendid, I think, if you're writing about those days."

Eddie looked down at her hands. She was amazed that for a moment she'd softened toward Cheney.

Cheney pressed again. "Why are you embarrassed, lover, to be writing about your deceased husband? Why are you embarrassed to have it known?"

Eddie looked at Dolan. "He resents it that I'm not writing about him."

"Ha! I thank God every night that you're not! You'd ruin me."

Bren was there. She had to stop Cheney. She simply could not allow this in front of her son.

"What exactly do you tell us about him?" Cheney asked, too earnestly.

"Never mind."

"No, really. We'd like to know. His brother would like to know. His son would like to know. His usurper would like to know." Cheney grinned at each of them.

"Hey," Dolan said amiably, "I've been gone a long time. I don't want to rush into the thick of contemporary American life too quickly."

"Oh, what you've been missing, friend!" Cheney went back on his chair again. "Social life in this country has become utterly barbaric. Marriage, for example. The state of holy matrimony merged with the State of Nevada."

"Cheney," Eddie warned.

Cheney turned to Bren and touched his arm. "Tell them what my motto is."

"Cheney," Eddie repeated, even more sternly. "Leave Bren out of this."

"No, really. He knows, don't you, kiddo? What's written on my shield?"

"Loyalty ties me."

"Binds me! Binds me!" Cheney turned to Dolan. "You may also have gathered that we are bound now by an infinitely entangled custody suit. We're paying our lawyers a fortune to confuse the issues. Or I am. Eddie gets hers for nothing."

Dolan wanted to get away from them both, wanted to keep on driving like a Swede at midnight. His dream of a new life seemed ludicrous. But what if Kitty Genovese was being stabbed outside his window? Was he only an evader after all?

Dolan put his hand on Cheney's shoulder. Even as he spoke he understood that his words meant he had stopped; he had joined them. "You know what? You'd feel better if you let it go."

Cheney looked shocked for a moment, and no one was sure how he was going to react. Then he nodded. "You're right." He nodded again. "I think you're right."

"Who wants coffee?" Eddie stood. Both men wanted coffee. She went to the stove.

"What brings you to Maine?" Cheney asked casually enough. But it seemed impossible for him to say anything that was not implicitly hostile.

Dolan reached across the table to pat Bren's hands. "Came to see my nephew." Bren ignored him.

"I never met your brother. What was he like?"

Dolan hesitated.

"Eddie never talked about him."

Dolan regretted bringing Brendan up again. He had no capacity for small talk or banter about his brother, and anything else would have been impossible. He sensed, though, that Cheney was on the edge of a dangerous mood and he didn't want to provoke him. "He was a nice guy," Dolan said. "Loyalty bound *him*."

"You like my motto? Duke of Gloucester."

"I thought you said king," Bren said.

"He becomes a king. When the play starts he's a

duke." Now Cheney put his arm on Dolan, mocking the very gesture that had soothed him, because after the fact it embarrassed him. "Loyalty blew him to smithereens, eh?"

Eddie said wearily from the stove, "Cheney, stop it."

He ignored her. "And you. What were you doing while your brother was getting wasted? Making it with Swedish meatballs?"

"Bren," Eddie said, "I want you to go upstairs."

"And I want him to stay!" Cheney slapped the table with his free hand, and then aimed his finger at Eddie. "This is his father's brother? All right. Let's do some research. For the kid's sake. For my sake. For your sake. You can use it in your book. Now, David, tell us what you were doing when your brother died."

Eddie crossed to the table and pulled Bren's chair out, but before she could take Bren's arm, Cheney took hers. He squeezed her so hard the pain registered in her face. "The kid is staying. I'm doing this for him."

Dolan was the only one who noticed the tears streaming down the cheeks of the otherwise impassive child.

"Get your hand off me," Eddie said.

"Calm down, for Christ's sake. This could be a nice family conversation."

"Get your hand off me." Her voice went up in pitch, not volume.

To Cheney's surprise and Eddie's, Dolan came between them. He grasped both their arms and separated them. Eddie was amazed that Cheney would let Dolan do that, but there was a firmness in him to which she responded too.

Eddie turned to Bren and took him by the hand out of the room.

"See what I mean?" Cheney said. "Barbaric."

"I've seen worse." Dolan sat again and leaned back in his chair, adopting, as his strategy, a much more relaxed posture than the situation warranted. "It's not the end of the world, you know."

Cheney smiled. He didn't need this guy's two-bit consolation, but he suppressed his belligerence. "Back to the subject at hand."

Dolan raised his eyebrows.

"Your brother."

"What about him?"

"When exactly did he die?"

"Exactly?"

"Yes."

"I don't know."

"I think if my brother got snuffed over there I'd know exactly when and how and why."

"I doubt it."

"Eddie wasn't informed of his death until 1974."

"Are you driving at something?"

"She was already fucking me by then."

"Don't try that with me, McCoy. Your issue with Eddie is your issue with Eddie. Don't dull your knife on me." Dolan still teetered back on his chair. He was swaying it slightly back and forth.

"She told me when the wire came that she was glad."

"I should think she would have been. My brother was dead a year before they said so. You know it, and I know it. She knew it. Why are you pushing this?"

"Because what she did to him she's done to me

now. Only I don't have the courtesy even to be M.I.A."

Dolan laughed. "The opposite of 'missing' is 'present.' I'd say you certainly have presence, Cheney."

Cheney smiled. "You know what, David? I like you." He put his arm around Dolan's neck again. Dolan did not react. "But you're so fucking Swedish. I'm standing here by the side of the road waving at you to stop because I'm wrecked, and you just keep right on going."

"If I stopped, you wouldn't like the help I'd have to offer."

"But I would. Know why? Because I like you."

"You said that."

"And because I do I'm going to do something special for you. I'm going to give you the gift of my art. It's all I have." He paused, then fondly caressed Dolan's head. "Would you let me read something to you? As an actor? I'd recite, but I'd rather find something to read. It's more of a challenge."

"Sure. Why not?" Dolan was not inclined to humor him, but he didn't know what else to do. He hoped by indulging Cheney's vanity to defuse his agitation.

He followed Cheney into the living room, but instead of going to the bookshelves, Cheney went to the desk. "Ah!" he said grandly, "here we are! I had a hunch it would be!" He picked up Eddie's manuscript and waved it triumphantly at Dolan. "The latest work of Edna Saint Dolan McCoy!"

"If that's her book, I don't think it's fair game." Dolan tried to inform his statement with an authority he didn't feel.

"Sit down!" Dolan didn't move. "Sit down!" Cheney roared.

"No."

"Suit yourself." Cheney riffled the pages open and began to read the text dramatically. " 'She wanted him to think she wasn't coming. But she wanted him also to wait for her like a sentry, with the alert posture of a front-lines watchman. She wanted him to grow impatient and wonder where she was and think she had forgotten him. All the while she drove madly through Virginia, Tennessee and Alabama, drove stopping only for gas, with the wind feathering her hair and the engine's blast filling her ears. All the while she stared down her road knowing that, where it ended, he was staring back. And that image seemed to her the only one for them, the eternal approach, and it explained her dread. They were perfect for each other as long as they were apart.' "

Eddie had been standing at the staircase, unable to move. The bastard would abuse anything that was precious to her, whether the book, her child or herself. Hearing him mock her writing and watching him flaunt her pages filled her with the same horror she'd have felt if he were juggling some priceless vase.

When he paused and looked up from the page at Dolan, she crossed the room and took him by surprise because he was angled away from her. She snatched the manuscript from his hands before he could react.

"Hey, Goddamnit, I wasn't through!"

She backed away from him. She didn't know how he was going to come at her, but she was sure he would. Instinctively she backed toward Dolan.

"It's picking up outside, Cheney," she said inanely. "You've got whitecaps out there."

Cheney looked. For miles out the waves were longer and breaking, but intermittently. What had been an eye-line shadow on the horizon was now a broad belt of black clouds to forty degrees. The front was moving in on them even while threatening to break open. Cheney knew he wouldn't be able to taxi off the water, even in the island's lee, once the wind topped twenty. He had fifteen minutes, at the outside.

"I'm sorry you can't stay," Eddie said.

Cheney smiled. "You're hoping for a real good Maine nor'easter."

"You'll be OK once you're up. You know it. What's more important, I know it."

Cheney looked at Dolan. "She cradles that thing like it's a baby, don't you think?" To Eddie he said, "You shouldn't haul the originals about. Is it your only copy?"

Eddie looked away from him. Her stupidity mortified her.

"Is there a part in it for me?"

"Have your agent call my agent. Please go now."

Cheney took a step toward the door. "Well, David, my friend, we'll meet again."

"Perhaps so."

"I'm sure of it. My lawyer will be in touch with you."

"Oh, Christ," Eddie said, sitting in the chair by Dolan. "You wouldn't."

"Call him to the stand? Of course, I would. David, I'm going to make you a star. You'll be the man who made a cuckold of poor old Cheney McCoy." He turned to Eddie. "You'll say his presence here was innocent, but in divorce court they will have heard that before. His presence is quite enough, and Bren can establish that for me."

"Cheney," Dolan said, laughing, "don't count on it. You should know something about me; I'm a hard fellow to pin down. I've been wanted in court for nearly ten years. Even if I show up, I can prove my whereabouts absolutely right through this morning. I can call the FBI to vouch for me."

"All the better. Fuel for the fire. All I need is the hint of scandal. Innuendo, man, is the name of the game. Fact is neither here nor there. Not to them, not to me. Whether you're getting it from her or not doesn't mean shit to me."

"What does?" Dolan asked. "I'm genuinely curious."

Cheney did not answer him.

Eddie said, "My having any life at all, apart from him. That's what he can't stand."

Cheney faced her slowly. He was aware of a muscle spasm below his eye. If he'd been rehearsing he'd have called it off to go into a dark room to relax. He'd have sent for a masseur. He'd have phoned Frazier. The wires of his body were stretched past breaking. But this was not the stage. This was life with Eddie. She was beating him, and he knew it. "No, love," he said. "It's the kid that worries me. Who gets him next? And for what price? I doubt you'll get as much for the next adoption as I paid for mine. You've got your own little white-slave trade going."

Eddie quite deliberately laid her manuscript aside, stood and crossed to Cheney. She slapped him in the face as hard as she could.

Cheney made no move to protect himself, because if

he'd made any move it would have been to bloody her. He had himself absolutely in check. He took her blow so rigidly that his head hardly moved with it, though in fact the force of it jolted him and the spasm under his eye came back.

He backed away from her slowly, aware of an impulse even then to do something nice for her. But there was only one kind thing left for him to do, and that was get away from her before the storm inside him broke. An acting coach would tell him later to recall that moment in its every nuance; he was to think of the gaping hole it left in him as the well out of which to draw entirely original renditions. Frazier would accuse him of having ruinously distanced himself by shutting off every feeling. But they would both be wrong. Cheney was not an actor now nor a patient. He was a man whose flight into numbness, that emotional weightlessness, no-feeling, the best foretaste of death, was a last quite deliberate, clear-headed and, indeed, saving act of love.

He turned and leapt into a run. He cut through the house. Eddie and Dolan watched him and did not move until from the far side of the ark, the kitchen screen door slammed loudly, like a film-maker's clapper, but, instead of beginning the scene, ending it.

"I'm sorry to have involved you in that." Eddie's hand trembled at her face. She knew she had finally held her ground against him. She felt no triumph though.

Dolan looked out at the sea. "Can he really take off in this?"

"He's very bold. And very good. I wouldn't worry about him."

"I wasn't." He nervously lit his last cigarette and balled the pack. "If he can't fly he might want a ride with me, and, frankly, I don't feature his company."

"I apologize, but you still must go."

"Of course. I'd still like to get in touch with you." He stopped and tried, unsuccessfully, to read his feelings with precision. "I want to get to know Bren."

"I want you to also. You remind me of his father. You're good like he was. You've changed, David. You used to be more intent upon yourself, if you'll forgive my saying so. Now you seem . . . Your being here helped me to stand up to him."

Dolan felt explicitly for the first time his old envy of his brother. The emotion that had brought him to Hunter's Island had not faded, and that was too bad, because now he understood it had to do with his attraction to her. Even the dreadful complications of her life with Cheney had not defused it. If anything, her strength against him made her more appealing to Dolan, and his own role as her ally had made him want to be her friend. But that was all for another time, not now.

Eddie put her manuscript on the desk.

"Is that really the only copy of your work?"

"Yes. I'm as insane as he is. I'm afraid of copies, I think. They fix what you've done. They make it permanent."

"They make it safe."

"You know what I'd make a copy of if I could? My son. He's what I worry about. Not this stuff."

At that moment they heard in the distance the roar of Cheney's plane starting up.

Dolan saw alarm flash in Eddie's face and under-

stood it. She took the stairs two at a time and he followed. She had ordered Bren to stay in his room, but
when she got there he was gone, and so were his cape
and sword.

CHAPTER 15

Bren had been waiting for him at the raft.

He'd been thinking about flying. The seaplane was a dream of his. Every kind of plane was exciting to him, but the seaplane, which broke the laws not only of the air but also water, was even more thrilling.

Bren leaned against the plane's left float to keep it from bumping the raft. The waters of the bay were choppy and every few seconds the raft and seaplane rose and fell and collided. It amazed Bren that he could hold the weight of the plane back, and doing so gave him a feeling of responsibility and partnership with his father. He liked the feel of the float against his rump, and as he pushed into it he was sure he was stronger than most boys his age. And how many of them had fathers with seaplanes?

So what if he hadn't ever flown in one?

Bren's mother wouldn't let him fly with Cheney anymore. She said small planes are dangerous, but he didn't think that was the reason. If small planes were dangerous they wouldn't let the President fly in a helicopter, which was even more dangerous because it couldn't glide down to a field if something went wrong. Besides, on t.v. only the big planes crashed.

In Bren's opinion it was his mother's business if she

didn't like Cheney anymore, but, for himself, he still did. He'd come down to the raft with his stick in his belt and his towel draped from his shoulders, in his mind a cocky sentry, so that he could give Cheney a proper farewell. Maybe he wouldn't ever call him Dad. Maybe he would stop thinking of him as his father even. But he could still say goodbye to him. They were still adopted, weren't they? That meant something. His mother had no right to say it didn't. And Bren was sure Cheney would need help pushing off. And there should be someone to wave when the plane left the water. And another thing: when his father arrived at Hunter's that morning Bren had started to tell him something. It was something undone between them and it had nothing to do with his mother.

When Cheney came running out of the woods, across the rocks and down the pier toward the raft, Bren wanted to think he was running the way he did himself when he was Jamal, running, that is, joyously. But Bren could tell from watching him that Cheney was running to get away, not to play. Bren wanted to stop him from leaving, but Cheney ran down the pier without seeming even to see Bren. He was making for his plane and Bren was in the way.

Bren stood up straight. If he'd been a lion he'd have roared, a cannon he'd have gone off.

"Halt!" he said.

Cheney kept coming.

"In the name of the crown, halt!"

Cheney was staring at the seaplane behind Bren as he closed the distance, already making his inspection.

"Seize that man!"

Cheney stopped abruptly. He looked quizzically

down at Bren, seeming not to recognize him. But then Bren spoke again, and a dramatic recognition drew across Cheney's face; he was an actor showing that he saw before him what he'd been looking for.

Bren flourished his cape and said, "Behold, I am the Prince of Whales!"

Eddie tore through the house, across the lawn and into the woods. When she realized that Dolan was right behind her, she yelled back at him, unnecessarily, "He's got my son!"

There was alarm in her voice but also, perversely, relief. Her convoluted battle with Cheney was coming down at last to a direct, simple, physical confrontation. If Cheney had taken Bren, then she'd been right to leave him and right to cruelly forbid him access to Bren. She was off the hook. The guilt and ambivalence were pushed aside now by the infinite righteousness of a mother out to rescue her child. To save Bren she could and would do anything. Cheney's power to demolish her will was gone; or rather, it was hers now.

It seemed to Dolan he had never run so fast, but he could not catch up with Eddie. She ran like a Chagall comet, a bright streak through the green woods, but he did not admire her. He sensed her vigor, but also a ruthlessness. He had never seen the desperate fury of a parent and it shocked him. He had imagined that an attachment like Eddie's to Bren was powerful enough to give an otherwise empty life joy and meaning. Now he saw that the same attachment was powerful enough to blind a parent with rage, blind her even to the true welfare of the child she wanted to save. Dolan worried because he sensed that in addition to the animal strength of her anger, she was going to need her intelligence too, and perhaps some restraint.

He was completely focused on her. His movement released him from all his own windmilling. Suddenly his guilt over his brother, his treason toward his country, his ambivalence toward Sweden, his job at NYU, his disappointment in Artie Rose, his flight from the FBI, his father too tired to die, his mother's defeat, even the prospect of jail—were all of no account. Only helping Eddie protect Bren mattered now. "I'm with you," he hollered, but he had no reason to think she heard him.

Eddie and Dolan both took the woods in great strides, and both perceived its details with unusual acuteness—pine boughs with the paler green tips of the year's new growth, cones like grape clusters, stains of night water on bark, wounds from which sap bled and underfoot roots arching out of the dirt. Eddie was conscious of her tight skin stretching over her muscles and bones, her charged hair, the moisture in the palms of her hands and the dryness of her throat. Dolan felt the manufactured breeze of his running and distinguished it from the ocean's wind coming from behind him.

Eddie led the way down out of the woods, over ledge, leaping two boulders, screeching a great Greek roar which was lost in the primitive wild scene of the broken waves cowed by the glowering sky. She hit the pier at full tilt. The wind, however, was a blast which slowed her, but without forcing on her consciousness the new fact that the long-threatened storm was at last breaking. The concealing gray clouds were gone. The heavens were an ebony sheet, suspended like a tent at a funeral. But Eddie could take in only what she had fixed upon.

The seaplane was a dozen or two dozen yards out from the raft, taxiing into the bay, lurching in the chop, with Cheney's ever-perfect profile filling a window, obscuring, but not completely, the terrified face of her son.

This is the rule in turbulent weather: get airborne and altitude as quickly as possible, then ignore the world outside the cockpit and fly instruments. Cheney longed to be off the water. Even in the most severe bumpiness a plane with air under it could be as tranquil and reassuring as a monk's cell. Downdrafts would make climbing sluggish and a jolt at low speed could cause a stall which would dunk them. Side gusts could sweep under a wing and pitch it over. Wind shifts could make controlled, steady ascent nearly impossible at first. Rain, when it finally broke, would dampen turbulence, but flow over the windshield like a river. An ascent through the clouds would risk St. Elmo's fire, a lightning strike which, if it didn't blast them out of the sky, would at least throw off their compass and make it impossible to know where they were headed. These were possibilities that awaited once they left the water, yet Cheney longed to deal with any of them because, as dangers, they all paled beside the danger of the takeoff run.

Even in the lee of Hunter's the swell system was extreme, long and fast, with white water at the crest of each wave. To take off on a heading parallel to the crests would risk a capsizing of the seaplane if one float fell into the trough of a wave while the other was on its crest. To take off into the face of the swells would involve a pounding that would make it nearly impossible to keep the plane at correct attitude. In that case, at takeoff speed the waves could sheer a float off, wrecking them instantly. In addition, if the natural rhythmic pitching motion of the plane as it rode the waves while gaining speed fell into phase with the swell pattern, it would become a violent porpoising which would end with the plane flipping over nose-first. If an obstacle or other craft crossed in front of Cheney once he'd started up-swell, it would be impossible to veer off without capsizing. But there were no water craft out. Every sane creature had taken shelter already.

A run into the swell despite its risks would be directly into the wind, and he'd get over the hump faster, and onto the step where the floats skim the surface and water resistance drops away. If he could hold the Cessna in attitude until it attained enough speed for firm elevator and aileron, he could be airborne with half the sprint.

Cheney had never run directly into the face of such a system before. But neither had he ever tried taking off in such turbulence. He was stunned by the rapidity with which the weather front had slammed down on them. Weather simply did not erupt like that in the West. Any Maine fisherman could have told him—their absence from the bay should have—that nor'easters are double-barreled. He forced his attention onto the preflight adjustment of instruments. He could not allow himself to take in how drastically altered the situation had become in minutes. The wind was topping thirty knots now and the sea showed it. But he focused on the effort to spot obstacles and debris. He reviewed his options, how far out to taxi, which way to run, how to take the water and the wind. Once he'd have cursed a pilot for a fool, a disgrace to the sport, who'd set out in weather like that, but of all the options he coolly considered while drawing out into the bay, none included turning back.

He was responding not only to confidence in his skill and trust in his flyer's intuition—he had exceeded stress limits before—but also to the extremity of what he had already done. He had finally acted on his months-old impulse to take the boy. Cheney had forced Bren into the plane. He'd had to slap him to shock him into subservience, but he had not struck brutally or insanely. What surprised Cheney most was how calm he felt and how right what he was doing seemed. The boy was afraid of him for now, but that was as much fear of the lurching, pitching plane as it was of him. Eventually Bren would be glad Cheney had taken him, and he would even forget that blow. Cheney had resolved instantly never to hit him again. From now on it would not be necessary. This rescue was what Cheney had come to Maine for, and he felt, despite the risks of their imminent dash across the waves, a profound satisfaction with himself.

Only one thing disturbed him, and that was his great urge to get off the water as soon as possible. His first responsibility as a pilot, having reviewed procedure and options, was to select a takeoff plan. All possibilities under complex sea conditions are undesirable, but the most conservative choice, the safest, would be for a long runout, which would allow a sparing application of power. But his gut-felt need to be airborne immediately precluded that. He chose the boldest plan, therefore, and he knew that what decided him was his desperation to be gone.

Perhaps it was his innate sense of the weather, his intuitive reading of what was happening. His acute instinct must have been telling him that the sky was about to break wide open and make the seas more dangerous still. Electricity registered in his stomach, behind it in the nodule at the base of his spine in which all of his best reflexes first scored. His left hand was firmly, calmly playing the wheel. His right, above his head, eased in the throttle as he prepared to make his turn. He had taxied far enough. The world was wide open before him. He quickly eyed once more his instruments, the fuel, tachometer, artificial horizon, glide scope, gyro, speed indicators, altimeter. His radio was tuned for the Bangor intersection, which he would contact at altitude for weather and bearings. Everything was under control.

He made the turn into the swell and throttled half up. The plane bounced off the first wave but breasted the second. The engine went up in pitch and volume. The turn was accomplished and he was about to gun it when he saw broad on his port bow a small boat, the Boston Whaler, coming at him from the raft. He knew then that it was not the weather that made him want up and out as soon as possible. It was Eddie.

There was no prudence in Eddie, no caution. She would have gone out without Dolan if he hadn't leapt in the boat just as she was casting off. She was at the wheel and she belonged there. Dolan knew he would not have had the nerve to do what she was doing. It was mad, but it was perfectly calculated and so bold as to transport him, apparently, beyond fear. He held onto the gunwales with two hands and watched as, in an ultimate act of impulse, they closed the distance. She had them headed not at the seaplane, but at a point well ahead of it.

Both machines were at full throttle. It was everything Cheney could do to keep the Cessna at attitude and watch the water-speed indicator climb toward twenty. At twenty-five he would be on the step, planing, and he would lift off immediately. The floats would strike successive wave crests, but with diminishing impact as he increased the nose-up pitch angle and slowly gained altitude.

He saw what Eddie was doing. Her abandon would once have stirred him, but now he simply took it in as another datum to factor. He tried to read her speed and angle. She was riding a wave crest parallel to the swell, and not against it as he was. He saw in an instant that, if she'd picked her point accurately, she would cut him off just when he made his speed. The hell with her, he thought, squeezing an ounce more out of his engine. Let her try. He was as concentrated on his purpose as she was on hers. And he was better than she was at risking everything. He was famous for it.

Eddie was gunning the Boston Whaler toward that Cessna to stop it. This was not the threat of obstruction, or a mere gesture toward it. She was simply not going to let that airplane off the water. If there was danger, it was in the chance that Cheney might take this as one more feint of hers and hold his heading. He might not understand that she was different now. She was serious, and she had her keen vision back. It enabled her to spy, among other things, the certain spot in the bay ahead at which to aim her boat. Once he abandoned his takeoff run and slowed, she would

be on him in seconds and he would have nothing
with which to resist her. She would go claw-to-claw
with him at last, and she would have her son back,
and her life.

It was the noise, perhaps the worst he'd heard, the
engine and the slamming of the floats against the
waves, around which Cheney's perceptions organized.
The noise was so loud it fostered inside him a kind of
silence. That relaxed Cheney enough, even as he
leaned against the throttle, so that he thought of
Bren.

Cheney looked at him. He was tiny in the copilot's
seat, pressed rigidly against the back of it, and he was
white as a piece of bread in water. His lips were
stretched in an expression of horror—in the engine
noise Cheney had no idea if he was screaming—and
his cheeks were clamped in the vise of his two hands,
which pressed against his ears. Terror of a kind
Cheney had never seen before, even on a trapped animal about to die, showed so starkly on the boy's face
that Cheney felt it like a slap, a slap that returned
him to his senses. For that kid Cheney would have
wrestled a bear.

And here he was about to blow him to kingdom
come in a collision with his mother. Bren was right to
be terrified because his parents' game of chicken had
finally become lethal. They were careening at each
other to kill. And why? Because of Bren, they'd have
said. For Bren's sake, they'd have said. Over Bren.
But Bren knew the truth of it, and made Cheney see
it. If they collided this time, Bren would die.

Cheney looked away from the kid and out at the
Whaler. He knew he could not make it. He had only

just come on the step and needed another seventy-five yards to clear, but in fifty his course and Eddie's would cross. She had driven at him expertly. Damn woman.

Since she was coming at him from his port bow, the surest evasion would have been a cut to starboard, but Cheney knew that a turn at his speed was going to throw the plane obliquely at the swell, which would tip the wings, one down into the waves and one up into the wind, and that would push them over. A turn, in other words, was certainly going to capsize the airplane. That was why he decided to cut to port, toward Eddie, not away from her. He would have to accomplish it perfectly to miss the Whaler, but if he did, when they went over, his side of the airplane would sink first. He did not want Bren trapped below him in a submerging cockpit.

Cheney closed the throttle, dropped flaps and reversed the propeller, then cut hard on the wheel, each step in controlled sequence, but so quickly and smoothly as to have seemed one move. The engine shot up in pitch, then gagged and spat as the plane shuddered, swerved, and Cheney shocked himself by praying. "God," he said "hold it together."

The seaplane went over and began to slide down a wave into the water. Eddie brought the Whaler around on a dime and cut the engine, dropping the bow, in which Dolan crouched, so that it slapped against the plane's float.

Dolan leapt onto it even as the float was sucked under. He scrambled into the struts and onto the fuselage, which for the moment held buoyancy. He had no footing and no leverage to ply against the cockpit door. The door refused to open until he realized he was lying across it. He adjusted quickly, hooked his legs around the aft strut and tried again. The door opened. Bren was strapped to his seat, and when he saw Dolan, he lunged at him, but the shoulder harness snapped him back.

The plane lurched suddenly. The sea crashed over them and swirled into the cockpit, driving the airplane down. Dolan had his hands on the boy's harness, trying to break it. He knew that he'd have to find the buckle to release it, and knew equally that he never would in time. The plane went completely under with a whoosh of suction.

Bren had Dolan by the neck in the panicked grasp of the drowning, and Dolan suddenly had a nightmare vision of himself pushing the boy's arms away, wrenching them off his neck because otherwise he too would drown. His dream.

Down the plane went. Dolan held onto Bren with one hand and desperately felt with the other for the seat-belt buckle, but futilely. The child was strapped in tight; he would never get out. Dolan ran his hand up and down the harness. The buckle simply was not there. He felt a wave crest and break inside him, the sudden expectation of death, Bren's and his own.

Then his hand closed upon, not the buckle, but another hand, another man's, Cheney's. For an instant, it relaxed in Dolan's grasp, then quickly pulled away. When Dolan tugged on the belt then, it gave. The belt was released and Bren rose out of the seat, floating upward as if, below the sea, gravity was not so much mitigated as reversed. Dolan understood that Cheney had been grappling from the underside of the cockpit to free the boy and that he had found the buckle and snapped it open.

Dolan allowed Bren to climb on him as if he were a ladder, a pole. The boy had him by the neck and head, was on his shoulders, and as Dolan pushed up away from the plummeting fuselage Bren was trying to push away from him. They kicked and clawed the water, rising, rising. The plane had taken them down farther than he thought. Was Cheney still in it? Did Cheney know that Bren was out?

Dolan could not hold it. He simply could not hold it anymore. He intended to keep a firm grip on Bren, but he pushed him away from his face and throat. Though he knew it would kill him, he opened his mouth to breathe.

They broke through the surface of the water and what he gulped in was air. He got an arm under Bren's chin. The boy was gagging horribly, but his agony filled Dolan with relief. He was alive.

Eddie was there, reaching for them from the boat.

But a wave crashed down, pushing them both under again. Now they had as much to fear from the boat as from the sea because it was upswell of them and would smash them violently if they surfaced under it or just in its lee. That act of mind overpowered all Dolan's instincts and his ferocious will to return to air immediately. He forced himself down, and the boy with him. Bren yielded as they went deeper again. Dolan felt him go limp, but refused except vaguely to register what that meant. He swam against the force of the water so that when they came back up, as it happened in the crest of a wave, the boat was safely below them. Eddie was leaning over the port side where they had first surfaced. The sea delivered them

to the starboard gunwale, nearly swamping the
Whaler, and Dolan hooked his arm over it. He had to
call out to Eddie to make her see that they had come
up behind her.

She took her son on board, but his body was inert,
all resistance, panic and apparent life gone. She
hugged him and knew that he was dead, but the sea
refused her the seconds she needed to understand,
much less react. A wave crashed and nearly broke Dolan's hold on the gunwale. To save him, Eddie put
her son down, propping him against the helmsman's
bench to keep his head out of the water that was rap-
idly filling the boat, as if the boy could take in more,
as if the sea could have done him worse.

She hauled in the exhausted, gasping Dolan, who,
when she turned back to Bren, feebly told her to get
the boat going. It was half-sunk already.

Eddie looked about as if for the first time. They
were less than a hundred yards from a curving spit of
rock, an extremity of Hunter's inside which the water
flattened out, but beyond which the mountainous
waves of open ocean waited for them. Outside the lee
of the island the Whaler wouldn't last three seconds,
and that was where the drift was taking them.

But Eddie, having seen through the chaos of gray
and white, her own blizzard of lurching, bobbing,
nauseating anxiety, saw also who was missing.
"Cheney! Where's Cheney?"

At that moment the storm with its slashing, pelting
rain pounced, destroying their visibility. The island
disappeared. She screamed Cheney's name again and
tried to see him. But she could barely see beyond the
edge of the boat.

Dolan raised himself, as if against her, and hooked

his legs under the seat to brace his weight and free his arms. He took the boy away from her, but not before she'd pulled back as if they were gulls fighting over the corpse of a fish. "Drive!" he ordered. But she crouched there empty-handed, tears mixing with rain on her face, about to scream at him, whether in Cheney's behalf or her son's, neither knew. Before sound escaped her he grabbed her arm and squeezed it brutally, purposely hurting her, defying her panic, inflicting on her, like pain, his sudden knowledge that he, David Dolan, and not killing weather or scuttling waves or hellbent Cheney McCoy or her cold terrors or his own habitual abstractions would this once prevail. "Drive!" he repeated. And he pointed the way and stared at her without pity until she nodded.

He held Bren up by the legs and bent him over an arm and slapped his back to force the water out of him.

Eddie fought the engine into gear and steered where Dolan had pointed. Rain lashed them. Several times the swell shifted and came at them from an angle, nearly capsizing them.

Dolan cradled the boy and tried breathing into him the way firemen on their ladders do babies. The gentler sea inside the curve of the island had its rhythm which lulled in time, and the wind filtered by trees was, compared to the howling ocean's, like a lullabye.

Once she collected herself, Eddie drove the half-swamped boat skillfully, despite her certainty and despair that she had just accomplished the death of her child.

She was wrong.

When they reached the shore Dolan leapt out ahead, leaving her to secure the boat, and he stretched Bren on a flat rock, closed his nostrils with one hand, arched his back slightly with the other, covered Bren's mouth with his own and, more proficiently than before, forced air into the child and, quickly to his own great joyous surprise, life.

CHAPTER 16

"The boy's mother and I were standing here on the raft watching them take off."

"You came out to see them off, that it?" The Coast Guard officer didn't look up from his pad. The act of writing seemed foreign to him, and he was as ill at ease with the interrogation as Dolan was.

It was just after dusk, but a gray light, the last light, clung to the broad, open bay. Mt. Desert, the outline of it, was just visible in the distance. The water was flat. The Coast Guard lieutenant, the Hunter's Island fire chief and one of the volunteers were standing around Dolan on the Brewster pier. They had shed their foul-weather gear, but Dolan was still wearing a thick blue sweater the Coast Guardsman had lent him hours before. The search was called off now for the night.

"Yes. The boy and his stepfather were going down to New York."

"Wasn't it already pretty rough by then?"

"Yes. Too rough obviously. Even at the time I wondered if he should be trying it. But . . ." Dolan shrugged and added feebly, ". . . It wasn't raining yet."

He had adopted a demeanor calculated to suggest

ignorance and innocence; what did he know about the sea or seaplanes? What he did know, but kept to himself, was that he and Eddie had caused the plane to capsize. He had to steer the officer's inquiry away from that. His inbuilt paranoia was serving him well.

"And when it went over you and the Missus . . . ?"

"Leapt in the Whaler and got out there as quickly as we could."

Dolan felt the eyes of the two islanders on him, an accusation? If they knew that he was lying, would they expose him? They would if the man who'd drowned was one of them. The two shared a hint of the idiot look he'd noticed on his arrival at Barrett's Cove.

"How long did the plane take to sink?"

"It went under just as we got there."

"That's surprising." The lieutenant looked up from his pad. His stare was openly accusing, but intimidated less than the fishermen's because he was no islander and lacked their strangeness. He'd come over in his cutter from Southwest Harbor. He waited for Dolan to respond to his statement, but it hadn't thrown Dolan, who refused either to speak or look away. The officer went on, "Usually they sink like stones. You must have moved damn fast." He looked off toward his small ship at anchor. Seventy feet below it his team of divers had found the plane. There was no corpse in it.

"We did."

"And you got the boy."

Dolan said nothing.

"And then you started looking for his father."

"His stepfather. Once Mrs. McCoy and her son

were on land, yes, I went back out, but it was useless."

"You didn't see him swimming."

"I couldn't see the hand in front of my face." Dolan paused. "What do you think?"

The officer looked up from his pad. "About what? Him?"

"Yes."

"Can't say. Anything's possible." He looked out at the cutter. "He'd have to be a damn good swimmer though." He looked sharply back at Dolan. "Was he?"

"I don't know."

The officer shifted his weight, and the pier creaked under him. He exchanged a look with the fishermen. "What do you men think?"

Neither replied.

The lieutenant studied his notes. "I should ask some questions of Mrs. McCoy."

"You should do that tomorrow, lieutenant." Dolan had to speak to Eddie first so their stories would jibe. "You have to come back anyway."

He shrugged. "Maybe not. They'll probably send a chopper up. That body, if there is one, could be anywhere by now. By tomorrow . . ." He shrugged again. He had a report to file. He was trying to decide how it would look if he hadn't talked to the other principal.

Dolan took off the sweater and handed it over, a gesture intended obviously to send them off. "She should be left alone tonight. And so should the child."

The Coast Guardsman studied the sweater, then

looked at the islanders again. He was from Rhode Island himself, and these Maine Coast sphinxes even after nine years made him uneasy. He asked Dolan, "How do you fit in, again?"

"I'm the boy's uncle. His father, my brother, died in Vietnam."

The officer's eyes fell shut for a second and a low groan escaped his throat. He slapped his notebook shut.

He nodded at Dolan, but couldn't meet his eye, because he felt he'd failed these people. His job was to find the corpse before the briny water turned it into a bloated blue sack of pus. That was always the hardest part for the relatives.

"Chief," he said, stepping toward the fisherman's skiff, which was tied to the raft, "how about a lift?"

The three climbed into the sixteen-foot boat, shoved off and chugged out to the cutter. None of them so much as raised a hand toward Dolan, but the volunteer stared at him continually for the moments it took them to reach the Coast Guard vessel.

Dolan backed off the pier slowly. He waited just inside the fringe of the woods, watching until the ship's engines caught, roared and spat exhaust, its running lights blinked on, and it began to glide off into the gathering dark. The fishermen steamed back toward Barrett's Cove. Then it was quiet.

Already Mt. Desert was gone. Only when it was completely dark did the clean fine air of the storm's aftermath and the night calm of the sea and the contemplative mood of the witness forest register on him as beautiful.

* * *

At the house he noticed a car next to his in the driveway, and in it the form of a large man hunched in the seat, dozing. He went past him quietly.

In the living room by the single light a sour-looking middle-aged woman sat in the stuffed chair, knitting. She looked up at Dolan, but did not speak.

"Who are you?"

"The nurse."

"I thought a doctor came."

"He did. Dr. Sawyer." She indicated a piece of paper on the desk. "That's his number."

"Is he on the island?"

She nodded. "This month he is."

"He's summer people?"

She did not respond, not even with a movement of her head, and that communicated that the doctor was not an islander. Why, Dolan wondered, did that relieve him?

"You can go now. I'm Mrs. McCoy's brother-in-law."

The nurse continued knitting.

Dolan climbed the stairs quietly and found Eddie asleep in a large bed with Bren. Eddie was on top of the covers, dressed in a brightly flowered housecoat. Bren was snug under blankets, his face turned away from his mother. Her face nestled in his back.

The sight of them moved Dolan, particularly that child into whom he had breathed life again; perhaps that act accounted for the strong paternal feeling that came over him. The boy was alive because of him. The joy in that was familiar, not because he'd ever had it, but because he'd yearned for it for so long.

After some moments he pulled up the folded blanket from the foot of the bed over Eddie, not that she seemed cold, but that he had to give expression to the tenderness he felt toward her and her son.

Dolan withdrew, closing the door quietly behind him.

Downstairs the nurse ignored him.

"They're all right?" he asked.

She nodded.

"The boy too?"

She nodded again. "Dr. Sawyer said I should stay until she woke up." It was the statement of her authority. She wasn't going to speak and she wasn't going to leave.

Dolan couldn't stay in the room with her. He found a kerosene lantern in the mud room off the kitchen, lit it on his third try, took a slicker and a blanket and went outside. He circled the house to the ocean side, spread the slicker near the cliff's edge, sat down and draped the blanket around his shoulders. The lantern glowed eerily. He listened to the ocean and watched the moon rise and tried to understand what awful thing had happened.

Certainly Cheney was dead, and that knowledge devastated Dolan. What an unnecessary death! In their absurd conflict Eddie and Cheney had ruined each other and nearly killed Bren; what a wasteland they'd made of their family life. Family life, he repeated, perhaps aloud, and shuddered. Yes, he felt a new strong kinship toward his nephew. He would willingly have died for that child. But family life? No, he didn't want it.

Later—he would have guessed from the moon's passage about two hours—the car engine started on the far side of the house. He listened to it fade as someone drove away. And then he heard the near door open. He did not turn.

"I saw your light." The crust of defensiveness was gone from her voice.

He faced her, realizing as he did that he would rather have been left alone. She was standing just outside the pool of the lantern's illumination, and he could not make out her features. From where he sat she seemed tall and large in her flowing gown. She had her arms folded, but in one hand she held a glass.

"Gin," she said, and offered it to him.

He reached toward her.

She stooped and gave him the tumbler, which was half full of straight gin, no ice. He took a healthy swallow while she remained crouched but not sitting in the lantern's circle of warmth. The liquor jolted and soothed him. He handed it back to her and she sipped it.

"Any cigarettes?" he asked.

She shook her head. "Sorry."

He shrugged, but his need for one clung. "Bren's all right?"

Eddie nodded and cupped the gin. "Sleeping it off."

"You both were." Dolan smiled faintly. "I looked in on you." Had there been meaning in the child's having faced away from her?

"I'm a somniac, you see," she said lightly. She sipped her gin and offered it again.

He declined. He realized that she was slightly tipsy already, and that irritated him. But he reminded himself, she had a right to be.

"I'm sorry I was useless in the search," she said. "Mrs. Roche told me you didn't find him."

"They'll send a helicopter up tomorrow."

"Jesus." She stared at the glass. Both were silent for some time. Neither was conscious of the stilted arrangements of their bodies. She remained stooping over him. He remained seated, twisted away from the sea.

"Mrs. Roche? The nurse?"

"Yes. I just sent her home. They give me the creeps, the island people. I've never liked them. They make me feel guilty for the quality of my chromosomes. I feel guilty for not chumming it up with them. My mother is fast friends with Mrs. Roche, from whom she will hear in detail everything. God." Eddie put her glass to her forehead and rocked herself.

Dolan felt another pang of annoyance at her. Her inane talk made it seem she thought nothing much had happened. "We have to talk about those details, Eddie."

She looked up sharply.

"I told the Coast Guard that you and I were standing on the dock when the plane went over."

"Why?"

Dolan checked his impatience. Surely she understood what they'd done. "Because the Boston Whaler—" he omitted the phrase "driven by you" "—caused the plane to capsize. It's a question of liability."

A blankness had fallen across her face. "I don't get it."

"Criminal liability, Eddie. Manslaughter." Eddie

stared at him. It was because her face showed him
nothing that he repeated, "Manslaughter."

"You think he's dead?"

"Of course he's dead."

Eddie began to tremble, at first faintly. The liquid
swirled in her glass. Then her shoulders shook and
gradually her whole body convulsed. When she fell to
her knees gin splashed onto her and Dolan took the
glass away from her. She crushed her hands and the
very muscles of her face against what she was feeling.

She saw everything, a brutally illuminated chain of
mistakes and sins, her mistakes and sins, which ended
with Cheney's death but began with her betrayal of
Brendan in David Dolan's bed in Quebec. So many
links to that chain bound her. The ease with which
she forgot Brendan once he died, the "gift" of her son
to her new husband, the ruthlessness with which she
snatched the "gift" back, her eagerness now to exploit
Brendan in her novel and, the most dreadful recognition of all, that she had nearly killed Bren and surely
had maimed him forever while killing Cheney. She
was a merciless bitch who had ruined everything she
touched, all in the vaunted name of her independence and her strength. A fucking bitch.

Dolan forced the glass back into her hand. "Here,
Eddie, take a swallow," he said, trying to calm her.

She drank and sat back on her haunches.

"No one needs to know what happened," he said.

"That I killed him, you mean?" She looked at him.
"That I nearly killed my son?"

Dolan could see her misery. He wanted to tell her
that what she had done had been accidental, not deliberate, unconscious, not so bad. But she had

destroyed herself, and she knew it better than he did. He could offer her nothing but his dismay.

Still, he had to speak. "In the morning, the Coast Guard will be back to see you. You must say what I said. You must forbid them to talk to Bren."

She snatched at his hand. "They will find him, won't they?"

Dolan looked away from her.

"I mean the body. They'll find it, right?"

Dolan thought of the helicopter that was coming up the next day, and knew that he wouldn't be able to watch it. He tried to keep the image of it out of his mind, but couldn't. He heard it even, whining up and down the coastline, futilely searching. Surely the corpse was sucked out to sea by now, but he had not kicked it from the skids of a crippled chopper. That was another dream, not this one. "Of course, they'll find it," he said.

"I couldn't stand it if they didn't." She said this dully, with defeat in her voice. He saw that she was ready to surrender every inch of ground she'd held against the events of that day. She had nothing left with which to defend herself against anyone or anything.

"They will, Eddie. They will."

"No one understands. No one understands. They give you letters pronouncing him dead and expect you to behave accordingly. If you have questions they resent you. If you're angry they say you've no respect. But their letters are not remains. What I need are remains!"

"I need them too," Dolan said. He was swamped by sadness. "Where can I go to pray for him?"

"Will the Coast Guard send me letters?"

"No, they won't."

"I didn't want Cheney hurt. I never wanted him hurt." She looked at Dolan, but blankly. "I didn't want him coming here."

"I know it. It wasn't your fault."

"Whose then? Whose was it?" She began to scream. "Tell me whose! Tell me whose fault it was! Should I have let him take my child? Should I have just stood there, watching? As if I didn't care?"

"No."

"Should I have stayed in California with him? Should I have been his doormat for life?" She stood abruptly and roared her question out against the quiet sea. She hurled her glass of gin in a spraying arc. It went over the cliff and there was no sound of it crashing. "Should I have found a way to keep loving him? Oh God, how I loved him! How I loved him once! I didn't want him dead!" She closed her arms over her face, over a long low moan.

Dolan stood. Overhead galaxies of stars had filled the sky behind the moon's advance. The air was absolutely clear. A soft breeze tugged at his blanket and, made aware of it, he thought of draping Eddie. But she was hugging herself. He tried to imagine what her pain was like, thought of fire and how, if he dipped his hand in it, he could not hold it there, no matter what his resolution. He tried to think of books he'd read, descriptions of suffering, grief, agony. He believed in books, had built a life inside them as if they were shapely stones, but like stones then they seemed opaque and harmless. No one ever burned himself to the elbow in a work of fiction or philosophy.

But to his surprise Dolan realized suddenly that his

life of books and thought, his exile, his decade of introspection had equipped him for this. He understood her. He saw her as she was and he did not flinch. He did not think she was contemptible. He sensed how dangerous her hatred for herself was. She was not going to survive it unless someone helped her. Him.

"Eddie, you said no one understands, but I do. I understand." He hoped she would turn toward him. When she didn't, he continued, but addressing himself to the sea. "I understand what it is to fail everyone who loves you. I've done it. Not because I'm evil, but because I've been confused and things were too messy and the times ugly and chaotic, and I was afraid. I blamed everyone but myself, like you did. And now, reversing it, you want to blame only yourself, as if you caused death itself to come into the world. Whose fault? Whose fault? Yours. That's right, yours. But also Cheney's. And in his time, also Brendan's. And also, maybe, Bren's. And also, certainly, mine. You know what?" He waited for her to show him that she was listening. She shifted toward him slightly. "We're in the same Boston Whaler."

They turned toward each other. "David," she said softly, "I'm so sorry. For all of it. I am so sorry."

Dolan remembered the gesture of priests, how they raised a hand and turned it palm toward you and waved it in a cross. He raised his hand toward her head, which she lowered, closing her eyes. He touched the crown of her head but could not speak. Who was he to pronounce an absolution? But who was he to refuse it? "Eddie," he said, "that time in Quebec? I regret it because of Brendan. But because of myself I cherish it. Our motives were far from pure. But, don't you see now, they never are. And they never need to be. I was in love with you."

She remained utterly still for a long time, standing before him with her head bowed beneath the light touch of his hand. He could feel, it seemed to him, through his fingers, from his life to hers and back, the transfer of healing.

When she looked up, her eyes were glazed but not overflowing. She stepped closer to him and he felt even before she kissed him the tremor of her offer. The very place, where the tide rose against the rock, seemed to shift under them, and he felt it roll slightly like a ship in a soft wind.

As she brought her face up to his, his hand circled her head and came to rest on those inches below the ear where a throat becomes a neck, and for once the line he followed slowly, exactly, with his finger and his eye and then his mouth was not outdone by memory, not memory of another woman but memory of his dream of how it could be perhaps with her. Their kiss was formal, swaying and prolonged, like a slow dance.

She pulled back before he did. "I nearly stayed with you, David," she whispered. "I wanted to."

"Why didn't you?" He cupped her face with his hands.

"It seemed disloyal, and not only to Brendan." She could not look at him. "To everything."

He raised her face so he could look in her eyes. "I don't have to defend what I did anymore. I can live with it, even here. That's why I'm back."

"I'm glad you're back." She did not add, "I can live

with mine too," but it occurred to her. They were laying Brendan's ghost to rest. And more.

He smiled. "Of course if you had come with me I wouldn't have had to picture you all these years in ski clothes." He let his eye fall over her flowered housedress.

"It's my mother's."

"It doesn't suit you." He stopped breathing.

"Should I take it off?" She asked him, as if for permission, but not coquettishly. Too much had happened that day for any but raw, direct emotion to be left her. She felt bashful. She was afraid, but whether of his saying yes or saying no she couldn't imagine.

At first it seemed he wouldn't answer. Then deliberately he let the wool blanket fall from his shoulders.

She stepped back from him half a step and unzipped the dress from her throat to her navel.

He unbuttoned his shirt slowly and took it off. He was thin. Even in the shadows cast by the lantern she could see that it had been a long time since his body had been exposed to the sun.

Eddie let him slide her garment off her shoulders and let it fall to the ground. She was fully unclothed, but suddenly not embarrassed or shy. She made no move to cover herself, nor did she avert her eyes while he took in the sight of her. It had been a long time since she had felt so frankly admired. Once, she'd have inhaled and held her breath to display her ribcage, but she had no need then for the tricks of an ingenue.

He read the curves of her flesh carefully, as if they would tell him secrets. They would, but not until he touched them. He bent to take off the rest of his clothes. When he was as naked as she was, he stood up straight again and faced her. Neither shivered. The light breeze seemed to warm them.

"It's been a long time," he said, thinking of Quebec.

"Longer than you know." She touched her forefinger to his lips. "We must be kind to one another."

He took her finger, then her hand, then her. He pressed his body against hers as if that passionate attachment was what he had come home for. And, of course, he saw it then. It was.

From Noah, that widow's tower on the roof of the old red ark of a house, the scene seemed primitive and liturgical, the moon bathing the stately sea with its pale light, the white tidal water stealing in quietly to the cliff's edge, and the two shadowy figures naked by the flame of the old ship's lantern.

Cheney McCoy watched them from Noah.

He watched them embrace where they stood and hold each other. He watched them kiss. He watched them sink to their knees, where they stayed for a time. How slowly they moved their hands and faces. How thoroughly they explored each other. Their movements were like a ritual choreography and it seemed beautiful even to Cheney McCoy.

He watched them help each other down to the blanket on the ground and he watched them kiss each other everywhere.

He watched Eddie settle herself over Dolan and begin to ride him. He admired the grace with which they accomplished a turn so that Dolan was on top of her, but their synchrony had increased, not broken. Eddie arched herself for Dolan, who drove into her again and again. Cheney watched their coupling as a man watches his dream of the end of everything. He thought he could watch it all, but when he heard, even through the glass of his hiding place, his wife's great, ecstatic cry and recognized it from a long, long time before, he looked away.

CHAPTER 17

Cheney recited quietly as he climbed down the stairs, recited repeatedly, ". . . Sad stories of the death of kings: how some have been deposed; some slain in war; some haunted by the ghosts they have deposed; some poisoned by their wives; some sleeping killed; all murdered . . ."

By the time he entered the living room he had to lean against furniture and the walls because the abrupt movement down the stairs had made him dizzy. He was barely aware of the throbbing in his head, but his momentary imbalance gave him the impulse to walk stoop-shouldered. His slouch was perverse in one whose figure was usually so graceful, whose face so becoming. He had always found ways to put his looks to use, and he still did, but now ironically, sarcastically even. He twisted his frame and wrenched his mouth and eyes into a sneer, a rebuke to his own appearance. It wasn't acting so much as a mockery of acting. He lurched about the room like an ape, deliberately slamming into things, now crudely stomping a foot, now dragging it, snarling, whipping his eyes back and forth in a parody of stage madness. He was playing to an audience of one inside his head, and it was difficult because that audience was distracted, couldn't have cared less about the playwright's notion of what was tragic, not even Shakespeare's. Every audience brings its own version of tragedy with it to the theater. The actor's task is to convince it that his character's fate matters more than the audience's own. Cheney's performance was manic and bizarre. It had to be if his character was to outdo, in chaos and fury, himself.

He bumped an end table and knocked over the lamp, which crashed to the floor. He turned to see if Eddie had heard or if her fucker had. The night, the sea, the loving couple, apparently, ignored his mischief.

What tale to tell now? Surely they heard him. He watched the door and expected their naked, beaded bodies to appear there. He was deciding what to hit them with. Another lamp? His misshapen arm? Cattails, if he's a king; a hundred lashes for the rogue, a thousand for the wench.

He backed into the wood stove and though it was cold, he leapt away from it, a comic bit. Laughs. Laughs. Let the fools conclude him their buffoon, then strike! He reapproached the stove and opened the firebox door. The makings of a fire were set: kindling, paper and two crisp logs. He took a match from the adjacent table and lit the fire and watched it flare. When the flame settled and the edges of the logs glowed, he put his hand into the box and lowered it and tried to touch the fire, but couldn't. Good. He was not insane.

He saw on the desk the manuscript Eddie'd snatched out of his hands as if he were a child playing dangerously with something precious. He stood and looked out through the window, hoping to see her. How could she not be thinking about him? It was too dark to see out. Perhaps she was watching him even now. An actor is always blind to his audience. He continued to stare out at the dark, as he'd been trained to, as if it had eyes. "What surety of the world, what hope, what stay, when this was now a king, and now is clay?" He raised his withered hand and stared at it for five long beats.

Then abruptly he turned and crossed down to the desk, from which he snatched Eddie's manuscript. He crushed it to his chest. He'd accused her of cradling it like a baby. "Despair and die," he said, and then limped back upstage to the stove.

He leafed the pages at random and read softly, " 'She could not close her window in the night against the tidal cries of the girl across the street whose newest lover brought her again and again to orgasm, even though the girl's ecstasy made sleep impossible. The next day she stared at every girl in the city. But they all looked too much like she did herself. She knew that in behavior, as in appearance, as in feelings, she had no capacity for the extreme, but for the first time in her life that seemed a fault. And that was why finally she decided to go to him, and to take gladly whatever he would give.' "

Cheney snapped the page out of its folder, balled it and threw it on the fire.

He did not wait to watch it flame, but turned to the next page. " 'She was forever outrunning herself. Was it any wonder she had outrun him? But he had refused to give up on her, which humiliated her and made her graceful. There would be other men, perhaps, but he would always be the one who'd caught her by surprise and kept up with her until she stopped running.' "

Cheney snorted and fed the page into the fire and then the others, in bunches. He did not read more of her scrawl, what was written on those yellow pages, because it was writing, frankly, the king did not admire.

He burned her book, fully conscious of what he was doing, with all due solemnity.

Dolan and Eddie smelled the smoke.

"Someone has started the fire," she said. She saw the glow of it through the living room window.

Dolan assumed that the nurse had not left after all. He wondered what she had seen and resented her. He had expected to lie with Eddie in his arms, wrapped in the blanket until the sun came up.

She rose quickly and donned her gown, zipping it as she made for the house. Dolan would have stayed where he was and waited for her to come back, but he caught her alarm. He dressed promptly and followed her.

Eddie opened her mouth to scream at the sight of Cheney, but no sound came out. But it was not Cheney! It was his ghost! He was bent over the wood stove. The sight of him horrified beyond any horror she had ever known. His body was twisted and shrunken; when he looked up at her he appeared to be drooling. He leered inhumanly at her distress, and that reinforced her perception of him as a ghost. It did not occur to her that he was mad, but that perhaps she was. He leaned toward her. Involuntarily Eddie took a step back from him.

He held the last of her pages up to her and waited for her to recognize them.

She started to move, but couldn't. For a moment her command of her body was gone.

He put the pages in the fire, which brightened, and then he looked toward her somewhat sheepishly.

She ignored Cheney. She could not look at him. Her hold on herself, on sanity, was too fragile.

When her authority over her legs returned she walked slowly to the stove, reached into the firebox and took her manuscript by an edge and pulled it out onto the floor. Fire scattered about the rug. To Eddie her book in flames was like a punishment, an act of God. She sank to her knees.

Dolan rushed into the room. What he saw made no sense to him. Cheney was alive? Eddie was inert on the floor before Cheney and paper was burning in front of her. It was like a vision, a nightmare to which, obviously, Eddie had succumbed. Dolan tried to think, to impose a rationality on what he saw. He could not. But the fire required that he act. He crossed the room and upended the rug, kicking it over onto the flaming pages and stomping on it until the fire was out.

Eddie didn't move. She stared at the floor.

Dolan looked at Cheney, astounded still that he was there, returned from the dead. Dolan had to resist the same fright of unreality that had put Eddie into shock.

"What the hell's the matter with you?" he demanded of Cheney. "You hid from us! We thought you were drowned!" Dolan was instantly aware of the inanity of such a statement. He had above all to keep his sense of what was real, a sense of proportion. But a visceral surge warned him. He was going to have to act again. He remembered that in *Richard III* the final combat was with ghosts.

"I want to know, Cheney." He tried to calm himself. He lowered his voice. "How did you survive?"

"Without your help, you son of a bitch!" Cheney lunged at Dolan. "You left me out there to drown!"

Dolan shoved him clumsily away. Instantly Cheney seized the iron poker from its stand by the wood stove and whipped around with it aimed at Dolan's face.

Dolan flinched.

"In God's name cheerly on, courageous friend, to reap the harvest of perpetual peace by the one bloody trail of sharp war."

Dolan backed away from him. The entire bizarre day, in its chaos, in its bitterness, in its release had been mere prelude to this encounter. He wanted commitment? Now he was going to have to commit himself as never before.

Cheney moved at him brandishing the iron pike. Dolan retreated farther. To his amazement, what he felt was neither anxiety nor fear. He felt relief. Cheney was not making some mere frivolous threat; this was not the academic life, playing at being radical or a game with the FBI. Cheney meant to strike with that poker. Dolan was going to have to do something now or be bludgeoned. Such a prospect would have paralyzed him as a young man. Now it did not.

Dolan raised his hand, continued slowly to backpedal, and said, "Don't come at me with that thing, Cheney."

The sneer drained from Cheney's face. His withered arm and idiot drool were unconvincing, but an awful corruption clung to him. It was the corruption of hatred and it shocked Dolan to discover that he was himself its object. Dolan moved continually, circling the room.

"Stop, damn you, and meet me."

"You don't expect me to stand still while you beat me with that thing, do you?" Dolan looked briefly in Eddie's direction, and he said to her in a quite different tone of voice, "You'd better call what passes for the police out here. I think he's snapped."

But Eddie didn't respond. She remained slumped where she was, with a bewildered look on her face. Cheney lunged at the desk as if she had moved toward it. He jerked the cord out of the wall and swept the phone onto the floor.

In his quick movement Cheney had dropped his pose and stood upright now. The withered arm, slouch and darting eyes had disappeared. If anything, he looked more sinister. He raised the poker at Dolan, gestured with it toward Eddie and said in his own voice, "I watched you fuck her. What kind of man fucks his brother's wife?"

The question slammed Dolan.

"My brother's dead," he said. It was not a denial, and it was not relevant.

"I'm not dead."

"You're not my brother," Dolan said.

A pained, animal look crossed Cheney's face, a pleading to which, in another circumstance, it would have been impossible not to respond with sympathy. "We're all brothers. Isn't that what you Swedes believe?"

"I'd love to believe it, but I don't."

Cheney took a threatening step toward him. "And you don't believe in fighting?"

"I don't believe in God, either, but sometimes I pray. Put the poker down and I'll fight with you." Not only did his voice lack bravado when he said that, but he was moving backward again. Dolan knew that even without the poker Cheney could beat him senseless. He reminded himself of that, not remorsefully, but in an effort to keep his mind sharp with what was real and what wasn't.

Cheney was moving as in fog. Dolan guessed that he thought the cameras were rolling. He came at Dolan now with energy, the poker up. He cut their circle short and lunged, swinging. Dolan ducked and swiveled by him.

The poker crashed down on a small table, demolishing it.

Eddie backed up against the wall behind the wood stove. Dolan tried to catch her eyes, as if she would tell him what to do. But she stared at Cheney. She was oblivious still to everything but his having returned. She was terrified, and that served to double Dolan's anxiety.

He raised a palm toward Cheney. "Hey, look, come on," Dolan said, but without authority. "Put the poker down and . . ."

Cheney swung at him again. This time Dolan felt the breeze of the iron rod as it whipped by inches away from him. He fell over a chair and thought as he went down that perhaps Cheney would leave him alone once he was vulnerable. Perhaps he should just sprawl there sheepishly. Would it help if he apologized?

When he looked up from the floor he saw the thing coming full force at his head. He rolled away only an instant before it smashed onto the floor, splintering the wood. He knew then that he could not back up anymore.

Before Cheney regained his balance Dolan was on him, but Cheney shrugged him off and sent him careening into the wall, then lunged with the poker, this time stabbing him in the side. It was too blunt to puncture, but it bruised him horribly and the pain in his ribs made him cry out, "Hey, Christ!" Instinctively he punched at Cheney with his right fist, striking him just in front of his ear.

The blow staggered Cheney, which surprised Dolan and encouraged him. It was the first punch he'd thrown as an adult, and it was easier than he'd expected. Unfortunately he didn't follow it up. He glanced toward Eddie. She was frozen against the wall.

Cheney swung the bar and struck again, this time a hard, vicious blow against the arm Dolan had raised to protect his head. Dolan thought his arm was broken. He scurried backward, holding it. The pain was excruciating, and his panic now was like a pack of wild dogs inside him. He knew that panic was as much his enemy as Cheney was, but he couldn't help it. He didn't have a chance. Cheney was at him again. The bar struck once more, this time on the back because Dolan had turned at the last second. It was the best Dolan could do.

Dolan found it impossible to fight back. He could only flee. He pushed a chair in front of Cheney and backpedaled. But Cheney caught him in a corner. He brought the iron down on him. At the last second Dolan moved his head. The blow fell on his collarbone. Dolan yelled, twisted away and fell against the wood stove. The pain of the scalding metal on top of all his other pain was too much. He wanted Cheney to finish him. He collapsed against the shelves to the left of the stove. A metal tackle-box clattered to the floor, spilling reels, flies, coiled lines and a trout knife.

A trout knife. He grabbed it.

The knife meant to Dolan that he did not have to die. That's all. There was no reflection, morality, metaphor, guilt or pleasure. There was only the urge to live, and the knife was how he could.

He slashed up at Cheney, who had charged again, and the blade caught him.

It caught him on the forearm.

Cheney reared back. He saw his blood. He saw the knife and kicked at it instinctively. The knife flew out of Dolan's hand and fell at Eddie's feet. But she only stared at it. Cheney raised the poker over his head to bring it down on Dolan one final time.

The child in the doorway said, "Dad."

Cheney McCoy froze.

It was Dolan's chance, but he didn't move. Neither did Eddie.

Cheney turned slowly toward Bren. The boy was clutching a sheet of paper. Dolan could see that it was a drawing, but of what he couldn't tell.

When Dolan looked back up at Cheney looming over him he saw an expression of anguish on his face that reminded him, inanely, of the definition of hell he'd been taught by nuns: infinite pain felt infinitely. Then Dolan saw that Cheney had forgotten all about him.

Cheney shook his head slowly and began to move toward Bren. The poker was still raised over his head. A male Medea. Dolan realized that Cheney was going to bring it down on Bren.

Eddie saw it too, and finally she moved. She scooped up the trout knife and lunged across the room.

Bren remained motionless. He watched Cheney coming at him and his mother coming at him. She had the knife up and aimed at Cheney. Just before she hit him, though, she dropped the knife. A decision. She could not plunge a blade into Cheney in front of the child who'd just called him "Dad." She slammed her body into Cheney with all her power: it would have to be enough.

But it was not.

Cheney lowered his arms to fling his elbow into her teeth. His perfectly timed jolt turned her momentum against her, stunning her. She fell. Blood gushed out of her mouth. But she clung to his legs as she went down. She held him.

Cheney raised his arms again and once more aimed the poker at Bren.

Eddie had not stopped him at all.

But she'd given Dolan the moment he needed. Dolan hit Cheney low with his good shoulder and sent him sprawling. Cheney got halfway up, but Eddie was on him, clawing. Then Dolan slugged him, a great roundhouse punch that knocked him down.

Cheney struggled to his knees once more and Dolan kicked him. Cheney got up again, but Dolan threw himself at him, driving him across the living room and through the screen door. Dolan stayed at him, churning his legs like a blocking lineman with his injured left shoulder turned down into his chest. Cheney crashed against the porch railing, collapsing it and sprawling backward down the four feet onto the grass. Dolan, still with him, fell on top of him.

And they lay there like lovers, spent lovers trying to breathe again.

Dolan's left shoulder was hurting terribly, and his heart was pounding madly, and he could feel Cheney's pounding too. They lay there in the dark waiting, it seemed to him, for something to explain what had happened. Dolan's face, the side of it, was on Cheney's and he felt the moisture of what he thought might be tears. He raised himself to see if Cheney was weeping, but he wasn't. What he saw in Cheney's eyes was not evil, corruption or murder. Dolan saw a plain unhappiness that was not altogether unfamiliar.

Cheney whispered something.

"What? I can't hear you."

He whispered it again.

"Kill you?"

Cheney nodded.

"You want me to kill you?"

He nodded again.

"Don't be crazy." Dolan got up and, with his good arm, brushed himself off. The bout was over. Dolan was creamed, but Cheney seemed barely alive.

Dolan stood back while Cheney slowly rolled over onto his stomach and then, as if he were climbing obstacles, made it to his knees and then his feet. Without a look back at Dolan or at the house, he staggered toward the cliff. Dolan thought he might throw himself off and he wanted to stop him. But Cheney found the rickety wooden stairs that led down to the tidal rocks and took them without hesitation.

"Who is the slayer?" That line from Sophocles.
"Who the victim? Speak!" It rang in Dolan's head.

He could not watch indifferently while Cheney
plunged down toward the sea, but neither could he
help him. Cheney disappeared in the darkness. No
one spoke.

Dolan turned and walked up the porch stairs. Every movement hurt his shoulder terribly.

The door was jammed open. Dolan walked into the
living room and stopped.

She rocked. How can I have done this to you? She
rocked her child. How can you ever forgive me?
When she tried to put it into words she said only,
"I'm here, my sweet," and then again, "I'm here."
And continued rocking him.

After a long time Eddie became aware of Dolan.
She wanted to turn and ask him, Can this be repaired? Will you come and help me with my child?
But she did not.

Dolan was afraid that they didn't need him. He
resolved to go. But he couldn't move. He simply
couldn't move. How vulnerable she was. How desolate. He saw that they were his. He said quietly from
where he stood, "I'm here too."

Eddie turned and opened an arm to him. "Help,"
she said. "Help me."

And he moved toward her. He would.

JOIN THE
DANIELLE STEEL
FAN CLUB

Just fill in the coupon below, mail it in, and you will receive:

• a personally autographed photograph of Danielle Steel

• sneak previews of all of Danielle Steel's newest books

• up-to-the-minute information on Danielle Steel's next visit to your hometown

---

Yes! Enroll me in The Danielle Steel Fan Club.

Name

Address

City   State   Zip Code

MAIL TO: The Danielle Steel Fan Club
                Publicity Department
                Dell Publishing Co., Inc.
                245 East 47th Street
                New York, N.Y. 10017

Dell Bestsellers

- [ ] **A PERFECT STRANGER** by Danielle Steel ..$3.50 (17221-7)
- [ ] **FEED YOUR KIDS RIGHT**
  by Lendon Smith, M.D. $3.50 (12706-8)
- [ ] **THE FOUNDING** by Cynthia Harrod-Eagles ..$3.50 (12677-0)
- [ ] **GOODBYE, DARKNESS**
  by William Manchester $3.95 (13110-3)
- [ ] **GENESIS** by W.A. Harbinson $3.50 (12832-3)
- [ ] **FAULT LINES** by James Carroll $3.50 (12436-0)
- [ ] **MORTAL FRIENDS** by James Carroll $3.95 (15790-0)
- [ ] **THE HORN OF AFRICA** by Philip Caputo $3.95 (13675-X)
- [ ] **THE OWLSFANE HORROR** by Duffy Stein ..$3.50 (16781-7)
- [ ] **INGRID BERGMAN: MY STORY**
  by Ingrid Bergman and Alan Burgess $3.95 (14085-4)
- [ ] **THE UNFORGIVEN**
  by Patricia J. MacDonald $3.50 (19123-8)
- [ ] **SOLO** by Jack Higgins $2.95 (18165-8)
- [ ] **THE SOLID GOLD CIRCLE**
  by Sheila Schwartz $3.50 (18156-9)
- [ ] **THE CORNISH HEIRESS**
  by Roberta Gellis $3.50 (11515-9)
- [ ] **THE RING** by Danielle Steel $3.50 (17386-8)
- [ ] **AMERICAN CAESAR**
  by William Manchester $4.50 (10424-6)

At your local bookstore or use this handy coupon for ordering:

DELL BOOKS
P.O. BOX 1000, PINEBROOK, N.J. 07058

Please send me the books I have checked above. I am enclosing $_____
(please add 75¢ per copy to cover postage and handling). Send check or money
order—no cash or C.O.D.'s. Please allow up to 8 weeks for shipment.

Mr/Mrs/Miss _____

Address _____

City _____ State/Zip _____